ABOUT THE AUTHOR

Luke Icarus Simon was born in Old Nicosia and immigrated to Australia as a teenager. He has a BA (Hons) in Australian Literature and Drama from the University of Sydney and additional degrees from both the University of Technology and Wollongong University. He has worked as an actor, playwright, screenwriter and as a principal in the tertiary and vocational educational sectors.

He is best known for his plays, produced in Sydney and Melbourne theatres and his teleplays for the AFTRS, SBS TV and ABC.

His poetry, reviews, essays and short fiction have appeared widely in national and international literary journals, newspapers, magazines and anthologies since the early 1980s, including in *Southerly*, *The Weekend Australian*, *Metaphor*, *Overland*, *Mattoid*, *Westerly*, *Antipodes*, *Good Reading Magazine*, *Famous Reporter*, *Outrider*, *Penguin's Australian Writing Now*, *Campaign*, *Outrage*, *The Union Recorder*, *Social Alternatives*, *Hobo*, *Akti*, *Rochford St Review*, *The Poetry of Men's Lives* (USA) and *Neighbours: Multicultural Writing of the 1980s* (UQP).

Simon is a Stage 4 cancer survivor. He lives in a small Murray River town.

THE ART IN MY PALM

Also by Luke Icarus Simon

POETRY

Latin

The Transit of Cancer

The Gospel of the Fallen: Selected Poems 1996-2006

Swimming in Words: New and Selected Poems

SHORT STORIES

Lost in the Last Divided Capital

PLAYS

Urban Tales of Utter Devotion

Fish Wednesday

Sir

A House on an Island in the Aegean

The Conscience of Narkissos

NON-FICTION

Michael Gow: A Thematic Approach

The Little Book on How to Stop Smoking

SCREENPLAYS

My Stamp Collection (ABC)

Schism (AFTRS)

English At Work- SBS TV (3 teleplays)

Event Cinemas TV (30 scripts)

THE ART IN MY PALM

LUKE ICARUS SIMON

STIRLING
PUBLISHING
AUSTRALIA

First published 2025 by Stirling Publishing Australia
© Luke Icarus Simon 2025

Enquiries should be made to the publisher:
stirlingpublishingaustralia@gmail.com

National Library of Australia cataloguing-in-publication data
is available at http://catalogue.nla.gov.au
ISBN (pbk) 978-1-7638915-1-7
ISBN (hardcover) 978-1-7638915-0-0
ISBN (ebk) 978-1-7638915-2-4

Cover art design: Luke Harris
Cover Painting by Lonias Efthyvoulou: from the author's personal collection
Designed and typeset in Garamond Premier
Headings: Larken

At Working Type Studio,
PO BOX 72 Eltham, Victoria 3095

Dedicated to:

The Missing of Cyprus
And
To all the Displaced Cypriots,
compelled to flee their homes

Acknowledgements

Excerpts from this book first appeared in earlier versions in the following literary journals:

Chapter 4 in *Overland,*

Chapters 12 & 13 in *The Famous Reporter,*

Chapters 36 and 48 both in *Southerly.*

The author gratefully acknowledges the support of the editors of these journals at the time of first publication.

'The coup of the Greek junta is an invasion and from its consequences the whole people of Cyprus suffers, both Greeks and Turks.'

President Makarios, July 19, 1974, UN Security Council

PROLOGUE

Anatheman din oran.
(Cursed be the hour that misfortune struck)
Cypriot expression

My full name is Demosthenes Evagoras Hatzinikolaou.

My surname would've been of fewer syllables but as my paternal grandfather had made the Orthodox pilgrimage to the Holy Land of Jerusalem, he rightfully then added the honorific *Hatzi* prefix. It would have been just Nikolaou, had he stayed put on our island. My surname though should have been my father's first name, as is the custom in some regions of Cyprus. It should've been Evagorou— his name changes its last syllable to indicate possession, as per the complex grammar rules of the Greek language and its cases.

I have also been known as *Lotta* (a sow in Greek Cypriot dialect), a moniker created by my older brother. Then *Zzavos*, on account of my busted nose. As *Demos* by my mother, on occasions— when she is too lazy to say all the syllables in my name or when she is angry; and *Mitsis* (the little one) by my twenty-seven first cousins because I was the youngest of them all. The one that hurt the most was being called *Bastard* by fellow school kids who were never ever going to be my friends.

The last moniker was bestowed upon me as throughout primary school I was the only kid in my class whose father was absent. In the eyes of my peers at school, he therefore did not exist. But he did. He was away. Working overseas. From the time I was a toddler. I never understood why.

I got used to responding, sometimes gingerly or pissed off, to all of the above names in several dialects for the first decade and a bit of my life. Then unintended circumstances, not of my family's doing, found me facing an avalanche of new names, most of which I thankfully (at first) did not fully understand.

This is the story of my life, as best I can recall it, from when I was a kid to just before my eighteenth birthday. I am remembering that period as I commemorate the tenth anniversary of the passing of a loved family member. So many people in our world are not permitted to tell their stories. For varying reasons. Even if everyone's story could be told, so many of us would not wish to listen.

My Greek forefathers may have founded the concept of democracy but that doesn't mean all people now live freely and equitably. Even in the most developed Western countries democracy is cunningly disguised and manipulated to suit the philosophies of those in power.

I have not been allowed by society to legally marry, or have children of my own or adopt. So, this story is written as testimony. My convoluted surname will become extinct with my passing.

If there are gaps in periods of time in my story or fragments floating untethered or even secrets left unsaid, it means I can't remember with any clarity. Or, I don't wish to remember that period or those particular events and honour them in words. We all have fragile pieces of truth hidden away so deeply within ourselves that we can't ever articulate those experiences in words.

We have to accept that words become useless sometimes. Even for poets. For safety reasons. In order for us to protect ourselves and survive. To continue to get up each morning, shower and get dressed and make our way to our working space. And *be nice*. If my mother or siblings were looking back at this period of our lives, I am sure they'd have their own perspectives. Their own version. Their stories to tell. For example, when I was three, I started to desperately miss my absent father. My mother, if she were sharing this anecdote, may correct me and assert that I was only a two- year-old or even a four-year-old. And that I wasn't actually missing my father but rather that I was simply being rebellious. To demonstrate to her I was not a compliant good son. If a hair was out of place upon my return from school, she'd scold me and complain that I looked *dishevelled,* simply in order to intentionally upset her.

I hadn't really known my father except in limited bursts of time on his lightning visits to our island, to our narrow streets with their elegant architecture. Streets filled with the unmistakable scent of jasmine and smoky olive leaves burning daily in every home in dozens of *kapnistiria.* I wish my father had put down in words his version of life, that of his own before we all came along and more crucially, what happened after that. I never had the chance to get an insight into his psyche as he did not stick around.

My father left us all before I turned two. In truth, I probably missed having *a* father, *any* father, rather than the sum of parts my own father was. I somehow got it into my head that I could fly to wherever he was working overseas—so I jumped from the top of the stairs leading to the rooftop terrace and landed flat on my face. My nose was crushed, cartilage gone. I suffered.

I suffered from that fall all through my childhood and teenage years as I was the only kid in school with a broken nose. Mother said it would serve as a daily reminder to me, when I looked in the mirror that, 'there are consequences when you don't listen to your poor mother.' Our pediatrician, Dr Daphne, advised that I had to wait until I was eighteen before the specialist doctors could fix it.

At the time, eighteen seemed like the fourth century BC to me. Dr Daphne might as well have been talking about the Dinosaur Age. I wanted to ask her if she believed dinosaurs had actually existed, as a way of testing her, to see if she were telling me the truth. But I kept quiet.

Like when adults said things.

Or did things to my body I was told to not ever mention. And I was an obedient little boy.

A perfect pupil, just like my mother had taught me. Never backchatted. Not an iota of insolence.

From the time I was a toddler I had a habit of hiding underneath the heavy dining table or inside an elaborate French armoire. I used to deduce from my relatives' dinner-table conversations that our island found itself in constant conflict, for hundreds of years. Some claimed for around 11,000 years but as a kid I could not fathom the idea or process what all these *thousands* of years entailed.

They all claimed it was because of where our island was located and the era of the Cold War we were living through when I was a kid. Each of the men had their own take on why we'd never find peace. The phrase *strategic location* was used a lot to explain why other countries wanted to own our island, but I had no idea what that phrase actually meant. And that we, the island's inhabitants, were nothing more than *collateral damage* to the powerful forces making deliberations and signing treaties about our island's future; usually without democratically canvassing the opinions or wishes of the people of our island.

Nightly on television there were plenty of programmes with

endless discussions about politics. The participants were almost always middle-aged or older. Grey men with hair growing out from their floppy ears, citing the British. Referencing the Turks. Blaming the Americans. Throwing about the acronyms EOKA and EOKA B. Arguing about the advantages and disadvantages of joining Greece as one nation. Like all the other Greek islands, spread across seas and archipelagos, and forfeiting our fledgling independence.

Our island had been an English colony for less than a hundred years. Only since 1878, in exchange for Great Britain's support of the Ottoman Empire during the Congress of Berlin. But our troubles had begun a long time before that. It was documented that our long history was characterised by serial invasion, occupation and outside interference by countries with vested interests in our location. For instance, in 1489, Cyprus was ruled by the Republic of Venice. The Venetian Governors fortified our cities due to continued Ottoman threat and around 1567 demolished the old walls of the city built by the Franks, (yes, we had a Frankish era too).

The new walls of Nicosia to this day, have three gates, to the north, Kyrenia Gate, to the west, Paphos Gate and to the east, Famagusta Gate. But even when we were declared an independent nation in 1960, just a handful of years before I was born, Cyprus still remained at the mercy of more powerful nations. The citizens of our island seemed to be given no clear authority to make up our own minds—always there were caveats and covenants and conditions to our sovereignty, notwithstanding what the majority of my countrymen and women wanted. A compromise was inherent, in whatever we actually wished for our lives at any given point in time.

Since the 1950s, people were being murdered for their political stance or for their heritage. Car bombs, letter bombs, purposely lit fires, shootings, executions, torture, dissidents being beaten to death, journalists bashed by those opposing their views. Cigarette burns as a threat that a worse fate awaited those who did not cease to fight for their political stance on *Enosis* vs Independence.

Our ethnarch had passed a law in 1967 entitled *Insulting the Head of State*; Article 46A provided for the imprisonment for three years of anyone deemed critical of the President. This applied in the event of his resignation and even following his future death. Our leader may have been dressed in the severe black garb of a Greek-Orthodox archbishop and was definitely adored by many, including my mother, but he ruled a totalitarian regime under the guise of democracy. And he feigned divine spirituality as if he were directly appointed by God. Like the Emperor of Japan.

And yet, the prescribed texts we read and learned from at school were all imported from Greece and had the approval of the military Junta ruling the Motherland. These military generals, were callous men who had deposed the very handsome king several years before I was enrolled in primary school. I thought The King of Greece looked like a Hollywood movie star as handsome as Cary Grant and Rock Hudson. And he was an Olympian to boot.

At school, we were taught how cruel, how brutal the British had been against our people, especially during the 1950s. Apparently, they executed those who fought against their colonisation. Ironically, it seems our religious leader did not have any qualms about adopting brutality against those of his own citizens whose total devotion and obedience he demanded. Was our cherished president and spiritual leader simply too self-deluded about his strategic intelligence and his insistent non-alliance? Merely self-aggrandising? Out of his depth? Did he get it wrong to play the USSR and the USA against each other? Were his bets placed on a game of chess he soon lost? Floundering badly and aggravating both behemoths of world power? I don't know as I was a kid.

This is my story of discovering the world of a new country as an immigrant with genetic trauma in his DNA. Coping with my father's decade-plus abandonment.

A displaced boy starting anew in a country with its own incandescent scents and landscapes and shoreline, and disturbing dark history of colonisation. My story of survival. Learning a new language as a tween. Always being asked, 'Where are you from?' which immediately destroyed my illusion, any sense of belonging to my adopted country.

And, to the best of my inner resources, trying to forgive everything that was done to me. To my body. Making a concerted effort to somehow erase the past, and hopefully, minimise its hold over me. And to work, instead, towards finding my true self. Allowing trauma and melancholy to hopefully dissipate, using Reich's Cloud Busting machine to blow them away. No one can dispute that my adoptive country could most definitely win an Olympic gold medal in brilliant blue skies. And another gold for its incandescent blinding light.

PART 1

A Small Island in the Eastern Mediterranean Sea

Pou tin yin os ton ourano
(from Earth to Heaven)
Cypriot expression

1

The first house I was taken to, a month after being born, was Areos 36. Our street was named after the Greek god Ares, who was the god of war. Many of the streets in our old city, a city built within fortified high walls, had the names of the Greek gods or of the Independence heroes of 1821. Evidently, we were proud of our Hellene heritage.

A month after being born, I say, as I had to stay in hospital a month and a bit because I was in a great hurry to leave my mother's womb and join the great world. It might have been because of the bombing raids our city suffered while Mother carried me in her womb. Perhaps babies *can* hear what's going on in the outside world. So, instead of being a Christmas-made baby, born in September, like my two siblings, I decided to sabotage family tradition and prematurely embark on this journey in the searing heat of July.

I wonder now if that was my first ever mistake.

'You ruined me completely. It was as if you were playing soccer,' Mother was fond of saying when she was in a martyred mood. Just for the record, I never used to play soccer when I was little (and Mother knew this as *she* was the one who forbade me from playing soccer). Still, I wondered whether she was right, as a dark brown birthmark, round like a soccer ball, was planted right in the middle of my chest. The humiliation and anxiety that birthmark caused me all though childhood and adolescence pretty much exonerated me—in my humble opinion—from any vigorous kicking I may have exerted within the miniature soccer field of my mother's womb.

In the middle of the old part of the city, two minutes' walk from the city's Venetian walls, stood our two-storey Neo-Roman sandstone house. On the left at street level was *Pappou*'s abandoned workroom. On the right, a ground floor residence that in later years, due to Mother's *economic mismanagement*, was rented out to well-screened families with whom Mother was connected.

We lived upstairs. There was a verandah which ran at an L-shaped angle all around the back two sides of the house. Potted Greek basil lining the balcony rail acted as a barrier for us, as if we got too close to the rail, we'd scrape our legs on the rough concrete surface of the pots. The verandah looked down onto the courtyard below, with its large concrete water tank which served us well on Cataclysm Day, when everyone had to get everyone else wet on purpose. Imagine! And all the mothers didn't mind us kids getting our clothes wet. Not even the kinds of mothers who would normally say at the first drop of rain, '*Thee mou*, get inside or you'll catch cold!' and do their cross at least three times, fervently eulogising against *To Mati*.

There was also a swing, which we weren't allowed to ride as our mother had an obsession-level fear of accidents. So, of course, to spite her, we had plenty of rides despite the extreme precautions she took. She preferred to insulate and cushion us from the real world of cuts and bruises and broken bones. And from friends.

Being high up on the second storey of the grand old house

and separated by heavy, bolted, wooden doors, outside shutters on every window, as well as by a staircase in the ground-floor foyer which led upstairs, we were quite physically isolated from most of the goings-on at street level. Despite the physical proximity of the neighbours' houses. All the houses in the streets around our own home had been built a long time before any of us were born.

On top of everything else that segregated us from the world was the fact our house had a hallway bigger than my bedroom, on both floors. These obstructed a clear view of the downstairs reception room to *Pappou's* tailor shop, so we could not even see what deliveries Mother signed for, or how much money she gave to the milkman or the baker or anyone else who knocked on our door. All these interactions took place downstairs, discreetly hidden from view, away from our inquisitive eyes. Mother could have met our Archbishop or even the English Queen herself downstairs and we would never have known about it.

'Who was that?' my sister would ask when Mother would reappear upstairs.

'None of your business, *koritsi mou*,' Mother usually said, discreetly placing a parcel in one of the many drawers of the elaborate three-metre-long chiffonier that took pride of place in our own foyer. Then, without further explanation she went back to her needlework, or to whatever she was doing in the kitchen, or to her bureau in her dressing room.

It was this forced isolation that led to my jumping off the window ledge onto the street below at age two (or was I older?) and the reason why I had to endure a broken collarbone. I cannot remember this event—I can only rely on my mother's memory.

However, this unauthorised experiment in gravity long before I had heard of any physics or kinesis concepts at school, did not act as a deterrent. In time, I found another source of constant amusement—the staircase which led to the rooftop. There we would eat watermelon sprinkled with fresh mint leaves and side plates of halloumi and bread, most days in summer. The door onto the roof terrace was locked but not the staircase. It was there for anyone's amusement and for experiments in flying without wings or with superhero pretend wings. It was a lot more accessible than the staircase that led directly down to Grandpa's workroom just beyond the large entrance foyer.

The staircase became my best friend. I'd spend hours there every day, talking to and playing with imaginary friends and contemplating my escape. But as mentioned, this obsession with escaping caused me to bust my nose.

I never actually saw Grandpa sitting at his *Singer* with its cast-iron wheel and foot pedal, or doing any sewing in his tailor's atelier. I don't recall seeing him at work measuring someone's inside leg. But his tailor things—spools, rolls of wool samples for suits, armless torsos—were all there, left behind. As if he might, through some kind of nostalgic inspiration, suddenly be drawn back to his former work den and pick up just where he had left off years before. It was kind of creepy. When on the rare occasion *Pappou* actually did magically reappear in his workspace, usually to drink cognac with his mates rather than to do any tailoring, it seemed as if I were having a surreal dream.

But I was recalling our accidents. I'm guessing my brother and sister and I all found having a broken limb to be a brilliant achievement, as it demonstrated we were rebelling against our mother's strict regime. My brother Konstandinos had to get stitches in his head or his leg as a matter of routine. Philadelphia was always declining invitations to birthday parties on account of a sprained wrist or ankle, even when she was perfectly fine. As mentioned, our mother's caution against any kind of outdoor activity extended to forbidding us from playing with other children on the street below, where all the kids in our neighbourhood played freely and unsupervised until dinner.

'Just think yourselves lucky,' Mother would say, reminding us that the other children who lived in our street did not live in a house the size of ours with its closed-off rooms, its many chandeliers, Pendeli-marble floors and high ceilings. It was a no-brainer why we were shunned by the other children, and as revenge we learned to scoff at their stupid billycarts and chalk games on the asphalt. Just in case they thought themselves better than us on account of their freedom.

Still, without friends my own age I desperately wanted everyone to like me. Anyone.

2

· · · · · · · · · · ·

The first significant memory I have is of once being driven to kindergarten in a long, black, chauffeur-driven limousine. I wasn't popular at kindergarten. Perhaps my broken nose scared off the other kids? Perhaps they had spotted my horrible birthmark in between my nipples on my chest and were horrified I was some kind of wolf-man? The limousine on my first day may have put them off. It was a one-off birthday gift from my godfather, who was a renowned surgeon with his own hospital.

Now and again he would organise special surprises. I remember for sure that on several occasions the limousine took me to my godparents' grand but dark house, next door to their hospital where my siblings and I were all born. Another time his driver delivered to our house sweets flavoured with coconut that I did not touch. Just reading on the packaging that coconut was listed as an ingredient turned my stomach.

My godfather was just like my father—not present. Always busy. I used to wonder, even as a kid, why he had bothered to agree to having a godson. Twice a year, I would be invited to have tea with my mostly silent godmother. Occasionally, I would catch a fleeting glimpse of my godfather in motion, but he never once joined us for afternoon tea. I would only ever see him in passing. As he passed the room I sat in or as he said goodbye to my godmother to return to his

18

duties at the hospital. Once or twice, I remember him patting me briefly on the head in the hallway when the driver would deliver me like a parcel or by the metal gate on his way out as I arrived, always asking me, 'How's your mother?' whilst unsuccessfully trying to put his arm into the sleeves of his white doctor's coat.

I have vague recollections of returning from the daily tortures of kindergarten in a minibus which first went out to several outlying suburbs before finally terminating in the city, where I alighted, the last passenger. The manual gears were always getting stuck, so I'd be wanting to throw up by the time we reached home. My godparents never visited me once in our house. Instead, a modest gift would arrive on my birthday. Mother would unwrap the present and without showing it to me first would herself assess its merit or suitability and usually take it away to one of the closed rooms, with the intent to donate it to charity—no discussion was entered into with me.

I don't recall whether the kindergarten bus terminated right outside our front door or nearby. Just the thought that I was allowed to walk free of adult supervision, even from the corner block, seems inconceivable. Kindergarten itself was totally boring. This may sound like an ungrateful attitude if you consider that this was not a public kindergarten and that Mother must have had to fork out quite a bit to get me enrolled. Unfortunately, never having learned to play with other kids, I wasn't interested in the sandpit or in chasings or the silly lunches the staff organised where the food was cut into weird shapes. My bag was well stocked with goodies, some of which were confiscated by the teachers. Just like at home there were so many rules we were daily reminded we had to observe.

One clear memory I have is of a squashed banana, whose ripe and compelling smell emanating from my satchel filled the classroom in the summer heat of Nicosia. It caused me great turmoil and left me in tears. The smell was intense, and I felt convinced that my classmates would think I had done an unspeakable act, which we were told, day in, day out, we were now *way too old* to commit.

I did not attend the kindergarten for the full year. I recall I had an awesome toy car which lit up when a lever was wound and released and which could ride over dirt, if the batteries were up to it. It was taken from me one morning by a brutal, out-of-town boy who looked and behaved like the child terrorists we saw on the nightly news carrying suicide bombs.

Being withdrawn from kindergarten did not upset me. I did not make any friends in the playground. Perhaps the determining factor of my withdrawal from kinder was a question of money. Father's finances could not have been inexhaustible. The upkeep of our enormous house must have cost a fortune. Mother never turned away any of Father's relatives who used our house as a free hotel when they had cause to come into the city. Cousin Panikkos literally lived at our house as did Cousin Marios when both were doing their police training. Cousin Panikkos had failed his entrance exam twice but with some help from his parents' connections, he managed to just pass on his third go.

'It's perfect,' Panikkos told us, beaming upon hearing the good news. 'I never have to worry about getting a job again. They'll even give me a pension when I get older.'

There were so many family men in uniform I actually thought

that every man in our family had to be a policeman or a fireman or soldier. Apparently, even our father had been in uniform once, working as a ranger. I never saw him in his ranger's uniform, but Mother would frequently show us photographs of a handsome man in uniform she claimed was our father when he was younger.

I looked forward to any male relative visiting and staying with us as they would pay me attention. Once, I recall sniffing Cousin Marios's winter slippers daily with a guilty, unexplained pleasure.

After my kindergarten career stalled, I was once again banished within the mostly dark confines of Areos 36; that is, I had to spend most of my day in my bedroom, daydreaming and drawing pictures. Even during siestas when I was supposed to have a sleep. In the mornings, if an adult cousin had been visiting, I would sneak into the still-warm bed where my first cousin had slept the previous night and feel a little less lonely.

I couldn't understand why I had to share a bedroom with Konstandinos, whose return from school I would anxiously await, when there were enough rooms to go around. Mother kept several rooms closed. We would sneak in there, in these out-of-bounds rooms, rooms smelling of strong naphthalene, to play hide and seek. I enjoyed the dusty-musty odour emanating from the covered heavy furniture, that looked like abandoned ghosts with the white canvas sheets draped all over it. Philadelphia bragged that one day both the furniture and the house would be hers and she vowed to let her children do as they pleased within the closed rooms.

The floors of our house were all of marble imported from Pendeli on the mainland, except for two rooms, one of which was for guests and where an old lady (who she was I don't remember) died. I also don't remember why she chose to die in our house. I was in Grade 1 so all I do remember is that we disappointingly, never saw the body being taken away all covered up or anything as shocking as that. Mother made sure of that. I was sure I'd be popular in school if only I had seen the dead body. Mother was always one step ahead of us. Bloody maddening. Why didn't we have a mother who was happy to *let the children be children* as all our village relatives used to say to her in exasperation with *her ways*?

Then, when I was in Grade 2, a young soldier came to stay in the same room for a while. He only had one leg. How long he stayed with us, I could not tell you. I do not recall if someone explained to me that he was somehow related to us. I do not think so because he looked different to all my first cousins. He was a tall, blond, strong guy and could easily grab one of us and pull us up to the single bed he occupied most of the day. His name was Panayiotis Doukas and I found his name very masculine. Unlike mine that reminded me of a wimp. I used to repeat his name over and over again, in a chant, as if I were saying a private prayer to God. I kept pestering Panayiotis, asking persistently if I would ever grow as tall and handsome as he was and when.

Panayiotis disappeared one day. No warning. No explanation was given by our mother. I tried to guess what Panayiotis's transgression or crime of impoliteness may have been. My brother did not care to talk about it and my sister Philadelphia, as usual, just ignored my questions. I dared not ask Mother. I returned from school one afternoon to find him gone. His room spotless. Not a single trace remained that he had ever been a part of our life. Somehow one of his long APOEL football socks was left behind in the laundry room downstairs. I do not know why but I took his sock when I was certain nobody was looking. I hid it in my chest of drawers, noting the flush of excitement on my cheeks and my pulse running fast.

The bedroom in which I slept had several marble tiles about fifty centimetres wide that could easily be lifted, but we were not allowed to do so. Rumor had it that in the fifties, long before I was born, Mother had assisted the Resistance against the British and she used to hide propaganda leaflets under them.

Hidden inside one of Mother's elaborate French armoires, I overheard, from a visitor who prided herself on having known Mother from the time she was a little girl, that our mother was actually arrested on her honeymoon, with Father at the wheel of a Fiat coupe (or was it a four-door Peugeot sedan?) with a boot full of pro-independence leaflets. What was more, that she was duly tortured by the British for she had claimed ownership and total responsibility.

Mind you, we chose not to believe this woman's allegations entirely because the British soldiers we came across driving south of the city in Cousin Dimitris's Triumph two-door coupe would always look so clean and polite. Nice-looking soldiers did not torture people—surely. Anglophilia was well entrenched on both sides of the family. I had to sing *God Save the Queen* every morning at assembly, admittedly, without having a clue as to what the words actually meant. The young Queen Elizabeth's picture, taken after her coronation in the fifties was hung bang in the middle of our classroom at the front, just like the Evil Eye in the middle of our church's altar.

Our Anglophilia could be logically explained because England, along with Motherland Greece, was our island's guaranteed protector, under the *Treaty of Guarantee* against any invasion by our enemy. So, I guess we were grateful. England did not have a whole British Empire for centuries for nothing. If needed, England could lawfully intervene and fight off enemies big or small. When you are a kid, you believe in absolutes. Foolhardy, but we don't know better.

In the bigger of the closed rooms was where Philadelphia and Konstandinos had committed their unforgivable crime when I was an infant. Apparently, they had tried to strangle me. This, I also definitely do not remember. Although, throughout childhood both Philadelphia and Konstandinos often referenced this event, whenever I played up or backchatted to them and reckoned they should have finished me off when they had the chance.

Now, on days when the reality of my history becomes too much, I too rue the fact they had not finished me off then.

4

· · · · · · · · · ·

The relative we all loved the most, even my stern sister, was Aunt Hara. She was really our second mum, our father's eldest sister. It's as if she were always there. Aunt Hara was good for many things; nobody could match the aniseed sourdough bread she baked, no one could upstage her at a funeral. She would beat her breasts with her tiny fists at the slightest tragedy. She would try and jump into the grave just before the coffin was lowered as a sign of her true grief. Once, when we accompanied her to a funeral service (behind Mother's back) she did just that. Jumped in.

We were aghast. Embarrassed. Hated ourselves for not realising that the dead man must have been, as Phil pointed out in a self-satisfied tone, Aunt Hara's *one and only true love*. Later, we fished for information. We burned with curiosity. We had many questions to ask of our aunt. But Aunt Hara recovered too quickly from the jump.

'Who was he?' we begged in unison, pulling at her black dress.

She shooed us away. Like she did with her chickens and her nasty geese. She wasn't in the mood to feed our fantasies. Just our tummies with her lemon potatoes baked in her outdoor oven.

'I don't know. Some stranger. An old man. I actually don't know,' she answered dismissively.

'So why did you jump in the grave then?' dared Philadelphia

and Konstandinos and I went crimson at our elder sibling's boldness. Mother had said never to challenge an adult. 'Especially an older relative,' conceding 'Even on your father's side.'

'They paid me good money,' was all Aunt Hara said walking away like the queen she was, and we were once again left with our mouths wide open in wonder and awe.

We usually had an ally when Aunt Hara came up to the city to visit for a few days. She had a certain cross-generational appeal with children, 'The poor thing doesn't have any of her own', Mother and other women, were fond of saying.

'She's *a divorcee!*' Konstandinos would proudly say, and Mother would fix him with a look which meant that Konstandinos would be getting yet another haircut, two weeks earlier than planned. My older brother only hated school more than getting haircuts at Kyrios Pitzolis's dark barber shop in town.

Aunt Hara always arrived early in the morning on the first and only bus from the village, just as were setting off to school. This made the day go past very quickly for us; we couldn't wait to get back home so she could drown us in her demonstrative love. We would always have to dust shadows of flour off our clothes after she had hugged us as she always baking sour cream pie or deep-frying *loukoumades*. Or making her famous *pittes*. For no matter what separated us from her lifestyle on her farm in the village and our *city-folk* ways, she was literally dripping with blind affection for us all, though Konstandinos was her clear favourite (as he gave her the most cheek). She made no secret of this because Konstandinos reminded her of her dead father whom none of us had met. Not even Phil had had a chance to meet our paternal grandpa. My sister who seemed to me to know everything and everybody.

At least that's what I thought then.

Aunt Hara smelled differently to Mother. Mother wore French perfume. Aunt Hara smelled of flour and sweat and of shredded wheat. And of chickens. Her skin was always warm to the touch. She was big bosomed, never wore a bra and forever dressed in black, on account of her deceased father and the two husbands who had died on her. Not literally 'on her' you understand. Not that we would have known really, because sex, the word Konstandinos was obsessed with, no longer played a part in our aunt's life. I did not know what *divorced* and *widow* actually meant back then but I knew both words had caused my aunt grief and that her reputation as a good Orthodox woman was forever tainted by them.

She always wore her hair in a bun which she wrapped like a snail at the back of her head and which she covered in a black scarf. She didn't wear her *kouroukla* right down to her forehead like *Stete* did in the village, but rather, courtesy of her rebellious reputation, just midway around her head. Her headscarf had some detail on it around the edge that she had painstakingly crocheted onto it. Aunt Hara had a particular reputation in her own village, and in the tiny villages which were scattered in isolation all around the island, as a bit of a rebel. For a start, not many women had been married twice, not in Father's village anyway.

She openly cheated on her fasts. Other village women, sick of having to fast themselves, craving a tahini pie, told on her (in confidence, of course) to the bishop. The local priest was then told, and Aunt Hara had to rush to confession. In no time, the whole devout village had found out about her shenanigans. Aunt Hara was god-fearing on the one hand but unrepentant on the other. If anything, she was more superstitious than religious. The priest gave her a talking to, but Aunt Hara had won him over and soon, loveless, gossip-mongering village women of a certain age had the two of them splitting a halloumi pie just before the services would commence on the holiest of days.

Just after my seventh birthday, while we were on holidays at *Stete* Virgin's house, my loved aunt predicted that an obnoxious neighbour who had visited us for afternoon tea would, out of envy, cast her evil eye onto us. Sure enough, not long after the woman's departure I was laid out in bed. The doctor couldn't find anything wrong with me. I had fevers and sweated. I ate lots and then threw everything up. Aunt Hara blamed herself. *Stete* Virgin vowed that 'that vile woman' was not to be allowed to visit in the future. To this day I still think of the Evil Eye and what it can do. Our village granny typically did not say much to us or to anyone else really except when something bad happened to her *horaitika* grandkids.

'What would I say to your father if something terrible happened to one of you?'

Without granny saying so, we knew her love was reserved mostly for our father, her baby son in absentia and that granny did not have much love left for us three. Nor for her other two dozen grandkids.

'Why is she called a virgin when she has so many children?' my brother used to ask. He was then given a slap on the back of the head by the adult closest to him in the room or, worse, was stared at so badly by Mother he would immediately shut up.

'It's just her name, you idiot,' my sister used to explain to him rolling her eyes.

When she was visiting us in the city, Aunt Hara couldn't understand why we had to be in bed by 8:30 pm and supported us in our protestations against Mother's rules. Philadelphia always maintained that the real reason was that Mother wanted to watch 'Peyton Place' on television in peace, without being disturbed.

Konstandinos was fond of sticking not just chestnuts into the fire but his own fingers. And mine too. Our aunt thought this was hilarious. She'd laugh out loud if we got a slight singe instead of acting like the world had ended, like our mother did. Aunt Hara would volunteer to tuck us in, and we would spend a couple of hours mucking around; her singing her renowned *tsiattista*, to us, her fat bosom the best cushion we could wish for to send us off to blissful sleep. I have spent many years since staring at women's breasts. Sometimes this gets me into trouble. For a long time, I did not understand why.

One day I found her sitting out on the verandah, staring at the radio, intensely. She wasn't listening to it. Just staring at it, turning it this way and that.

'How do they get in there?'

'Who?' I asked, not sure of her question.

'The people who are talking.'

'They're not in there,' I laughed, feeling smart. *Were they? Nah...*

'Well, how come they can talk to me then, hmm?'

'They're talking to lots of people, not just you.'

She wasn't convinced. Mind you, I wasn't quite sure myself where the announcers were, but at eight, I knew pretty much for sure that they weren't inside the actual radio.

'Come here,' Aunt Hara encouraged. She turned the radio around and showed me the lit fuses you could just see inside, through the crack of the hard plastic packaging. 'Isn't that the light from their house?' She was unrelenting.

'I don't know. But I don't think so *Theia*.'

'Well, you have a think about it and if you find out the answer you can tell me. Then we'll both know, and I could explain it to your *yiayia*. Slowly, of course, so she has a chance of understanding. She's not very quick, anymore, bless her.'

I agreed and hurried off to grab the encyclopedia, wondering if my aunt was a complete intellectual moron or if she were just tricking me into studying to find out the answer by myself. At that age, I couldn't accept the first proposition, for adults always knew everything, (or so they made out). And as for the latter, I didn't think Aunt Hara so cunning.

5

. . . .

To Mati saw everything we all did even when we weren't in church. Wearing an evil eye pendant acted as a deterrent against the Evil Eye but I was convinced if I wore one, it may also witness events I did not wish anyone, including myself to be reminded of—our teachers repeatedly warned us that it even witnessed stuff you couldn't imagine telling anyone. Like pilfering Panayiotis's sock.

In the same room Panayiotis had occupied, I saw Cousin Panikkos doing something frantic to himself with his right hand in the re-classified out-of-bounds room. He seemed simultaneously in pain and in ecstasy. He looked shocked when he realised I had been hiding behind the magenta velour Luis IV armchair, watching him, fascinated by the sounds he made and the half-pained expression on his plain, normally quiet face.

'Not a word to anyone or else I'll kill you,' he warned me.

Our first cousin Aliki, who was our mother's brother's first born, was also a big Anglophile and she held great influence over my sister Philadelphia. She kept a hardcover exercise book full of Beatles lyrics she carried around with her most places. I did not like music when I was little. Mother only allowed me limited access to the radio and certainly no access at all to the gramophone.

Aliki was the only one in our immediate family (the people we saw every week) allowed access to the English radio programme at eleven pm and since she didn't live with us, we couldn't sneak into her room and listen. Philadelphia used to have sleepovers now and then at Aliki's and she would come back full of exclusive experiences gained from being free to do what she pleased after dinner including staying up until midnight listening to the British radio programme. Our uncle Pericles had a *very relaxed approach to parenting* as our mother was fond of saying.

'Just go outside and play together and leave me in peace,' was his favourite line. Our mother was very fond of rolling her eyes in disapproval whenever her brother's cool approach to parenting was mentioned and we knew she would be *having a word to him* when she heard of liberties and privileges extended to us during our visit to our uncle's. Mother was very fond of saying, 'I'll be having a word to your uncle about that,' most days. So much that my siblings and I were always impersonating her tone and laughing ourselves silly. I hate to admit it, but my older brother Konstandinos was so good at impersonating Mother, pursing his lips like she did and sometimes, wrapping a bath towel around his head, to signify her double-storey bouffant hairstyle. I loved my brother the most when he was game to do and say things that showed he had the courage to try and take on Mother even when he knew that he'd lose and be punished.

We were asleep long before ten pm in our house. Mother had lots of rules. And we obeyed them for we didn't appreciate the repercussions that most certainly would ensue if we dared to transgress. Rules and strict discipline were our lot. It got very boring but, we had no choice.

We only had our mother.

Areos Street was a very narrow street where only one small Fiat could pass at a time. Some of the larger Mercedes-Benz taxis had to drop off passengers on the corner. Everybody who lived in our street knew who was coming and going into anybody's house. Only one of the mothers in the street worked but all the other mothers did not respect her for this. It didn't help that she had her hair done twice a week and always looked immaculate. The rumor mill had Kyria Aspasia being anything from a defrocked nun to a murderess. Her husband was apparently working overseas but the neighbourhood gossips remained unconvinced. They were certain Kyria Aspasia was capable of foul play.

Her two sons, Panos and Lefteris were attending the same private Grammar school as my sister Philadelphia. Panos was even in some of my sister's classes but, according to her, both brothers, like their mother, kept pretty much to themselves at school. Panos sometimes grunted a greeting at us if we passed him in the street. His version of Hello only had one syllable and sounded like a wounded bear was having a hiccup.

'Just because they've lived in America for two years doesn't make them special,' my older sister had told me, many times. Once though, when I sneaked a look at her diary, there was an entry, which read, *How handsome Panos looks when he smiles.* And on another page, *Panos speaks English so good even the teacher told us this to be true.*

I would think of Lefteris and Panos, when Mother turned off the light and told us to go to sleep. Trying to decide which brother was the one I most longed to be hugged by.

6

· · · · · · · · · · ·

Pappou had chosen to mostly abandon his atelier. Either before I came along or when I was so young I cannot remember the actual event. Like Father he too was absent. It was *Pappou* Demos who I was named after. I suspect the reasons for his sudden withdrawal were rather messy and *emotional*—Mother's visitors would bandy around the Greek word equivalent of emotional or *upset* each time they popped in for an unscheduled Nescafe with Mother.

'Go to your room,' Mother would bellow at us, 'Your *Theia* and I are going to have a quiet Nescafe. *Einai anastatomeni.*' Occasionally, my brother would dare retort that the *emotionally upset* visitor was not actually an aunty, as we were not related.

Uncle Pericles was proud of his dad's success at finding a second wife. When we'd visit him, he'd tell us, 'And do you know what your *pappou* said? "I am still a man".' Uncle Pericles loved nothing more than sitting in his armchair smoking a pipe, sipping cognac and telling stories. I understood, even then, that some events or decisions in life are seen as positive by some and as something to be ashamed of by others. Since his absconding, Mother and *Pappou* rarely saw each other except for awkward one-word telephone conversations to organise our infrequent visits to see him.

Or when *Pappou* appeared like an apparition in the atelier. Without notice.

'Her corpse was still not cold,' some family members whispered about the second marriage in disapproval. Sipping her Nescafe, our mother would nod but keep quiet on the subject, occasionally making a long resigned, breathy sigh. For Mother's mother had been a much-feared matriarch and a well-known identity of our walled city. She wasn't just any old thing. *Kyria* Konstandia Lavrentidis was a blue blood, born and raised within the best street within the ancient walls. Others could only dream of such lineage, such impeccable pedigree. No matter what lies people tried to promulgate in an effort to promote their so-called heritage, everyone from small children to old spinsters knew the names of the eight or so families born into this exclusive club.

'Look! She has a Mercedes now.'

'But she's still from Larnaca,' Nicosia born-and-bred neighbourhood women would scoff as they jumped onto the foot-wide footpath in order to avoid being mowed down by the aforementioned Mercedes driven by Toula—a *newcomer* to the city who married a Nicosia-born man, twelve years earlier.

'A Mercedes Cabriolet is no comfort to you in bed at night,' more forward-thinking neighbourhood women declared and suddenly Toula's Mercedes could have been a Lada for all anyone cared.

But Yiayia Konstandia. She had been a woman feared by local priests and shopkeepers alike. She wasn't one for hypocrisies of any kind. Apparently, she had had a cheeky sense of humour that was simultaneously wicked and self-righteous (we saw remnants of this in Mother's sometimes vicious tongue) and which got her into trouble. From the stories I heard when we were allowed to be in the same room as grown-ups, or when I surreptitiously eavesdropped, our maternal grannie had been larger than life, and people did not forget her easily.

I could only imagine what life might have been like had Grandmama Lavrentidis stuck around to see us born. Imagine her and Aunt Hara as a voting block against Mother! Uncle Pericles often admitted he was disappointed our mother had inherited only some of his mum's traits. 'Perhaps not her best ones,' he'd say, sounding despondent. Shopkeepers liked Mother for her consistent custom but were well aware they could not make a risqué joke like they used to freely with *Kyria* Lavrentidis. And they were most certainly not invited to the second-storey drawing room to play cards with Mother.

Sadly, Grandmama Lavrentidis's replacement, *Pappou*'s new wife, was a peasant from a village. We were under strict instructions to never address her as *yiayia*. Or the village word for *yiayia*—Stete. *Grandmama* too was definitely ruled out. Especially after Philadelphia had explained to us all that her English teacher had taught her class that adding an extra *-ma* to *Grandma* made that particular grandmother just that extra bit loved. Extra special.

The new wife had a huge dowry on account of her family who had been orchard farmers for a long time. *Pappou* was no fool. His first wife had spent her inherited money as if it were rice, throwing it to the wind. 'It's where I get my extravagance from,' our uncle would enthusiastically admit, pointing to his two motorcycles and to his own version of a closed room in his own modest house—a room filled not with treasured furniture but with extravagant purchases he had made but had never used.

'The fields are only full of cabbages and bitter lemons,' the Nescafe ladies of Nicosia sitting *en masse* around Mother's polished dinner table were quick to point out dismissively. Others reported that the old *karakaxa* wore too much make-up. That she did not have a clue how to cook.

'I tasted one of her *flaounes* once at the *Paniyiri*,' said Kyria Paotta, 'and what can I say?—it was hard to stop myself bringing it up. Right there, in front of the bishop!' Once, visiting this old woman everybody disapproved of with my uncle, our step-grandmother cooked us all fried eggs and chips but none of us could eat the food. It looked as it if it were swimming in olive oil. It was more of a soup of oil with two eggs drowning in it.

All the same though, she owned fields. Property. *Pappou* was *set,* people said viciously if Mother had rejected their application to join the Nicosia Ladies' Committee. Ownership of property, fields and farmland, so far away from the city did not mean you would be immediately welcomed by the closed set of Nicosia society. Farmers in general did not enjoy a great social standing in the late 1960s in our capital city and all agricultural pursuits were seen as simply a poor man's occupation by those who had been born and lived in the handful of streets within our walled city.

Mother was simultaneously disgusted and disappointed in her father, whom she had previously adored. Whenever we mentioned we wanted to visit him, she seemed alarmed. I don't believe she ever recovered from the shock of *Pappou*'s decision to re-marry. The men closest to my mother, like her father and her own husband seemed to have let her down her so badly she was inclined to always find fault with the behaviour of anyone of the male species. This extended to us, her two sons, most of all. My sister too, ever since I could remember, adopted the same attitude as our mother.

The new wife whom Mother never called 'mum', not even 'step-mum', was always referred to in conversations with Uncle Pericles as '*I misismeni*', the hated one. Grabbing the opportunity presented to him each time, our uncle's playful admonishment to our mother to 'Not use such strong language in front of the children' (when he himself would use full-on swearwords!), made our mother crack a smile that showed us how much she loved her brother. Still, uncle was unable to get our mother to move on—Mother kept insisting that this peasant woman had stolen their father away. And that *Haros* had taken their mother much too soon from them.

Worse, life had stolen her husband and banished him overseas. Our mother would often be found crying on her brother's shoulder. She'd never cry in front of us. Our uncle would morph from *incorrigible* to *You're my angel* and he would stoically comfort her, admitting he was *no angel*, addressing our mother by a nickname only he was permitted to use. Making jokes about stuff that had happened to them in their childhood that none of us ever knew.

I suspect our mother was not so much opposed to the second marriage on moral or religious grounds but rather on social ones. This 'Peasant from a godforsaken village no one has ever heard of' wore garish dresses, overbearing cheap perfume and what was worse, could not speak properly, never having learned to use correctly the plural form of you to address people politely, as Greek grammar rules dictated. Mother spoke to her using the formal mode of address and even in *Katharevousa* rather than demotic Greek. Instantly making her point that social class would perpetually separate them.

Mother never attempted to bridge the gap that existed between her city ways and that of a farmer's daughter like *our new grannie* as my older brother cheekily called *Pappou*'s new wife.

Our mother was not the kind of woman who liked the fact that men were different to her. Worse, on the rare occasions that Mother and Father were together in the same household, ours or in one of his sisters' houses, I never saw any demonstrated physical affection between them. I had seen other kids' parents give each other a kiss hello or goodbye. Our village relatives would always stand close to their spouse or have a loving arm around their husband or wife's shoulder or back.

But not my parents. I vowed I would be different to them.

Unlike my parents, I wanted everyone male I met under the age of thirty whom I considered handsome to give me a hug. And a kiss on both my cheeks. I can't say if my father ever gave me a hug or a kiss. I do remember him messing up my hair with his enormous palm when he would arrive from overseas for his brief visits. When I was really little and could hide behind large armchairs without being seen, I witnessed with my own eyes that Mother seemed to be always angry with my father, whenever he visited us. They would always be aggrieved when in conversation with each other and they thought none of us kids were listening. Mother always looked at Father as if he had done something truly terrible and that she would never find it in herself to forgive him.

To top it all off, apparently the lack of well-paying jobs on our island had forced him to go abroad, a long time ago, to various dusty countries in the Middle East. I say a long time as I did not have a memory of him ever living full-time with us in Areos Street. Monthly, a weird-looking stamped aerogramme envelope would be sent to Mother. The letters' contents were never directly shared with us. 'What is he saying?'/'Does he miss us?'/'When is he coming back?'

All three of us would fire these questions at our mother each time a letter was received but she would not say much except, 'Your father is working hard, and it is very, very hot where he is. He misses all his family.'

'When can we read his letters ourselves?' my sister would ask.

'When I decide you are old enough.'

'And when is that?' my brother would ask, buoyed by my sister's insolence.

'When I say so. And watch your tone, young man!' Mother would then walk away and as an afterthought announce that she'd be posting a letter back in three days. She would ask us to draw the outline of our palm on paper as our father wanted to know how much we had grown since his last visit. 'It's your father's request,' she'd say, displeased. 'If it's not done and on my bureau by then you'll have to explain yourselves to your father.'

'But he's not here,' my brother would remind her, totally unafraid.

I do not know what happened between my parents. To make my dad leave us. That is not something I was told. I guess that's my father's story to tell. And my mother's. I can only share with you how I felt about his leaving us. I felt cheated. I knew I would never leave my children willingly to seek work overseas. Everybody else in my class had a father who was present. All except for Socratis Melas, whose father was in prison for treason—and I was way too scared of Socratis to dare speak to him or ask him to hang around with me in the playground.

So, all our expectations, all our disappointments, our small failures and triumphs only had our mother as a judge to arbitrate on and pass judgment. Often, we would find fault with her because we imagined our father would have handled a situation in a better way. Although, we watched in awe when our mother would break bad news to someone in a very pleasant way, like a diplomat. Or listen to their bad news or grievance attentively. In a soothing tone call them *kaimeni* or if it was someone from the village relatives the more colloquial *kakomazali*. Offering a handkerchief that was always pressed. And a second or even third cup of Nescafe, served in fine bone china, or minted water and lemon slices if it was really hot outside. Cookies that were strictly allocated *for visitors only* by the large label on their canister. This prevented even Konstandinos from claiming in defence he didn't know they weren't for his daily consumption.

Our mother's voice and manner made the listener smile even when the news she was sharing was far from pleasant. We knew our distant father, our Uncle Pericles or even our beloved Aunt Hara all lacked this delicate social skill. The patience it took to attentively listen to all about other people's major or minor peccadilloes. Make the right noises of acknowledgement. But we still wanted to have our father there. We knew life would be better with both of our parents present.

Truth be told, we loved our mother the most when she wasn't being our mother but a good friend to others. Her ability to treat neighbours, relatives and acquaintances and even strangers so kindly and yet be very mean to us was something we were aggrieved by. Our sister insisted we were the reason for Father's choosing to leave us and work overseas. And it followed then that our mother blamed us for his leaving.

'But what have we done?' my brother would ask.

'That I can't answer,' my sister would say, almost sounding sympathetic.

8

· · · · · · · · · ·

The other pleasant memory I remember clearly of our neighbourhood is the cinema just past the corner of our street and Achilleos Street, in Marikas Kotopouli Street, directly parallel to our street. It was called *The Royal*. Its back exit was just over our ten-feet high backyard fence. It was a splendid-looking palace of dreams with chandeliers, deep carpet and gold-leaf furniture. The theatre was just beyond our mostly concreted, internal courtyard, which had three dwarf lemon trees, an almond tree and various overhanging branches of trees from next door providing shade. Like the fig tree that was so large it looked as if it were actually growing in our own garden.

The sunny side of the yard was taken over by giant pots of old-fashioned sweet-smelling big roses. On the other side of the yard, always in semi-shade was a small, L-shaped garden bed rich with basil, spring onions, thyme, oregano, parsley and mint. The yard was mostly taken over by the giant water tank and had no grass or playing area for us kids. We'd sit with our backs against its coolness when having watermelon, crusty bread and fetta on summer afternoons if doing so on the rooftop terrace was too hot. To this day, enjoying this simple summer meal always makes me lose it emotionally.

Mother used to take the three of us to the plush cinema once a month on a Saturday afternoon. She would be openly rather displeased if the *wrong kind of people* managed to buy tickets to the dress circle where we always sat. Mother was annoyed at the clicking and spitting these out-of-towners would make as they cracked open their salted pumpkin seeds incessantly. Worse, they spoke loudly throughout the picture. Even I knew, at eight, that talking at the cinema was strictly forbidden. How was it possible that adults did not know this?

Mother and the three of us in tow loved watching a newly released film. I remember fleeting glimpses of Melina Mercouri, Sophia Loren and most of all, Greece's *prima donna* of film, Aliki Vouyiouklaki. I was a big fan of Dionysios Papayianopoulos, the older actor with the huge eyebrows and the metallic voice who always played Aliki's businessman father. He was forever rescuing her out of whatever pickle she had found herself in, with equal measures of classic stoicism and parental anger.

I read that after his death they erected a statue of him in the village where he was born in recognition of his contribution to countless films. But that he had died alone in Athens. As did the comedian Sapfo Notara with a burned-out cigarette butt still in her hand and discovered days after passing.

In all the films we saw, Aliki's dad would always have lots of money and give his daughter whatever she wanted. He was always loving and affectionate. Even when he and we the audience knew she had had done something obviously wrong. I felt very envious of Aliki and did not approve of her misdemeanours as I desperately wanted to have a dad just like that. Even if he didn't have any money. Instead, I had *a missing-in-action father*, as Philadelphia referred to our dad.

And one we did not get to see often.

We loved Thannasis Vengos's films too, because of his slapstick routines, constant gags, his funny voice and his disaster-prone ways. So many other comedians, male and female whose faces and names now escape me. I do remember Rena Vlahopoulou's name, because she was hilarious and spoke so quickly that that in itself made us all laugh—but I am sure she has been dead now for a long time as she seemed old to us even then.

The mainland Greek actors, people like Konstantaras, always spoke way too fast and I never understood much of the colloquialisms they used. Still, I perceived an ambience of exhilaration and of joy in these comedies, sensations which were mostly absent within our household. I recall just being in the celluloid company of these actors made me feel that life could be happy. I associated going to the cinema with possibilities of joy, with storytelling.

I wanted to tell tales too. I had lots of stories to tell. Nobody wanted to hear them. I wanted very much to tell stories to my schoolmates, but I wasn't given a chance. Not only didn't I play soccer, but I also never had enough pocket money to bribe anyone into being my friend.

'Demosthenes *do* be quiet,' was Mother's most oft-spoken phrase to me. I did not know then that what she wished for she was going to get before too long.

On the corner of our street was where *Yiayia* lived. We called her *Yiayia* although she was not a real blood grandmother to us. She had grown up with Gradmama Konstandia. She might as well have been our grandmother though because we saw her more often than we saw Father's mother who lived in the village still. Our daily *yiayia*, *Yiayia* Efthimia lived with her peculiar, middle-aged daughter who *had visions*, adults explained, which, surprisingly, always came true. She forecasted the Turks coming in 1963 and sure enough they came. She knew the British would leave their colony here and they did. She knew whose husband was cheating with whom and what we would get for New Year's Eve from Saint Basil if we were good.

She wasn't born peculiar, Mother reminded us often. She became 'like a child' after a certain male relative 'interfered' with her. The meaning of this word was never explained to us and was always spoken about in a low, discreet voice by the older women who gathered so Eftihia (her name meant happiness) could read their coffee cup once a week. No one called her by her name behind her back. She was always called *I kakomazali*.

I thought she was a little crazy and was quite afraid of being left alone with her even for a wee bit. Her unpredictable nature frightened me, despite her jocular personality and the yummy chocolates she sneaked to us, surreptitiously, behind Mother's back. Perhaps she gave Mother chocolates too. Mother would always honourably defend *Yiayia* Efthimia's plight and that of *Poor Eftihia* in public. She kept *yiayia* employed as her unofficial ironing lady and always made a fuss of her when she visited us to deliver the pressed clothing, Manchester and handkerchiefs.

The men in the street mostly hated Eftihia with a vengeance but she steadfastly ignored their malicious catcalls. They didn't wolf whistle because she was attractive. Perhaps getting her own back for being treated as unworthy by them, she concentrated her efforts on telling every woman in the street all she knew about their husband's comings and goings, without being careful with what she said, or how she said it, like our mother always did.

49

9

By the time I was nine, I was a plump boy with breasts bigger than those of my girl classmates. Still with a broken nose and ashamed of the hairy birthmark on my chest.

I noted the presence of handsome military policemen standing guard on our flat rooftops around the city. Looking down on us in their splendid uniforms as we went about our business below. These young men in uniform with big guns scared the living daylights out of me but fascinated me at the same time. Sometimes, just before I fell asleep, I would think how fantastic it would be to be up on the rooftops with them, wearing the same glorious uniform, working alongside them, sharing meals, laughs, learning how to hold a cigarette. I would have imaginary conversations with them out loud and piss off my brother Konstandinos who was trying to fall asleep.

No matter what day you looked the young men would be there. Even if it was a public holiday, they would still be there on the rooftops of buildings three or four-storeys high. The UN soldiers of the peacekeeping force too. Danes mostly. Always obscenely tall, early twenties, fit and with machine guns at the ready. Especially when the Archbishop was out and about in his cavalcade. Being dramatic in nature, I sometimes imagined myself their target, via friendly fire, of course; for I was mostly a good boy.

My imaginative plots notwithstanding, I expected that all

adults were *civilised* (one of the first words I had learned from Mother). That they had to behave in a grown-up way at all times so I trusted that nothing could possibly happen that adults could not settle. Even so, these young men were on duty, day and night, watching us all, watching me. My questioning mind kept nagging me at night, making me think of things I could *not* articulate out loud for Konstandinos to hear.

Enosi (Unification with Greece) aspirants and EOKA B followers had already attempted to shoot down our Archbishop three times, each time without the success they craved. But never without bloodshed for the security men, the driver or the helicopter pilot. It also didn't help that one of these assassinations took place only a stone's throw away from our home and Miltiadou Street, the latter being where our favourite babysitter, Melpo lived. In 1967, sixty-six people died when a BEA flight to Nicosia exploded. General Grivas, a key figure in securing Cyprus's independence from the British Empire, was thought to be booked on the flight. The British Home Office sealed classified documents until 2067 so no one knows who was behind the bomb. If it were an assassination attempt on Grivas, it failed as Grivas changed his plans at the last minute.

On the way to Ayios Savvas church on Sundays, its ringing bells guiding us towards it, I would eagerly look for my secret friends in their glorious uniforms but sadly realise they were not on duty.

Sunday was for going to church, even for these young soldiers and afterwards, if you were lucky to be in a normal family, with a father that is, a father who drove a car, you would find yourself sitting at a Cypriot taverna. By the sea. Heartily tucking into your meal of fried red mullet and salad and side plates of tahini, olives and cucumber salad with plentiful crusty peasant bread flavoured with aniseed.

A jukebox would rotate bouzouki and *rembetika* (and now and again, an English pop song by *The Beatles*. My sister's favourite was *My Little Angel* by William Shakespeare who she insisted was not the great English playwright but a young guy from the land of kangaroos at the bottom of the world map.

It felt like heaven on earth when one of our first cousins would surprise us early on Sunday in his Triumph or Wolseley (Cousin Panikkos) and tell us to get ready— heaps better than going to boring church. Dimitris liked to take us to a different taverna each time, as he had an ambition to have his own seaside taverna one day and he wanted *to check out the competition.*

'Get a girl, then open a Kentron together and then buy a German car, that's my dream,' he used to tell me. Our eldest cousin Panikkos, who was dour, mostly silent and *not very bright* (Mother's estimation) just wanted to be a public servant of some kind, 'In or out of uniform, I don't care—as long as I am home by 4 pm, and have my meal prepared, I'll be happy,' he'd say when Mother would ask him about what he wanted to do with his life as we drove towards the village or to a monastery on the far northeast tip of our island.

I felt I was a silent traitor, for no matter how hard I tried to fathom it, I could never envisage my boring cousin's dream as my own. I knew, even at nine, that when I grew up, I would want very much to cook my own meals and not necessarily have to eat dinner at four o'clock. At least not every day. And I imagined someone, in or out of uniform, who looked like Panayiotis Doukas, would be sitting across the table from me. Effusively praising my culinary achievements. And smiling at me brimming with pure love.

10

· · · · · · · · · · · ·

Stete Parthena was not as cunning as her firstborn daughter; rather, it seemed to us that she had been in a bad mood for a long time. Perhaps since she was fourteen and was forced to marry *Pappou* Filippos. He was almost twenty years her senior and died long before I arrived on the scene.

Stete was old and mostly deaf even before I was born. I don't recall ever seeing her laughing or even smiling. Except once when an older male cousin, perhaps one of Aunt Skevou's sons, sat on a donkey and rode the donkey right up to where *Stete* was sitting in the sun.

'What do you think old woman?' he asked her.

Stete didn't miss a beat and dryly said, 'A donkey on the bottom, a donkey on top.'

We usually spent Easter holidays at *Stete*'s house. It was built out of mud and wheat stalks. The toilet was a hole in the ground outside the main part of the house on the side. To get to it you had to pass by the chicken coup and several virulent roosters who aspired to be great Lotharios. They screeched us all awake with their calls at *ungodly hours* as Mother complained, each morning.

The mostly black and brown chickens roamed freely during daylight within the mud side fence, but their coop had an inside wing to it too, where the chickens slept. Up below the eaves of the

53

roof, homing pigeons lived in square wooden cages. I couldn't tell you who may have built them into the wall or even when—they had always been a feature of the walls on either side of the very tall front door, a door that I do not recall ever seeing shut.

Just like everything else at our *Village Yiayia*'s place, the pigeons, the piglets, the kid goats and the chickens were not for bucolic decorative purposes—no, they were raised as food supply. I must have eaten pigeon meat hundreds of times when I was a kid, but I can't recall now how it tasted. The pigeons too kept us city kids awake throughout the night with their weird nesting soundtrack and flutter of wings. Weirdly, when we returned to our home in the city, we found that we missed all the sounds of *Yiayia*'s house. That we missed the sounds of birds and animals in the same way we longed to hear a traditional folksong sung by Aunt Hara to put us to sleep. She didn't have a good singing voice, but she *sang with aplomb* as Mother used to say diplomatically.

Inside, the main room of *Yiayia*'s house was a huge hall-like square with incredibly high walls. Each corner of the room served distinct purposes. Aunt Hara slept on a single cot in the right corner of the house, just outside the kitchen, which was off the main room and elevated by three steps. The kitchen had no benches or sink, nor pipes. It was just called the kitchen for there was a tiny stove, the sort you take on a camping trip with its little blue flame. Nothing like Mother's giant Leisure rangehood. By the tiny window, facing the front yard where the ducks ruled during the day, was the weaving apparatus, the *ergalio* where Aunt Hara spent most of her time during the day. It looked like a museum piece but was, all the same, perfectly functional.

Stete slept in another corner of the main room on a small bed, which was an improvement on Aunt Hara's camper-cot. A huge, medieval-looking tall bed with brass bits stood like an abandoned ship in another corner. We could not jump onto it without the assistance of chairs and a push on the bum. This was *Stete*'s marital bed which was now unused unless there was a big celebration like a wedding, when one and all arrived to stay, and people slept literally tenfold across it. Finally, Aunt Hara's wardrobe stood in the fourth corner. People guessed that she kept lots of money stashed in its bottom drawers but all I ever saw were some silver coins and a ring, which no longer fit her, stored there, wrapped in one of her hand-woven ornate handkerchiefs.

A massive dining table made from sturdy wood, not in the least bit elegant, but that still had, in our mother's opinion *a certain bucolic charm about it,* stood in front of the French armoire. The table had served on occasions as a bed, an ironing board and as a birthing station. We were banished from the house should such an event take place. Usually to Aunt Skevou's higgledy-piggledy homestead next door.

Normally, the table was covered with one of Aunt Hara's colourful woven creations. Or a crocheted tablecloth one of my other aunts had made. If we arrived early enough on a Friday afternoon to spend a long weekend at *Village Yiayia*'s house, we were surprised to find the table bare. Our aunt, always messy in her own personal grooming was a stickler for carrying out household tasks that all good village women had to carry out.

'What would the neighbours think if they didn't see me doing the washing every Friday? I'd be the talk of the town.' We were impressed with our aunt as she never failed to surprise us. Just when we thought we had figured her out she would say or do something entirely opposite to what we expected of her. She was never boring.

A jug of water, covered with a frilly cloth napkin (also made by our aunt) and always filled to the brim stood on the edge of one corner of the enormous table. It never ceased to amaze me just how many people could sit around this table when all the family would gather together for the many baptisms, engagement parties, funerals and weddings celebrated regularly.

Women always outnumbered the men at such gatherings. Even as children we knew that the men's absence was not a subject of discussion. A number of aunts had lost their husbands very early and some of their daughters had taken a leaf out of their mothers' books and had husbands who were *away*. Aunt Hara did not care to respond to my daring and constant questions about these AWOL men's whereabouts when I found myself by her side in the kitchen as she dished platters. Instead, she would hand me a piece of roasted goat or a chicken drumstick *yiahni* and prod me to eat it while it was piping hot. She had taught me well by ignoring my questions and asking me tricky questions instead. I was trying to trick her into sharing information I was convinced she withheld, but I never once managed to get her to spill the beans. Not even about her youngest sister, Aunt Tzeni (baptised Eugenia), whom she could not stand and referred to as *a jezebel*.

A first cousin usually collected us from Areos and drove us to Father's village. It was either Cousin Dimitris, who had the looks of a Mediterranean matinee idol, a moustache and a cute Triumph

Herald Sports to boot or droll Cousin Panikkos, driving his old sensible, four-door Wolseley. Panikkos thought Dimitris was *a show-off.* Dimitris thought Panikkos was *a boring pain in the arse.* Philadelphia would throw petrol onto the fire by telling Panikkos that he was simply jealous. That Dimitris was so handsome. That he could afford to buy a British sports car. This would make Panikkos grow even quieter than his normal withdrawn self, allowing us the pleasure of listening to pop music all the way to the village at a volume level Mother would have never condoned.

Mother, I remember, didn't come with us to the village. Perhaps she came later, just before Easter Saturday or something. She arrived in a Mercedes service taxi, some days later. I never once saw Mother catching public transport. She most certainly never caught the coach to the village. I always wondered what Mother would get up to in the city while we were gone. I imagined her to have a whole other secret life. A grown-up, secret life she could live during those weeks when she was freed of looking after her children on her own. Indulging in her whims, briefly untethered from responsibility as single mum.

11

· · · · · · · · · · · ·

We were ecstatic to be staying with Aunt Hara on her home ground with her lax rules. 'Remember: just stay away from the bulls,' was all she advised us. Mother knew better than to interfere. Perhaps that's why she left us alone for a week or two before she joined us. To give childless Aunt Hara a taste of sole authority over us.

We loved eating different food, especially as our *Village Yiayia* had a mud oven where lemon potatoes and goat would be succulently cooked, along with other game and fowl we normally weren't served at Areos. The meat of these dishes would melt in our mouths, and we would eat much more than we imagined we could.

However, we hated two things about the village: one was no television; but we got over that fairly quickly. The second was having to bathe in the shed where the wheat was originally stored but that now served as an all-purpose barn, and a bathroom to boot. We stood naked (we, who had a bidet at home) on the mud floor, hoping Aunt Hara would soon put an end to our ordeal and that the chickens would be less curiously forward than last year's lot. We screamed and screeched and cried if a chook, especially a big rooster came within three feet of us. Poor Aunt Hara cajoled and castigated us, all at the same time.

'*Soot vre*! They're only chickens.'

58

'I want a real bathroom.'

'Aunt, why don't you and *Stete* have a bidet?'

'Bidet? What? *Theleis pittes*?' Ssh. Come on. Almost over.'

And another bucket of soapy scalding hot water would be tipped over us without any concern. Konstandinos complained that there were tiny feathers in the bucket and that Aunt Hara just wanted us all to smell like her chickens.

'Now, where's Philly? Philadelphia? Where's your sister?'

'I don't know.'

Philadelphia, had taken it upon herself, being the eldest and female, to bathe next door at Aunt Skevou's place. She, courtesy of her husband's rich sister through marriage, had had a 'douche-shower' installed. Aunt Hara turned a blind eye to this revolt among her troops because it meant less buckets of hot water for her to boil in the giant *kazani* and then carry to the barn. But she was insistent that we boys could not make use of the modern shower in her sister's house. She was always going on about *toughening us up a little*. Konstandinos and I *were men*, she often told us. We had to be toughened up, even if it was only for a couple of weeks.

In fact, all the village relatives were worried that as far as boys went, Konstandinos and I were much too clean, far too well-spoken, and much *too soft*. I never understood then why they called us soft because to me only the yellow baby chooks were soft. Konstandinos even made the unforgivable mistake of succumbing to sunstroke after having been made to accompany one of our older first cousins on a shepherding expedition for the entire day in forty-five-degree temperatures.

'Nobody must ever find out he got sick being in the sun. Not even your mother.' Aunt Hara made us all promise and we did for we could never betray the one person in the world who showed us love so freely. We knew she loved us even if she was admonishing us for having broken a terracotta urn or refusing to go to church with her. It was something in her tone that we picked up—we knew she would let us get away with anything.

There was also a third thing about the village which worried us all; but it was in a different category to the aforementioned two. This third thing was far more grisly and more graphic than our worst dreams. There were no frozen chickens in the village. The local general store did not sell chicken. If you wanted to eat chicken in the village there was one choice available to you: you just ate chooks you killed with your own hands. Or you didn't eat chicken. Aunt Hara did not usually take an active part in this when we were visiting. She might have done this intentionally so as not to insult our city sensibilities—she knew first-hand how precious and squeamish we could be.

Stete was the killer. She would run after the chickens (who must've known what was coming), until she had grabbed one. She would then proceed to kill the unfortunate bird with her bare hands. This was a woman who was almost blind and technically deaf. The head of the unfortunate chook would be thrown lifeless to one side but the body of the bird would be let loose to fly here, there and everywhere, fluttering in the air, (like a cat I once saw get run over), blood spluttering and spilling all around onto the rocky yard, until, with a frightening thump, it would fall dead on the ground. The rocks were like the giant formations of grey stone one sees at the bottom of the sea at beaches like Salamis, where Dimitris often took us for a dip. Apparently, proof that water had once covered *Yiayia's* entire village.

We touched a corpse once. Well, more like prodded it. Konstandinos reckoned it was still warm. A bucket of hot steaming water stood waiting. The bird was dunked in a bucket of boiling water and soon *Stete* was plucking away. Philadelphia and I usually hid during these cruel ceremonies of life on the farm, but Konstandinos never missed one. Despite his frailty with the sheep under the hot sun he enjoyed village life the most, (for he didn't have to be neat and clinically clean for a change) and he usually stood by the scene of the bloodied crimes, urging *Stete* on.

The absolute annual highlight of our village visits was staying up way past midnight for the amazing Easter Saturday service at the new church, which stood next to the more picturesque ancient one that was falling apart.

We would fill our pockets with red-coloured eggs which we were supposed to use to wish everyone in the church a *Hristos Anesti,* but which Konstandinos ate furtively instead during the service. We didn't blame him, for Philadelphia and I were hungry too, but we didn't have the guts to do the same thing. We admired Konstandinos's boldness. We had to fast you see. Usually just for a week, although Mother made us forego the pleasures of certain foods for the full forty days. Philadelphia would sometimes threaten Konstandinos that she would tell on him and would put on a disgusted face that she sadly, would keep on standby for the rest of her life. I never knew why, but I too acted disgusted, taking my cue from my sister, who, for a while, was my role model for everything.

I was in Grade 3 before I realised, painfully, that boys didn't get their fingernails painted. Or shave their legs. And the social repercussions of doing so would taint a boy's reputation for the entirety of their school career. But nobody had bothered to forewarn me about such things.

A veritable banquet awaited us when we finally returned to *Village Yiayia*'s house in the early hours of the morning. A couple of times, I got lost in the huge crowds and had to find my own way back to *Stete*'s alone, in the total dark as *Stete*'s village didn't have streetlights. All the village dogs would growl as I walked by and sometimes give chase to the boy from the city. Every house had at least two dogs minding the sheep during daylight hours and acting as fearsome guards at nights. As I scattered and ran, careful not to trip on the countless stone formations which jutted out without warning in the fields, I felt certain that had I lived in the village permanently, the dogs would have been as friendly as the docile dogs presented in the books I read about quietly in my bed at Areos Street.

As a first plate, we usually had egg lemon soup followed by boiled chicken with chicken livers and giblets—at four am. We then went to bed until eleven am when we would wake up to find Aunt Hara in the midst of things. Her *fourno* would be full of food; meat mostly of every kind and prepared in a variety of ways.

Relatives of Father's would also present themselves both from next door and from several neighbouring villages. It was like waking up to a boisterous dream. I would sit on Dimitris's knee and be in seventh heaven as he smiled his perfect smile at me throughout the day. Panikkos would dare me to drink more KEO beer and Mother would look at me murderously.

One last thing I recall from my village sojourns maybe because of all the amazing colours in the dark: outside the church, boys, young, middle-aged and old, would burn an effigy of Judas. A giant fireball burnt throughout the night. We had strict instructions from Mother not to go anywhere near this display of *gratuitous pyromania*. Such *déclassé* things did not occur anywhere near Areos 36.

I was the only boy in Grade 3 who knew what *déclassé* meant. Our Mother used that word a lot to indicate displeasure with anything. Konstandinos would cop *déclassé* a lot. He'd point to a sports car sprayed in a Ferrari-red and Mother would look disappointed. 'Konstandine, that is very *déclassé*.'

One year, coming back for the first day of school straight from our Easter village break, we were greeted with the news that the smashed car we had passed earlier on the highway coming into town, contained the remains of Nikiforos and Elena. They were the only children of the second-grade teacher, whose husband operated the mechanic's workshop near our house. Elena was in my class, with the much feared (and loathed), Kyria Androniki, at the helm. Nikiforos was in Grade 5, so we didn't know him as Grades 5 and 6 were separated and had their own playground which was out of bounds to us.

We prayed at assembly. Kyria Androniki who had a moustache and a goatee, openly cried and for once didn't tell anyone to tuck their shirt in. Didn't call anyone a *peasant's son* or a *farmer's daughter* for an entire week. School was silent that morning and we were home by eleven.

A month later, Nikiforos and Elena's dad, Kyrios Mavris, drove me to hospital in his Rover coupe with the woodgrain dash, after Konstandinos had chased me with his water pistol around the courtyard. Trying madly to run away from him I got caught on a steel fence handle, nearly having to have my arm amputated as a result. To my busted nose, my hairy birthmark, I now had added the deformity of an eight-centimetre ugly scar on the inside of my left elbow. Mother later bought Kyrios Mavris a shirt to thank him. I recall it was a black shirt.

Father never once spent an Easter holiday break with us in his mother's house.

12

There was commotion at Areos 36.

Visitors had arrived from the villages in preparation for the imminent arrival of Father, who was to visit for three days. Little round, metal baths normally used to soak white linen tablecloths and bedsheets had been filled instead with bottles of alcohol, Coca Cola, Fanta and 7UP. The kitchens, both the one downstairs and our own upstairs, as well as *Yiayia* Efthimia's down the road, were all utilised. All brimming with delicacies and home-made efforts, some, admittedly, of dubious quality as Father's sisters would make all sorts of things with fried dough.

Dubious was another word Mother used very often. *She is of dubious origin* was a favourite expression of hers.

Overwhelmed by the horde of village relatives, Mother would call upon several of her city matrons to do combat on her behalf, so as not to be outdone or find herself totally defenseless and outnumbered, at the total mercy of Father's village relations. It was one thing visiting the village three times a year for eighteen hours or two days at a time and putting up with village ways; it was an entirely different matter having them visit you and stay in your own house for days.

Our father's relatives did not seem anxious about arriving *en masse* at our house. Always bringing along with them extras, people who had never actually even met our father. For instance, some *kotziakari* who was on her own and had known *Yiayia* in passing, or mates of our teenage first-cousins. All of these people arrived on our doorstep, supposedly to welcome Father back to our island. Many brought with them a sleeping bag or slept on cots we used to pull out of the sheds in summer to take to our cabin by the beach in Kerynia.

Aunt Hara would arrive at our house three weeks before Father's arrival. She loved our father the most and never missed an opportunity to show it. Conversely, most of his other sisters all seemed fearful of expressing any emotion in public. Only Aunt Areti was perpetually jolly and full of laughter. Even before she had her morning coffee. We did not know any grown-up who was jubilantly happy to chat away to us in the morning like she did. Aunt Areti was laughing in her high pitched piercing voice even before she'd had a Nescafe or two Greek coffees, like most adults needed.

'They've brought with them the meat from all the piglets they have slaughtered in cold blood,' Philadelphia would snigger disdainfully.

Our father was in fact the baby of the family, the last-born, but to us he might as well have been the eldest. He had six sisters and a brother, Uncle Socrates, who had had white hair forever. Except for Aunt Hara and Aunt Skevou, we hardly saw Father's other sisters as they lived in far-flung villages where the service taxis dropped you off on the main road and you had to make the two-kilometre or more trek to the actual village, on foot. Our city shoes soles were not suitable for traipsing through red soil. Not having a car and more importantly a male of our own who could drive us there, we lived in isolation from most of the relatives on Father's side. Mother could have learned to drive but she was never as progressive as the scorned Kyria Paotta who drove the narrow streets of our city in a burnt orange Fiat 124 coupe. Still, now and then, out of duty, we would visit our aunts.

On rare visits to the villages, Mother always took gifts. The aunts too, gave us presents in return. Besides their bottled, syrupy fruit and bottled whole walnuts we gulped down without munching, they had the habit of giving us chickens—live chickens!—despite Mother's polite protestations that one was not allowed to keep poultry in the city, especially on the second floor of an *Arhontiko.*

Konstandinos loved getting chickens as presents. He would take his chicken, and mine and Philadelphia's and organise what he called flying competitions where he would try to make the chickens fly in the expansive yards of the village relatives. So, as it usually turned out, our aunts had to pluck the failed athlete chickens first, thanks to Konstandinos's genius, and the decapitated chickens never got to see the Big Smoke.

On the day Father was due to arrive from Damascus, Bahrain, Tripoli, or Abu Dhabi (I never was very good at geography and could not keep up with Father's postings) the busloads of relatives and non-relatives descended upon us. Even Mother's closed rooms would be opened for occupation.

We kept out of the way of the grown-ups as Mother had instructed us.

Children were meant to be seen, made to kiss old people of both genders twice on the cheeks (very often unpleasant) and then on the hand, look clean, speak properly and be invisible to the adults in the room.

It felt funny being banished in our own house for the duration of the relatives' visit. I often broke Mother's rule and in the middle of the night would creep into the room where my older male cousins slept and edge myself between them.

Many a time, I would wake up in the middle of the night to find an adult male's arms around me and feel secure. Wanted.

13

. . . .

At the new Nicosia International Airport, we used to have a giggle at all the strange, hairy, swarthy men who were dressed in *djellabas* and who were darker than anyone we knew. Darker even than the *Hojahs* who would climb up the minarets and holler their call to prayer each day around sunset, in the Turkish quarter, five blocks from Areos. I was fascinated by the automatic doors, opening and closing as if by magic and exhausted the patience of whichever adult was entrusted with my care for the day. Mother was always *emotional* (that's what the adults used to whisper about her at least) on such days and would abandon control of me in my harness.

It was a relief to be left off the leash, like a bolting pony and wander freely for farther than a few feet around the terminal unrestricted by mother's controlling tug halting my movement. Instead, I could go pretty much wherever, an adult relative or older cousin trailing me. Castigating me if I dared to run like a freed gazelle around the enormous, cavernous space the West German architect firm Dorsch and Gehrmann had brought to life. I'd climb up onto the huge round red pouffes and hope the day would come when I'd be tall enough to simply sit on them unassisted. I'd marvel at all the framed posters on the walls and wonder where all these exotic places were, who or what Yves Saint Laurent was and be reassured by the familiar, local Bata Shoes poster. I'd look up at the enormous circular light fixtures and wonder how the light tubes borrowed natural light from the rooftop, funnelling it down into the enormous pendants, their ring of grey making the light fittings seem like clouds of white illumination, as if all of us standing underneath were lit by our very own spotlight. Making me half-expect God or one of the Saints were about to descend to earth, and parachute down the light tube tunnel and into our lives.

No matter how many times one of the adults had telephoned the airline company to confirm the flight was on schedule, we always had to wait. And wait. Finally, a group cheer and a frisson of excitement would break out as the aeroplane landed. If the plane's tail did not show the Cyprus Airways logo, I would ask whoever was around which airline it was, and which country owned it. I had never been to Bahrain or to Syria or Libya. I wanted desperately to finally go beyond Customs, wave my passport and ticket to the always-tetchy looking staff and walk on the tarmac and onto the plane. Take my seat next to my father.

Another wander through the sleek terminal would ensue as we always had to wait for ages for our VIP visitor to go through Customs.

'They're delaying him on purpose,' Aunt Hara would propose, without anyone having asked her for an explanation. 'It's a plan they have,' she would add, 'they're no fools, they know we're here. One of Aristides's nephews is the manager now. God knows why. He is doing this to spite me, for divorcing his wretched uncle, may God rest his soul. I know it.'

We nodded. We really didn't care that much. The most exciting thing for us was the fact that we'd be drinking Coke for a month after our VIP had left. Mother always over-catered as she did not want to be criticised by Father's sisters as being tight and unwelcoming. But she never pleased them as they thought her a spendthrift for throwing their brother's money away without a care whilst he sweated bullets in some Middle East petroleum mine.

Aunt Hara always made sure, even if she had to kick someone else aside, that she was the first to greet the visitor with shouts and wails and her ready tears. She caused a scene on many an occasion, reciting as she did her rhyming poetry that she could put together on the spot, about any subject. It was one of her many creative talents. After having greeted the sea of villagers, the VIP then hugged each of us in descending order, according to our birth status.

'Say hello to your father,' various people would order and push me forward. I resented being told what to do by people I only saw twice a year. This was the man who regularly asked in letters sent from various cities in the Middle East, for us to trace the outline of our palms onto thin aerogramme paper to send to him but who never once sent back a tracing of his own hand.

I traced my hand carefully, like a surgeon making an incision. This was no simple, rushed, school drawing. Father had requested our aerogramme art. I was convinced that I needed to trace my palm with absolute precision, to demonstrate to my father how much I wanted to please him. To show him my love.

Why couldn't we have our father to ourselves?

In peace?

Why couldn't he ever drive me to school or walk me home, just once?

Why didn't he have a car like the fathers of the other boys?

Why didn't he come to church with us on Sundays? If he had,

I could sit on the male side of the church and get away from all those bloody *kotziakares* Mother made me kiss until I was sick in the stomach.

'*Ate re, pigaine*, go say something to your pa,' Aunt Hara would order and when that tactic had failed, she would simply push me towards this stranger with cool blue eyes.

But it was too late.

My shyness was rattled. I wanted to hide, something I was fond of doing in times of distress—not just under dining tables and polished French armoires, but also behind the school shed, under beds, in a giant toolbox in a mechanic's garage. Any place where it was dark, and people could not touch me. Men wanting me to do things. I obediently did what all adult men told me to even if I had a weird feeling that what was being asked of me was not right. I was told clearly not to talk about it.

Father was not demonstrative in his love. Was not enthusiastic in his quick embraces that left me wondering if there had been an actual embrace. His rare presence made me see how empty my feelings were for him. Standing before us at the terminal, Father would simply pull at my cheek, like all his damn relatives did and that would do it. I would vow not to speak to him for the entire period of his visit and just ignore him. The way he ignored us by not being there. What paternal rights did he have over us anyway?

I wasn't the only one unimpressed by Father on his visits. Konstandinos used to be pissed off too, because the three of us would only be allowed to eat after all the grown-ups had finished and had moved to the living room (the women) or the enclosed courtyard below to smoke (all the men). To Konstandinos, eating his barbecued souvlaki cold and never getting a drumstick was a much bigger grievance than having to kiss all the old hags from the village.

I noted though, Philadelphia and Konstandinos were slightly more friendly towards our father than I was. I guess they had known him longer before he left to work in the Middle East. Had memories, of him of shared experiences.

I kept promising myself that when I got older, I would confront him and ask him to explain why he had left. All the other boys in my class had fathers who managed to find a job in our city. Why didn't he try harder to find work on our island?

Why couldn't my father be rich like the dad in Aliki's films? Other boys' fathers, their hair slicked back, in their best suit, took them to church on Sundays and then onto a seaside taverna for lunch. Father never took us to a taverna for Sunday lunch. As hard as Dimitris tried to be a substitute father to us, we all knew he was way too young.

Nicosia International Airport has been abandoned since the 1974 invasion. It is in the UN buffer zone. It would eviscerate me to see it ruined. I'm no engineer but I am pretty certain the automatic doors would no longer open on approach.

The day after Father's arrival at Areos Street, his sisters and their entourage would have lunch with us and then several of them, along with their brood, would pile onto their regional buses for the return trip to their village homes. In the late afternoon, Father would sometimes borrow Kyria Panayiota's husband's car, a two-door Colt and take us to the outskirts of the city. To the edge of the forest. He would proudly point out the area where he had once worked as a ranger. He'd be mostly quiet so when he did actually speak, we listened attentively.

'I told your mother we couldn't afford three children, but she kept wanting to try and have another girl.'

As hard as I tried to picture it, I couldn't see Father as a ranger. He didn't look young enough, wasn't tall enough, had never worn a hat in my presence. He had never been in uniform I decided as I had never seen him in one, in the flesh. Unlike my Uncle Pericles, in his crisp, sergeant's uniform every morning and with his hair slicked, his stiff hat, popping round for a quick lunch with Mother or regularly stopping by for a Nescafe chat with our teary-eyed mother, on his way home from work.

Father looked nothing like the heroes in the comics Konstandinos stashed under his bed. The comics I got to read second-hand had shown me that real rangers had dense moustaches. Even though I knew by then that I couldn't rely on those comics much for reality. The heroes in my brother's comics could fly, could do anything they wanted to set things right. I could not.

Without any notice, Father suddenly hit the brakes of the borrowed Colt, got out of the driver's seat and beckoned us to hurry to his side.

'Look!' he said, excitedly. 'Over there!'

Trees were falling. One by one. Thunderous thumps echoed in the silence of the dense scrub. At first, it seemed to us that the trees were shrieking, protesting in excruciating pain. The trees fell safely at a great distance from us, fell apart and away from each other. When they were down on the ground, dust settling all around them in slow motion, I noticed the space between each of them.

I desperately wanted to reach out for my father's hand.

I watched him standing there, in the gaps of the felled trees, floundering badly in the narrow messy gaps, losing his footing, not really knowing what to do with us, helpless, not knowing how to bridge the space between us.

14

Uncle Pericles's three children were from three different wives. Somehow the siblings, Aliki, Petros and Alekkos (who arrived on the scene much later) all loved each other and got on more famously than Philadelphia, Konstandinos and I ever did. Aliki and Petros were considerably older than me; Philadelphia being the only one who was close to their age. I was generally lumped in with Alekkos, who was two years younger than me and a pain to boot.

He sulked. He threw tantrums. He boasted that his mother was rich, (but we had eavesdropped on Mother discussing rumours that the woman in question was nothing more than a gold-digger). Alekkos, when he finally learned to speak, also wrongly claimed that their house in the suburbs was better than ours because they had more lawn to play on and heaps of birds in the aviary.

Alekkos's claims were pure fantasy, total bull, because we'd been to their rented home. It was nothing special, looked like all the other houses in the street and was not very private. It didn't even have a fence. There were no huge wooden doors with a knocker on, just a small door with a buzzer that rang like a fire alarm when you pressed it.

'The only marble in that house is the chipped ashtray,' Philadelphia reassured me when I asked her once if Alekkos was right.

The *déclassé neighbours*, Mother often commented, kept an eye on everything that went on at Uncle's and would routinely ring the police if they saw a car parked out the front that they did not recognise.

It was at this house that a meeting was once held between my uncle and all his wives. I have no knowledge why such a meeting was held. I am guessing it had something to do with custody of my first cousins. I would have loved to have been there on that day when the two ex-wives were introduced to the third, much younger wife. Mother had only shared with us that 'It was a humiliating fiasco,' and that she didn't know 'How a boy with a private French tutor, a Madame no less, and even a pianoforte teacher, could ever grow into such a pig of a man.'

Mother was quietly hard done by, had her own grievances we guessed. She was raised at a time when having a son was something to boast of. Having a daughter? Not so much. Her mother had been a real society rebel by smoking openly in front of everyone, men included, and by keeping separate bedrooms from Grandpa Demos, something that was *avant-garde* at that time. By holding card nights at Areos Street where real money exchanged hands and the ladies and gentlemen had more than one glass of sherry. And so, my poor mother grew up to be a nice but self-righteous girl without any discernable vices. Perhaps in an attempt to counteract her own mother's socially unacceptable behaviour?

She joined the Ladies Committee at the church as well as the Philanthropic Ladies' League so as to compensate perhaps, through her charity and community work, for the terrible transgressions of her mother. Perhaps she may have done all these things in an attempt to counterbalance Uncle Pericles's behaviour too. He rode around the narrow streets of our old city in the biggest BMW motorbike Nicosia had to offer. His second bike, the reserve machine, was primed and ready to go should his primary bike be needing a service or a part that was ordered from BMW genuine parts suppliers only.

He *flirted shamelessly*, Mother said often in her disapproving tone. It was clear to us that our favourite uncle had definitely taken after Grandmama Konstandia.

'How could she have been so selfish as to die years and years before I was born?' I would moan, asking this of Mother, sulking. As usual, she would just ignore me. Then, after some time had passed and I had thought Mother would say nothing more on the subject, as an afterthought she would add, 'Why don't you go ask your uncle what caused your grandmother's premature death?', and I inferred even then, that our uncle's *shenanigans* had probably driven *Yiayia* to an early grave. Personally, I was of the opinion that Grandmama got bored to death with our ineffectual tailor *Pappou*. I may have been baptised after *Pappou* Demosthenes, but this didn't mean I had to like him.

Pappou Demos never paid us much attention, even when we would visit him. He never told us any stories or gave us chocolates or coins behind Mother's back. Weirdly, even though he was a tailor, he incongruously never made a suit for us or even a pair of trousers. The suits Mother made us wear for the family photos that never included our father, were always made by a swarthy tailor in the Turkish quarter of town.

Aunt Hara reckoned that Grandmama Konstandia had been

poisoned by one of her over-zealous card-playing buddies for being *too good at pilfering all their money*, but that's another story I cannot personally confirm.

Once, it happened that we were all sitting down to have a meal, even *Pappou* and Father. I noticed that both adult men were silent and focused strictly on the plentiful food on their plate and on their heavy tumblers of cognac. Looking at both of them, it struck me that my own father was a younger replica of my distant Grandpa and guessed that may have been the true reason why Mother had married him. She had only known how to deal with an absent male as she was growing up and I guess she learned that all men were distant, even when present, and went about seeking such a man to marry.

I shared this theory with my Uncle Pericles once, but he didn't support or refute my point of view. He just pulled my cheeks and falsely admonished, '*Re, esy eisai alepou, loukoumoudi mou*' (*You're a little fox, my sweet Turkish delight*), before advising me to hold on tight to his broad back. The smell from his leather jacket was overwhelming as we cruised the streets on his loud bike. I don't recall ever being frightened of riding on his motorbike way back then. It worried me though, that I never actually wanted to have my own motorcycle one day, despite loving riding as a passenger behind my uncle on his very loud beast of a machine.

My passivity made me anxious. I felt immense joy when my uncle would drop by and collect me before taking me to a police function. Once a year, all the police families would be fed a Christmas banquet and Santa Claus would parachute down and give us all beautifully wrapped gifts. I thought my uncle was the ants' pants. He would feed me *pastourma* and tell me to stop whining when I would protest that the chilli of the cured beef was too hot.

Once, when Aliki, all of seventeen, was left in charge of all of us whilst our mother attended a charity meeting and uncle was showing his prospective new wife from the mountains in Paphos around his favourite haunts of our old city, cousin Petros made us pretend we were his patients. He'd give us a squeeze on our arse and pinch us hard on the arm.

Petros was an idol of mine because he was as rambunctious as I was passive. In company, I retreated into my shell of doubt. I never felt I would grow up to be as strong as Petros, who resembled his father in miniature form. Or as handsome as Panayiotis Doukas or Cousin Dimitris. Petros was very fond of me, always looking out for me. But he bossed me around too. Making me tell lies to the grown-ups about where he was when he was smoking. I prayed to God to help me to grow up and be as confident as Petros.

15

At the beginning of summer in 1974, my life changed.

It was the fifteenth of July and like always, very hot. Mother had left early for her monthly trip to Barclays, in town, to collect the money Father used to send each month from Libya, Lebanon, Bahrain, or from wherever he happened to be that year.

I was listening to the radio and Philadelphia was sitting nearby practising the conjugation of irregular verbs. She was attending English classes two afternoons a week at the Nicosia Institute of Technology. My brother and I were envious of this and tried to eavesdrop on her learning so that we could parrot a word or two in English, and by doing this, piss her off a little. We loved stirring our sister.

By mid-morning the heat got worse. In a week or two, we would be sleeping in our thatch cabin by the beach at Kerynia and we looked forward to this two-week break all year. The cabin meant we would have opportunities to swim, eat *kleftiko* from the seaside, open-air taverna and try to get on with other children our age. In the city, the reason Mother gave for not allowing us out to play in the street was that it was *too common* and because: *all sorts of horrible things may happen* to us. We absolutely believed that had we played hopscotch on the narrow ancient streets, brigands would snatch us away only to sizzle us like giant souvlakia or a kid-goat, skinned and thrown on charcoal at Easter.

The radio went dead. I suspected it was the batteries again, as lately, Philadelphia would sneak the radio into her bedroom late at nights to tune into the English Hit Parade from London.

To our surprise, the radio started playing the Greek National Anthem. I knew then that something was not quite right. Because the anthem was seldom played on the radio, well, unless it was Independence Day or some old hero, like an old archbishop or a former government minister, had died. A muffled, female announcer's voice then came through the airwaves telling us all that our President had been killed, ('*O Makarios einai nekros*') and that there had been a coup d'état by the Greek Junta.

Our own people, the dictator military rulers of our Motherland, had killed our leader—the only head of government in the democratic world to also be the head of the church. Our countries shared Dionysios Solomos's 1823 anthem. My island had adopted the anthem officially in 1966. At one hundred and fifty-eight stanzas, *The Hymn to Liberty*, our national anthem, set to Nikolaos Mantzaras' stirring music, was the longest anthem of any country in the world. Now, people who spoke the same language and ate *tyropittes* and *diples* and *bougatsa* for breakfast like us, our countrymen, who worshipped the same movie stars as we did, were killing our own soldiers. I blamed the young King Constantine II for not having been strong enough to quash the generals' coup. These older wily military men had tricked the naïve King and easily deposed him in 1967, sending him into exile.

The announcer's voice went on, assuring us all that what was unfolding was to our advantage. It was for the future good of our country. Calmly warning us that anyone caught outside their home after four in the afternoon would be shot dead, on the spot. This rather unsettling and sinister announcement was repeated at two-minute intervals, in between which, rousing patriotic marching tunes were let loose. We had only heard this kind of music when the army used to march through the city streets on March 25, and all of us, in our best school uniforms, would stand on the footpaths, sometimes in the rain, clapping, waving paper flags and being patriotic Greek children.

Philadelphia and I were petrified. I somehow guessed that our mother would not be bringing home the customary treats of white chocolate that day. We stayed huddled inside the house, funnily enough in a room that was usually out of bounds to us. Perhaps its darkness, its ghostly, covered furniture and mustiness served as comforts. Normally, I was curious about what may be hidden in the out-of-bounds room but that morning I did not peek under the painting sheets to investigate, not once.

We waited for Mother.

Our Father of course wasn't with us.

I don't know how long Philadelphia and I stayed huddled together in the forbidden room but when we heard the downstairs door slam shut, out of habit, we rushed out of the forbidden room, fearing repercussions for being in there.

We naturally expected Mother to reassure us that everything was fine. But Mother seemed different. A triangle of redness formed between her neck and her ample bosom. There she was, hair half done, carrying her bag, the brown stiff leather one she always carried when going into town, shouting to us to stop talking, mumbling Konstandinos's name over and over again. We knew Mother was not well, for she never left the hairdresser's salon before she was done. It suddenly dawned on us that our brother was not with us, having left for his first high school summer camp that same morning.

She started crying.

Mother had never cried in front of me before. She sobbed, while my sister and I stood by, quietly watching her in silence. Embarrassed. She kept asking us where her tablets were. We couldn't find them. Our brother's name kept popping up. He was going to assemble opposite the Presidential Palace, where the *Gymnasio* was that same morning to board a bus to Troodos for his year's annual camp. Mother had heard that there had been a lot of shooting in the area given its proximity to our Archbishop's home. I wasn't too worried about Konstandinos because I didn't think anything bad could happen to him. I mean, he was my older brother, he was indestructible. Like his comics heroes. He might hurt his knee, it might look ugly and be bleeding for a bit but then he'd carry on, not noticing.

Mother kept wishing out loud that Father could come home right now. My sister and I just looked at each other, worried. I was not an adult and even I knew that he was overseas.

Father had never been there with us when he might have been useful. Like when Konstandinos hit his head on the corner edge of the armoire and needed stitches in hospital. Or to clap loudly when I got a prize for drawing at school. He'd never as much as bought me a pencil, let alone a set of pencils or art paper, to encourage my creativity.

He was missing even when I desperately needed his strength.

Like when men's arms and hands would hold me tight, and I could not extricate myself from their hold no matter how hard I tried.

Mother said nothing more to us and walked away. She went to her room. She closed the door. I was starving and told Philadelphia. For once, she didn't tell me I was a pain or a big fat *lotta*. She actually prepared some food for us. It was news to me that she could cook. She took a tray into Mother's bedroom, but she did not eat anything, except for taking a few sips of her peppermint tea. She asked for a Coca-Cola which we all knew she wasn't supposed to drink.

Later, my sister and I tip-toed around the big house hoping we might find Mother in the kitchen making her egg-lemon potato soup (*entrada*) or the *pastitsio* everyone kept begging her to make. But no. Mother stayed in her room.

Five days later, I found her in the courtyard, near the water-tank, busily sweeping sun-dried leaves. Her firm furious strokes across the concrete paths were reassuring, as she was in control, once more, collecting the mess and debris. I felt that things were going to be okay again.

What did I care about a stupid coup?

Grown-ups were always behaving in strange ways.

Emboldened by Mother's routine task, I asked whether we could go to the *bakkali* and buy some *lountza*. But Mother seemed preoccupied. She gasped. In the way she did when my brother, aggrieved over some punishment she had metered out, would say something bad to her about her cooking. She ignored my questions, brushing me aside and walking past Philadelphia who had come to offer her a cup of Nescafe made with condensed milk.

We shook our heads. Puzzled we followed Mother into the kitchen. We watched her drink a full glass of water and then, suddenly calm, she pointed out through the bay windows, up to the clear blue of our sky somewhere out west; it seemed to be raining there. Raining white, unfastened umbrellas, which had substantial packages hanging from their handles. These gradually drew near us, so much so, that I thought they would actually be landing in our courtyard below in no time, maybe on top of or behind the huge water tank where we used to play hide and seek. We were petrified, for Mother didn't say a word to us, just kept repeating Konstandinos's name. The thought of having to deal with the large, live packages, made me forget that I was hungry.

16

We listened to the radio. The same radio, which had Aunt Hara fascinated. A female announcer's voice, breaking with emotion, was telling all who listened, that as a result of the coup, we had been invaded. Our enemy claimed some clause in a treaty allowed them to interfere to restore order. Their troops had already disembarked on our northern coast, at Kerynia. Had killed locals. Not knowing how serious all this was, I asked Mother if I could still go to Zoë's birthday party that evening. Mother didn't answer my question, just looked away, sighing.

I loved Zoë. She had a way of smiling that made you think she was smiling just for you and nobody else. She was the cleanest-looking girl at school and pretty too, with long, blonde hair held off her lovely face by two ponytails, which she sometimes twirled and curled. I liked her best when she took my hand in her soft small hand underneath our desk and the teacher didn't know.

Mother's sigh was enough to make me realise that something nasty was going to happen or was already happening and worse, Mother could do nothing, it seemed, to stop it from happening. Mother usually had a plan, an answer for everything bad that happened. Everything she was aware of that is.

I heard the plane engines drawing closer, their revving only amplifying the earlier quake-like noises, becoming more frequent.

Mother called her doctor. The radio kept repeating that anyone spotted in the streets would be shot dead. It seemed very confusing that there were two groups of people who were raging an outright war against us. No matter how hard I thought about it, it seemed illogical that one of our enemies spoke the same language as we did and had learnt the same national anthem at school. Followed the same religion as we did. Had undergone the same rites of passage as us. Got baptised in church. Wore an eighteen-carat gold cross gifted to us by our godparents or our own family. Knew about the *Evil Eye*. Looked like us.

I felt that things had irreversibly changed, just like that; in just a handful of days, my small world was changing. As we were setting the table, glad to be doing so for a change, as it gave us a reason to be in the kitchen near Mother, the house shook with the loudest noise I had ever heard. I had learned about earthquakes in Geography lessons and honestly thought that this was a major one. I wondered whether I would be buried alive, if I would die before I was able to grow a moustache and look like the movie stars I saw at the cinema just behind our house. Mother instantly drew the heavy curtains but not before we saw, through the shutters, that the streetlights had fizzed out. Blackness swept our summer city. And our house. I was still hungry, but we never got around to eating that evening and I felt like a traitor because Konstandinos not being there did not satiate my hunger. But I never let on.

The enemy had disembarked all its mainland military power, and without any resistance had already taken the north ports of Kerynia and Morfou and was advancing south to the capital and west to Famagusta and Karpasi. The radio announcers sounded discombobulated with having to read often conflicting news reports. 'So, if we dare go outside, we are going to be shot by the Greeks and if we stay inside our houses we are going to be killed by the Turks,' my sister tried to explain to me, but I just could not believe this was happening to our home.

Soon I had other things to worry about, other worries which took over my hunger—physical pain and absolute terror.

Without any kind of announcement, my older brother returned full of adventures. I found him sipping his condensed milk with heaps of Milo at the breakfast table. My mother kept her hands on his shoulders the entire time Konstandinos had us all enthralled with his experiences with the Greek military personnel. His age had spared him and saved his life. Relieved as we all were, that same day, a week after the first invasion, we had to leave our house.

It was then that Mother started to change. It was then she started not to notice things. About us. We moved to a rented, as yet unfinished two-storey house about ten kilometres out of town. It was the furthest Mother had lived from the neighbourhood she was born in *within the city walls*. She couldn't take anything much with her. We took some clothes with us, but since it was summer, we didn't overpack. We were certain we'd be back in our own house fairly soon. We all honestly believed that this *war*, as Mother called it, would not last very long and that everything would soon be the same again.

Out of nowhere, there appeared on our doorstep half-known and totally unknown faces, all seeking refuge, sleeping on the floor in our rented house. They too were optimistic about seeing their homes and villages again. Everyone kept saying that England would surely do something soon because according to some important treaty, the English had an obligation to protect our island's sovereignty. Everyone, young and old, concurred that Greece had betrayed us—that the fascist generals who ruled Greece were only concerned with power over us. At all costs.

It was then I started to keep to myself, more so than before. I was by now, way too large to fit into an armoire. There were no beeswax-polished armoires in our rented house. It felt as if I could no longer produce whole words or phrases. Mother did not notice.

Father was typically absent. He was not there to lend us a hand packing and unpacking and repacking and carrying bags to taxis and relatives' cars as we were compelled to move from temporary accommodation to a safer place. And then as that place became unsafe, we repeated the process. Until nowhere was safe.

17

At night, men's hands would touch me. And more. I didn't know the words I could use to describe what was going on. Touching, kissing I knew. But the other stuff, no. I was very popular with these men all wanting to *sleep* next to me. All of them told me it was important for these games to be kept secret. I did what I was told. I did not feel like what they did to me was a game because games were supposed to be fun, not painful.

Rumbling noises kept coming from above. The sky had not been blue for days. One day it was so black outside during the day, the air smelling like burnt rubber that I thought the end of the world was coming. I dared to wonder what would happen after. Each day brought more arrivals into our already packed temporary household. One man even taught me to look for a falling star.

A couple of weeks later, around five in the morning a sudden deafening noise threw me against the window, and I cut myself. The walls of that rented house were also unfinished and were still rough concrete. If you were pushed against or just bumped into a wall coming out of a room, you would scratch yourself on its rough surface. One woman who was sleeping next to Philadelphia was squashed underneath a wall, which had collapsed on top of her. They took her to hospital but her son, a twenty-year-old soldier with big biceps, left in tears. I had never seen a soldier cry before.

Two days after the second bombing raid another soldier knocked on our door commanding us to leave. We told him that we didn't own a car and half-heartedly he said he would try and find us a means of transport. But he warned us to *prepare for the worst*. It seemed most of the other residents had left this suburb well before we had even moved in. A few miles in the distance we could see fires burning on the hills and lots of us were coughing from all the billowing smoke. Up there on the cliff, in the hills that stood facing our incomplete house, the sky was blacker still with shades of vehement red. 'God's wrath against man. God is punishing us all for our sins,' Kyria Panayiota kept sermonising in her martyred way and made everyone even more nervous and touchy.

I too had done things that now brought on copious guilt. It was my fault, I was told by men who had hurt me. It was my fault for not being strong enough to push them away.

Several long hours after the corporal's visit, an old pick-up truck appeared outside, and a dog's bark got our attention. It was our lift. An ancient man who'd refused to leave his house and his companion, Mavros, who was the ugliest dog I had ever seen up close. Instead of being relieved, I remember being instead peeved that the man who saved our lives had unimaginatively called his black dog, Black.

He kindly drove us to Terra Sancta, a boarding school run by Italian Catholic brothers, which had been taken over by the government as a refugee camp. Our cousin Adonis, whose father made a fortune selling cheap loans to people in crisis, used to go to school there. I had always wanted to study there. Now was my chance. I had got what I had wished for. This was my first tangible lesson that sometimes when you finally get what you want, it comes at a cost. Or you find you don't want it anymore.

I felt really embarrassed taking my clothes off in front of dozens of other men. Showering without any privacy using buckets of cold water in open cubicles. Trying to use a toilet that was always filthy, and which offered no toilet paper. Most of these strangers were peasants from out of town. The enemy had already taken over their villages. 'They're displaced,' Mother would tell me and my sister in a condescending tone, steadfastly refusing to accept that the same adjective could be used to describe our homeless, fragmented family.

We were allocated two canvas cots in one of the three dormitories. I made a lot of fuss about having to share my bed with my brother but there was no choice. Mother told me to *Shut-up* for the first time. There were no curtains so you could undress in privacy like at the hospital. The cots we slept on were placed almost right next to each other with just enough legroom between them to stand up. The one thing that remains vivid in my mind isn't the people who had blood on them and who were moaning all day but the stink of hundreds of bodies and the fact that we couldn't even have a proper shower.

The nights, the savage nights, when my body was not mine, were the loneliest. My father wasn't there to protect me. But men touched me and held me and made me feel like someone strong was there looking after me. My Mother did not see any of this. Or notice my moods. But I felt compelled to cut her some slack as she was mostly preoccupied with trying to find ways to save us. Get us out of the camp.

One night I sat on a filthy toilet bleeding from down there for a long while. I can never forget that particular moment. No matter how much time passes, it takes only the smallest disrespect, the first whiff of humiliation to take me straight back to that terrifying moment in time. I have never forgotten that all-consuming fear that left me breathless. On my own.

18

Australia was so, so far away. New Zealand even more distant. We imagined we knew more about New Zealand than Australia, as occasionally, Mother would serve us tinned butter from the Land of the Long White Cloud as a treat. I cannot explain why there was a need to import New Zealand butter to our small island. Our school gave us free triangular-shaped milk cartons some mornings. Our island had lots of wheat, lemons, figs, oranges and beautiful shallow beaches—this we all knew. Fresh milk? Not so much.

We were going to Australia.

What in God's name was Father doing in Australia? His English proficiency extended to a handful of words. What kind of foolhardy man moves to a country so far away from his extended family when he's already fifty? Did he secretly hate all his relatives, even his sisters who all adored him? How can anyone ever afford the cost of a return flight ticket to Australia? He might as well have moved to Mars. So far apart from the wife he was supposed to love? (Perhaps married people stopped loving each other after they had children). Did he ever spare us or our mother a thought? Could *he* sleep on a camper cot with hundreds of others all around? Even for one night?

In the camp, a female village woman had dared to challenge Mother as to how much water Mother had used for bathing. She accosted our imperious Mother in the doorway to the dorm.

'We're allowed two buckets and that is what I used,' Mother explained calmly in her superior voice. Konstandinos was punched three times for speaking with a 'city accent'. Philadelphia was called an *appomeni,* a *snooty little bitch.*

Australia seemed unreal. So far away from the old streets of Nicosia. But Father wrote it was pretty. With lush green lawns everywhere, even on the footpaths. Our footpaths in Nicosia were covered in sandy dust. Manicured lawns were the prerogative of luxury hotels like Ledra Palace where the bourgeoisie used to hold their wedding receptions by the poolside. I had been a page boy at a number of these long, torturous affairs and had gazed at the gleaming water in the pools with glee and envy. At times, I wanted to either push the bride into the water so I could see if her hair, done in a French roll, could survive intact. Or I wanted to throw myself in the clear water and hope never to surface again (as my Mother would have then killed me for *causing a scene*). But the luxury hotel was now turned into army headquarters, right by the Green Line that separated our city.

On the dock, we had been sandwiched in by people as if we were sardines, packed tight. We waited there, being shoved and shoved. It stank. We felt asphyxiated, starved of oxygen, by so many people around us for almost five hours, before finally being allowed to board. Mother had, after many telephone calls, somehow managed to book us on this small ferry. It would take us to Athens, so we could then catch the Olympic Airways plane to Sydney, where Father had been living for less than three months.

Getting on the ferry took so long because people without a ticket were desperately pushing and shoving and getting us all squashed, trying to get on board. In the early part of the morning, we couldn't even get near the dock. There were barricades. The port officials in rumpled uniforms and unshaven faces looked as if they would rather be anywhere else than on the docks at Limassol. Mother sat us down and made us eat cold hard-boiled eggs. She peeled baby cucumbers for us all, in her careful accomplished manner, just as if she were in her own dining room or kitchen at Areos Street.

Konstandinos threw an egg at a boy who teased us, calling us names I did not know the meaning of. Later, finally on board, staring unknowingly out of a tiny porthole, I saw hands waving and then start to fade in the distance as the boat pulled away from the port. Delusional with fatigue, I imagined I saw Aunt Hara waving at us, but it could have been anyone.

I realised we were leaving our island.

There were no goodbyes.

19

In Nicosia, I hated the sirens warning us of another bombing raid. I hated moving house every other week, each time being allowed to take less and less with me.

I hated being touched in the shower block in the makeshift refugee camp and made to do things with my mouth and body. Sometimes I'd be rewarded with some flavoured-milk or an ION chocolate bar. I hated my father for not being with us. For not ever protecting me. Was he that self-involved that he thought being in a refugee camp might be a positive experience for his children?

I thought about all that had happened to me. With no one to help me. Was that how my life was going to be—with no one to help me? On my own, I did not feel strong enough. My sense of guilt for what I allowed the strangers to do to my body, ate at me, made me paranoid. Even on the happiest occasions. For decades after.

But at the time the ferry pulled away from land and the port started to disappear I knew nothing about the future. Or that, in a matter of a few days, I would have to enrol in a new school in Australia. I did not know that we would all be cramped into a room. That we would no longer have lots of empty rooms in any of our new houses. Like in Areos Street.

The last few weeks in the refugee camp had felt nothing like a game; at least, not the sort of game I felt like playing ever again.

I was always paranoid about my safety, always looking over my shoulder.

For my last birthday on our island, Mother had bought a shambolic nougat cake from a local shop. I celebrated my new year in a rented house in an area we had never set foot in before the coup and the war. Even Mother, letting down her diplomatic veneer admitted it was the worst cake ever made.

To this day, I cannot sleep unless there is a light on just outside my room.

'We don't have to eat it Demostheni-*mou*. Just blow out the candles, my boy.'

Leaving our home on the ferry needed a celebration too. As a symbolic gesture of gratitude at having been spared by the bombs, at not having been made prisoners of war like so many relatives, and to say *Goodbye* to the place of my birth, I let go of my one and only personal possession—my beloved pair of sunglasses. Dimitris had bought them for me from a *Paniyiri,* only a few months earlier. Every village had its own fete and Dimitris loved taking us with him. Everyone used to think he was my father as he was in his late twenties. Nothing made me happier than when people would make that comment.

I loved Dimitris more than anyone else in the world. So much, that when he came to the city to say goodbye I wailed and would not let go of him.

A week later, Dimitris was captured by our enemy. Disappeared. We lost Uncle Sotiris too. He was executed in front of his sons. Dimitris had kept me safe. Made me feel I was secure whenever he was around. Without him ever saying anything I knew there was no chance anything bad could happen to me while I was in his company. He made me feel better about myself just by being there. With his beautiful smile. And he was tall. And strong. Like some kind of Mediterranean matinee idol. A Cypriot version of Alain Delon who made my sister swoon.

Dimitris was a living, breathing superhero. Demonstrated to me how strong I could be if I exercised and worked hard. Once, he let me watch him shave with his old safety razor and I was entranced that he did not cut his veins and bleed to death.

*

PART II

The Big Island at the End of the World

Yia to hattirin tis vasilijias pinni j'i glastra to neron
For the sake of the basil, the pot drinks water
Cypriot proverb

20

The excitement I had experienced on first hearing the news about Australia was now starting to turn to constant anxiety. The jumbo jet had landed much too soon for my liking.

I would think of Dimitris, wondering if he were still alive, when the boys at school called me *Dipstick* and talked down to me. I'd chant his name in a mantra and believed if I kept at it long enough, Dimitris would magically appear in the streets of our new country. Dimitris was the only grown up who loved me like a father should love his son. The day he had gifted me the sunglasses I'd wanted for so long, now kept coming back.

'One day, when I open my own taverna, you'll need to wear these when you're eating at the outside tables because the reflection of the sun on the water will be too strong. Just keep thinking about how relaxed you'll be, sitting at the best table by the sea, not squinting like all the rest of the boys, hey?'

He gave me a last hug and kissed me. I do not know how my young mind knew this, but my instinct told me that whenever it was that I saw Dimitris again, at his new taverna, the sunglasses would be way too small for me. That he'd be different. That I would be different. That he might reject the version of me he saw in front of him.

When we first were told about leaving our island, Mother had sat us down and told us calmly that Australia was so far away that it would be next to impossible to visit our island again as the cost would be astronomical. Our tickets to fly here from Greece were bought with money someone lent our father.

I knew nothing about having to learn a new language. I knew nothing about feeling weird and apart from the other pupils. That I would be called bad names daily, and that nearly all the other pupils would snigger and laugh at my expense. Landing in Australia, in a huge aeroplane, is not in itself significant. It is what happens to you *after* that's important. As an immigrant, no matter how old you may be on arrival, you don't suddenly change—discarding the self you have known and all that you believe in at the boarding gate of your own country—and morph into being *an Australian* (whatever that may be—is there such a thing?) the moment you arrive here. You don't suddenly become a new person as you clear customs. There is no way you can evolve magically into a person who can easily and successfully manipulate the systemic functional linguistics rules and prescribed scripts of every interaction in your new country. You cannot instantly master the skills required to communicate and relate successfully and effectively with other people who are already Australians, with people whose grandparents were born here, simply because you get on a long flight from overseas and land in Sydney, Brisbane or Melbourne airport.

We arrived from the airport in a taxi. Father had been living in an old boarding house with many rooms with lots of other people, most of them really old men. It was not fun living in one room, all five of us. It was fun for about a day and then it was horrible. It was freezing too. The toilet was used by everyone, and it was just as filthy as the toilets at Terra Sancta. The men would listen all day to their small transistor radios, listening to the horse races and to other programmes in weird-sounding languages at night.

The boarding house was in Hunters Hill, a beautiful part of Sydney, and if we walked far enough to the main road, we could see the water of the famous Harbour. Father bought us fish and chips wrapped up in newspaper for our first dinner. He said this is what people ate here. Mother was at first suspicious but soon she got used to our new food. She continued making us drink our Nestle condensed milk with Milo in the mornings, but we had it cold as we didn't have a stove or a kettle.

We arrived at Kingsford Smith airport on a Friday, and I found myself in a classroom the following Tuesday. The school year calendar was different here and even though I had finished school for the year back home on our island, I had to re-do three months of the same grade here. But of course, what we learned was very different. And in English.

On that first day, Mother told me to have a shower and then, when she combed my hair, she put some lemon in her hands and patted down my hair.

The woman in charge at the school did not seem very nice. She kept talking to us in a manner which made me feel she thought we were dirty or bad people.

In the three primary schools I attended in quick succession, all the headmistresses and headmasters we met seemed to behave in the same way. On the surface, they were polite, but their smiles were insincere. Mother understood this, despite not knowing any English, and was clearly angry. I wanted her to protest, to talk back to the headmistress in her usual calm, measured way. But Mother couldn't, it seemed, say anything. This shocked me. All she could say in reply to the silent accusations which were thrown at us was a pitiful, *Please*, as if she were some malnourished, unkempt beggar, pleading for any loose change outside a church. Trying to enrol at that first school was the first of many times I would feel embarrassed by my mother.

Within a couple of years of our leaving, I would find myself cursing the war, the Greek Junta, King Constantine II, the British government, and all the authorities for not stopping the war, as the *Treaty of Guarantee* set out. I blamed the ruthless dictators of Greece and the Queen herself personally for not abiding by the treaty they had signed to protect us. I would curse them all each time I glanced at my mother, seeing her in freefall, grappling with her new identity in the outer-western suburbs of Sydney and simply not recognise her. The trauma of this stayed with me for decades.

It was at that moment, in the headmistress's office in my first of many schools that I started to see the world differently. It was on that day, that I felt totally lost and angry and decided that my new life, my mother's life, all our lives were going to be very different going forward. Consumed with fury, I wanted to make a fuss and break something and raise my voice. I have fought this feeling ever since. Quietly seething. For I wanted to gain my new country folks' approval. I wanted to fit in. I wanted desperately to be accepted. I wanted that horrible birthmark to disappear. To be eighteen so I could get my broken nose reset.

<h1 style="text-align:center">21</h1>

The entire class fell into an inquisitive silence. When the teacher said my long name, everybody laughed.

'Let's call him *Dimwit* for short,' said a boy sitting at the back row of the class and the whole class broke out in raucous laughter. I knew it was at my expense. A freckle-faced boy then called out, 'He's a flaming Reffo! Straight off the boat!' and everyone again laughed out loud. 'Look at his clothes!' I heard many bad expressions and *Bloody wog* numerous times during my brief stay at this school; so, they may have been the first few words I learnt in English.

After everybody stopped laughing, I sat down where the teacher indicated, next to a large girl with pimples and funny steel-looking caps on her teeth. Maybe children had horrible teeth here, I thought, for looking around I saw she wasn't the only one who wore these ugly teeth guards. The girl smiled uncomfortably at me and was red-faced.

I recognised sums on the board and took a pencil out of my yellow rocket-shaped pencil case (a present from the aeroplane). It must be Maths. I pretended not to notice that all eyes were fixed on me. All the other boys and girls wore a grey and blue uniform matched with a V-neck jumper. A darker grey V lined the neck of the jumper on either side. I only had my yellow t-shirt. A pair of blue shorts. I was pleased that the class was doing Maths as that did not involve knowing English or having to speak. I could just show the teacher my answers. The numbers were the same but the sign they used for division was a little strange.

At recess, some of the kids stood around me, forming a circle, watching me. I felt threatened. I was a new species, and they were curious. I hated being looked at. I desperately hoped nobody would touch me. They each took turns at interrogating me, but none of them had the sense to use the right language. They made funny sounds when I told them my name slowly, syllable by syllable. They seemed angry when I kept quiet. In the end, they poked me and pushed and shoved me and finally when they got bored, left me there, all by myself.

I desperately wanted to go to the toilet but had no idea where it was.

I wanted a cold drink but had no money. It took me three days to understand that everything from the canteen needed to be pre-ordered the previous day.

One of the neighbours' children walked me back home on the first day at my new school. He did not want to, I gathered. I am guessing the teacher made him do it. He had a funny haircut, very long like a girl's and he kept talking when he knew I couldn't answer him back. The next morning, he left me outside *Administration* and an old lady of about forty beckoned me to her office where she too proceeded to rave on and on and to smile at me as if I were dumb. I think she said my hair was nice and stroked it but perhaps she was checking for lice. I didn't understand anything she said except her hello. She gave me two textbooks.

A week later, things were not any better. Nobody bothered to be friendly. I remember being so desperate for someone to talk to that at recess and lunchtime I went around the yard asking every male student who had dark hair if they could speak my language.

'*Milas Ellinika?*' I would ask them earnestly. They would all sneer as if I were a bad smell or laugh at me and push me out of the way. I hid in the toilet cubicle most breaks, hoping nobody would harm me. Late one afternoon, two weeks to the day I had started, I ran out of the classroom in tears. The boy who had called me a *reffo* on my first day, had crushed my yellow rocket pencil case to pieces, stomping on it on purpose. A chant of *Dipstick! Dipstick!* erupted in the class. The teacher didn't seem to notice.

I kept on running. I called out for Cousin Dimitris. I called out for my father. I wanted to run back to my island, back to where I belonged, where people liked me, where they spoke the same language. Back home to Areos and into Aunt Hara's comfy, flour-smelling arms.

Nobody came after me. I felt very alone. I feared that I would never have a friend in this new country. That my parents would not have the means to visit our island and those who had loved us, even if peace ever returned. Humiliated too, that since all the other pupils already spoke English, I would have Buckley's chance of ever coming first or second in my class. Even my mother would be ashamed of me from now on.

22

· · · · · · · · · · · ·

Polixeni Lavrentidis-Hatzinikolaou sits in silence.

Today, she is preoccupied with the peeling of muddy, new potatoes. It has just gone eleven-thirty, and the midday sun is streaming through the back windows, covering her in strands of warmth as she sits there, on automatic pilot, preparing the evening's meal. There is no radio, no television, no telephone in the empty house. There is nobody to talk to or keep her company or distract her.

Her youngest will be home for lunch. His primary school is only two blocks down the road, through a bit of bush. Cheese-spread sandwiches again today. Demosthenes can't complain and she gets to keep the bonus drinking glasses the stuff comes packed in. She's collected four in just six weeks. One more and she will have enough for all of them. She has no idea what is in the jar, nor can she read the label. She knows it is a cheese product and hopes it has some nutritional value as there is no way they could afford to buy real cheese, a block of Havarti or Jarlsberg (her second child's favourite), or halloumi cheese in a bucket of brine. She has not seen any of these cheeses in the narrow Flemings at the local shops, but she has read in the Greek newspaper that delicatessens in the Greek and Italian areas of Sydney stock European cheeses. But she'll need three buses to get there. She wouldn't have a clue how to find these delicatessens. And where would she find the money? Perhaps she can convince Philadelphia to accompany her one Saturday.

Her eldest speaks some English. Polixeni's investment in the private grammar school all those years back home has paid off—Philadelphia impatiently explains and translates all forms and documents to her and her husband. When she is not in one of her moods.

For lunch, this cheese in a jar is all there is. She knows the boy needs to have a bit of tomato or some olives or a slice of cucumber but all these extras cost money. She also hasn't seen any olives in the local supermarket and the cucumbers here are fat and watery and have seeds that upset the kids' stomachs.

She doesn't have the language skills to ask at the local supermarket if they might be able to order some decent cheese for her family. There is no delicatessen at the local shops, just a supermarket, a butcher's, a cake shop and a Chinese restaurant. Polixeni dares not enter any of these establishments. Since arriving here, she has been metamorphosed into a mute imbecile.

If my brother Pericles were here, he would die of hunger, she thinks to herself and a half-smile forms on her pinched face. Her brother had smoked hams hanging in their entirety in his kitchen, so large that to buy one here would probably cost their weekly rent. She abandons the potato she has peeled, and it dives into the sink. She rinses her hands and wipes them on her apron. She uses the brown wrapping paper as a plate and takes two slices of bread from the breadbox. It is bread from two days ago and Demosthenes is bound to complain: this she knows as her youngest has always been a difficult boy, and at times quite sullen. She tries calling him Demosthenes, but these days he doesn't like it, and he sulks. Many days, he refuses to eat his sandwich, saying it is stale. Making her feel inadequate and humiliated. Who would eat two-day-old sliced, white bread back home? The wretched supermarket down the road only sells white sliced bread. No loafs of sourdough or loaves with aniseed are sold here. She and the kids crave some olive bread or even a tahini pie, a halloumi loaf. But the cake shop here sells creamy puff pastry stuff, with cold apples inside.

She took Demosthenes to the front office of this new school over a week ago on Monday. Not a word of English, besides *thank you* and *please*. Demosthenes had somehow managed to convince the headmistress that he had finished fifth class. She was a very unwelcoming woman who seemed obstinate and not very kind. When they had walked in through the steel-fenced school entrance her little boy had asked if this was a *Grammar School*. At home, when she had told her children the news about the decision to go to Australia, Demosthenes had declared he would go only if he were enrolled in a *Grammar School*. Philadelphia had been going to a private Grammar School for several years and Demosthenes aspired to follow in his sister's footsteps.

'Yes, Dimo-*mou*, Australia, I am certain, has many Grammar Schools,' she had reassured him back then.

Now they were here, she could not lie. 'No, my boy, it is not a Grammar School. But when you are ready to go to high school, we will find a very good school for you, much bigger than this one. But look over there, it has a sandpit.'

'But you said I was not allowed to play in the sandpit, remember?' Demosthenes retorted petulantly and Polixeni blushed. Demosthenes stopped and would not budge just as they had reached the headmistress's door. The headmistress noticed this and looked impatient and already fed-up before even a word had been exchanged between them.

'We've never had any refugees at our school before. Now, I don't want you causing any trouble young man. This is Australia and you will have to abide by our rules. Your family lives down the road you say...' Demosthenes explained the lady wasn't friendly and wasn't sure if she had said that he could enrol at the school or not.

'I stay?' he asked boldly, and the headmistress admonished him.

'You should say, "Am I welcome to enrol in your school Mrs. Higginbottom?"'

Polixeni had met hundreds of unhappy, middle-aged women in her time and had been effortlessly able to cajole them, to assuage their bitterness with her well-bred manners and choice of gentle words, but this situation was quite different. She could not speak this woman's language. Unfortunately, Polixeni, an only daughter of one of Old Nicosia's best families (*Only a handful of families were born within the city's ancient walls ...*) did not know how to plead in this new language. She didn't understand exactly what the headmistress was saying but at the same time the woman's tone clearly showed her negativity, the resentful nature of this educated woman, and Polixeni understood all she needed.

Polixeni knew this was a government school and that it was almost free to enrol. As the school was down the road from their rented, empty house, she guessed the headmistress had no choice but to accept her youngest. She had no idea where other schools may be, if the woman refused them permission to enrol.

Her instinct told her to just grab Demosthenes and take him to another school, a private school, wherever that may be. She had seen advertisements in the Greek newspapers for Catholic Schools and if they were advertising in the Greek press then they would not refuse her boy. But how much did they cost? She kept looking at Demosthenes's bright yellow T-shirt, which was a size too small for him these days and just wanted to sob.

Her beautiful boy standing there ill at ease, being judged by this woman, no wedding ring on her fingers, grey hair a mess, her blouse not ironed, her fingernails bare, no lipstick—*was she really the headmistress or an impostor trying to dupe them*? Polixeni wondered. Here was little Demosthenes with his long jet-black hair like a Prince from the Orient and his perfect smile, a boy who had always come first or second in his class, now being looked down on by this stick of a woman who Polixeni at first had mistaken for the cleaner.

'The boy will have to abide by our uniform rules. We have uniforms here in Australia,' the woman shouted at them, stressing every single syllable, slowly. The headmistress now looked pleased with herself, relieved almost, as if she had accomplished a complex brilliant mission to the Moon.

'Uniform?' Demosthenes asked timidly. 'What is this?'

'It is what good boys and girls wear to school here in A-U-S-T-R-A-L-I-A,' the old woman answered, and Demosthenes shook his head disparagingly at his mother. They both stood there facing this woman and Polixeni wanted to slap her.

'Tell her we're not deaf,' she said to Demosthenes and from that moment on, Demosthenes would swallow hard and learn, through trial and error, not to translate frankly whatever it was his mother had told him to say in English to their interrogator, whomever it may have been. Demosthenes quietly confided in his mother that he wondered whether it was in fact English the headmistress was speaking because the way she spoke English didn't sound anything like any of the British teachers at the Nicosia Institute of Technology where he finished a week-long course just before they left. It had taken a war to convince his mother to let him go along with his brother. Polixeni suggested to her son that perhaps in Australia people spoke Australian, a different kind of English.

'Just like in our country people speak in Cypriot dialect, different to Greek but still Greek. So, it must be the case here too with Australian English.'

'Well, obviously we're going to have some problems communicating,' Mrs. Higginbottom said with a false little smile. 'There's no Special English class at our school unfortunately. We don't get many ... er ... *ethnic* students from overseas here. In fact, you'll be our first ever refugee, Dimo...' the woman trailed off.

'Di-mo-sthe-nes,' her boy sounded out and she was proud of him.

'Please ...,' Polixeni pleaded when it was the last thing she wanted to do, and she was well aware that with the uttering of this word, her social status had now changed forever. Demosthenes too, looked as if he was going to burst into tears as the woman suddenly stood up and came around to where he and his mother were standing, wrenching him from her hand without further ado. They were out the door in a flash. She had wanted to kiss Demosthenes first, tell him to be a good boy and wish him good luck. But the headmistress just took him away and Polixeni felt like screaming. *She didn't even ask us to sit down, the whole time,* she realised. She was immensely thankful it wasn't she who was walking into a new class so soon since the last school where her boy stayed less than a month.

Our bloody country and its politics. I've lost my mother's house. My grandmother's house. I've lost my language, my pasta maker for God's sake. I even must start calling my own children by different Christian names now. What next?

She wanted to swear in the most offensive phrases her brother Pericles used but collected her anger. She counselled herself to bear in mind that despite everything that had happened, there was still a God who may take offence at blasphemy. Polixeni decided to curse all the morbidly obese old men, the useless, self-serving politicians who had willingly, through their stubbornness, corruption and complicity, allowed her island to be taken over.

If only I had followed my first cousins to England before the children were born, Polixeni sighs. *Why did I trust him to bring us here?* Thank God she had the safety of her silent home as a retreat. Konstandinos and Philadelphia had to catch a bus to a high school, but they decided that between them, they could manage going to their new school by themselves.

'You know something Ma, that beehive you have, is not very popular here,' Konstandinos told her on his return from his first day.

The house was empty, save for an old blanket covering the middle of the living area, spread as a makeshift coffee-table, dining table and oriental rug. At night it became the boys' bed too. Today the kitchen is sunny. This small mercy cheers her up tremendously.

Already, she misses the climate of her island. The kitchen window looks out onto a field of less than lush, overgrown green.

Just like the villages, back home, Polixeni thinks and feels homesick for her old, narrow Nicosia streets. The streets she had known so well. The streets with their scent of jasmine filling the air. Those coveted streets encased within the surrounding walls of the Old City. She thinks of her beautiful house and what became of it after the second bombing raid.

She spots a horse grazing on the horizon and for a moment she kids herself that they have moved to a farm, near her husband's village. But she has not seen wild freesias growing here on the side roads. And who knows if they'll ever afford a car. To go on a country drive. To pick wildflowers.

She had found some abandoned plates of assorted sizes and patterns underneath the sink when they had first moved in, but they were still in need of an extra dinner plate. Her husband had his meal served on the lid of their one and only piece of cookware. Making soup was out of the parameters of possibility. Tonight, they'd have the potatoes her husband had bought from the Flemington Markets on Saturday. Half of them were rotten brown inside. She had thought that keeping them in a dark place might make them last longer but maybe she had been wrong. Since their arrival, she had started to second-guess about housekeeping stuff she knew or could do in her sleep.

All she knew with certainty was that at home, all she'd had to do was telephone the shop, ask the store-owner how his lovely wife was, ask after his elderly mother who hadn't been coming to church lately, and once he, in turn, had asked about the children and whether she had received a letter from her husband, she would order her fruit and vegetables. Then, Kyrios Thanassis, obligingly, would have his boy deliver everything on his bike, in an hour or so. You gave little Miltiadis five cents' tip, and everyone would be happy. Once a month she'd go down to Kyrios Thanassis's shop and he would tally up all she owed with his tiny pencil which was stored permanently behind his left ear and that would be the end of that story. All she had to do was pay her bill in full and wish Kyrios Thanassis a good day.

Having finished rinsing the potatoes, she begins to cube a brown onion, two sticks of celery and three carrots, devising a new recipe for stew. A meat-less stew. She finds this perversely amusing and smirks to herself, remembering that back home all she had to worry about was deciding what to cook. Here it was what *was there* to cook. She picks up the boys' stuff off of the floor, wondering if they should borrow some money to buy a pillow or two, some sheets. The Greek newspaper was only on sale in the city. She made a mental note to get the children to ask the local newsagent about ordering one in for her. Demosthenes could pick it up in the afternoon once a week.

She wants to vacuum the (formerly) cream-coloured carpet clean but she has to make do with an old broom she found in a shed in the backyard. She dabs at some build-up dirt with warm water and gets a laugh at finding herself on her knees like a charwoman. Determined, she finishes the task, her knees burning a little, drinks a glass of water from the tap, acknowledges that even water tasted different here and goes to the front door. Outside, she goes down the three steps of the front porch, painted in a claret red, and on the left of the front lawn, she takes in appreciatively the only plant, an old thorny rosebush with thick trunks. It is covered in pink flowers today. As she manipulates her hand carefully to avoid the thorns she hears a rustling noise beneath her step. She tries to ignore it. Next door, they have a kind of jasmine crawling a little over the fence, but it has a sickly sweet smell unlike the intoxicating jasmine back home.

How lovely of God to send me a rosebush, even here, where I have nothing else. It truly is a lovely day today, she says out loud.

Perhaps Demosthenes could have his sandwich and his cordial out here? A picnic, of sorts. The two of them sitting on the front steps. It was certainly prettier out here than inside the bare house.

Just then, Demosthenes comes rushing in puffing from his run home. He has been putting on weight at a time when they had nothing to eat, Polixeni acknowledges perplexed. She then hears a rumbling croak, heavy, near them. She looks down and screams. A huge, moving lizard, like a small crocodile, a horrible, dark tongue, like none she has ever seen, is staring up at her. Without thinking, she reaches for the old brick, loose from the fence and in a rush of adrenaline and panic, begins to batter the creature with all her might, repulsed and terrified at the same time.

A neighbour, sipping from a teacup on her front porch two houses up from them, watches her in silence. The creature makes a shrilling noise so intense it drives Demosthenes inside. Polixeni continues with her vehement assault until the reptile expires. In her utter disgust, with the use of two bricks, she shoves the corpse timidly behind the rose bush where the children would think twice about going. She would put some soil over it later. She can't bring herself to look at the mangled corpse right away. Women from either side of the house are now looking at her disapprovingly, shaking their heads.

She thinks of Kyria Panayiota's constant disapproving looks and reminds God to bless her soul. Lost in the second bombing raid. She was in the middle of castigating a soldier who had peed near her front steps when they were both struck. Her boy Prokopis, miraculously, was spared and only lost two fingers.

She goes inside, somehow ashamed. Demosthenes has his sandwich. She notes that he seems agitated.

'I am not going back,' he announces, calmly. 'I am not going there, ever again.' He stresses the syllable of each word. She thinks to herself, *He's so stubborn just like his father.* She sits down on the floor, puts an arm around her beautiful boy and starts to convince him that he has to go back to school.

'All little boys have to go to school. If you don't go to school, then my boy, you can forget about Grammar School.' Demosthenes drinks up the last of his cordial. Asks if there's any more when he knows there is not, says he's still hungry. When he finally goes, stopping first to pee, she feels lonely and very much alone. She wonders why none of the neighbours came to help her.

She gazes around the bare house. She has no shelves of books, or figurines or Limoges display plates to wipe clean, no cushions to puff up, no vase with flowers that needs the water changed, no elegant Luis IV armchair which may look better in a new position, not even an iron to while away an hour or so. The children came to Australia with just the clothes on their back. Her husband bought them all two t-shirts and one polyester jumper each, all *Made in*

China. It was winter when they arrived here. *Evagoras is clueless,* Polixeni thinks and suddenly her brother comes to mind, and this overwhelms her with emotion.

Demosthenes insisted his jumper was making him itchy and refused to wear it. A day going by without hearing Demosthenes sniffle would be unusual. The local menswear shop sold school jumpers, and she had put that down as a priority on her list for next Thursday's pay. She has lost all her jewellery, her pearls, her earrings, her bracelets. Thankfully, the kids all still had their crosses. She has been lucky in that she still has her wedding ring and four gold bracelets her husband had brought her back from the Middle East when he had first started working there. She couldn't remember now if they were bought in Libya, Bahrain or Syria.

It didn't matter now.

She is crying now and doesn't have a clean handkerchief to wipe her bitter tears. How on earth did this happen? How did they all get here? What was her blasted husband thinking in deciding to come to Australia, the end of the world, when she had four first cousins living in London and three in Rhodesia? All of her family had done well overseas. Her London cousins had a clothing business and would have found something for her Evagoras to do. Maroulla, God bless her, always with a heart of gold, promised to send the children a parcel of clothes, once she had an address. Polixeni would count and recount the days, asking Philadelphia how long it took for packages to get to Australia from England.

'Mother, you've asked me a thousand times. I don't know. Why do you think we suddenly know everything?'

'You go to school. You learn new things every day. How am I going to find out being here all day, on my own?' Polixeni snaps back, simultaneously feeling sorry for herself and defending her right to ask things of her children. Why did one have children if it wasn't for the guarantee of them helping you when you needed them? Poor Philadelphia, she had so much to learn.

Had they gone to England, she would have had someone to talk to during the day, the children too would have had six cousins to play with, go to school with. All of them would have had a sense of family, community. England may have been better for the children to grow up in. And if everything sorted itself out in Cyprus, the plane ride was only three and half hours from London rather than twenty-six and costing a small fortune, as it was from Sydney. Here, they had nobody and nothing. No hope of ever going back even for a little break.

Why did I listen to Evagoras, Polixeni castigates herself but stops her mantra when she hears the postman's motorcycle. She leaves the children's dirty clothes soaking in the kitchen sink, rushes out the front, stepping on a pebble in her rush, sways to regain her balance, hoping for news from home. At the same time, she cannot avoid the fact that she has yet to send this new address to anyone except her cousin. She checks for mail nevertheless and finds two colour catalogues, one from a shop that seems to sell everything. The other entices people to enter a 'Beautiful Home on the Gold Coast' competition. A simple leaflet listing all the specials from a nearby Jewel supermarket has fallen to the bottom of the letterbox.

She throws everything away because even though she has no English proficiency (her vocabulary extended to: *Yes. No.*

Please. Thank you very much—that was it) she can recognise the dollar signs and the numerals. She thinks of her husband trying to earn a wage working in construction. Perhaps he might make the early bus tonight and be home in time for them all to have dinner together. She worries about him, but at least he can find his way around the city, can go into a milk bar and ask for cigarettes. She needed a new bra but couldn't possibly imagine herself in one of the city stores miming what she wanted, what size. The sales assistants would ask her questions, and she wouldn't be able to answer them. She'd look like a stubborn child, a dumb kid.

I am now a child in society's eyes. In my own children's eyes. I cannot do anything in this country. I may as well have perished during the bombings. I should have not agreed to this new life. Bloody Evagoras. He never did like my family. What the hell was wrong with him? Britain was so much closer to home.

She also needed new clothes herself. Begrudgingly, she accepted that Demosthenes wasn't the only one putting on weight. She blamed the bread she baked once a week, or fried, served either as an appetiser or an accompaniment to the meal or as dessert with a bit of sugar sprinkled on it. She'd feel puffed just by climbing down the seven steps to the backyard where the washing was hung on a strange square but practical clothesline. She'd never seen a square-shaped clothesline back home. Konstandinos was fond of jumping on it and swirling around and around, flying as if he had wings, all the time laughing to himself whilst Philadelphia raised her eyebrows in disapproval and shook her head.

It's such a shame God never allowed me to give her a sister

to share the burden, Polixeni thinks and a new, bleak wave of melancholy envelops her for the fourth time that day.

She puts a tiny bit of cheese spread onto some bread and has that as a snack. In Nicosia, she had never baked bread. The baker offered every imaginable type of bread one could want, and all the loaves were fresh daily, seven days a week. Why would anyone waste time baking bread? Only her husband's village relatives baked bread because they were too stingy to pay for it at a bakery.

She needed a check-up too, down there. It had been quite a while since she and her husband had shared the same bed and now, they were together every night. She couldn't expect the kids to translate what she wanted to ask of a doctor. No, that would be too humiliating, for all concerned. And doctors were expensive here too. Her husband had asked one of his fellow Greek bricklayers.

No, seeing a doctor shall have to wait. Right now, the urgent things were the children's school uniforms that weren't cheap even second-hand, and a set of plates, a simple cutlery set, a carving knife, a large pot. An iron would be a godsend. An ironing board could wait.

Spring in Australia was glorious. Yes, despite all that she had lost, she was sufficiently fair-minded to admit this. And yet, as her gaze looks down at her dress, she feels desolate. Wants to reassure herself that she will survive this too, that this stage of her life is temporary.

She tries to scrub clean the bathtub, but it is too old for cleaning to do it any good. She wipes the sweat from her brow and measures the space to figure out what length the shower curtain needs to be when she has the money to spare to buy one. She then closes her eyes. Starts to imagine she is giving a dinner party, a black-tie affair. Cultured pearls around female necklines. Stiff-collared, white shirts for the gentlemen. She sees herself descending the marble staircase in her mother's house, chandeliers all lit up like Christmas trees. Young, handsome waiters mingling with silver trays and people laughing and smiling and gossiping about who has done what to whom, where and how. *Dinner is served, Ladies and Gentlemen.*

The door thumps shut, and she knows Konstandinos and Philadelphia must be home. They don't talk to her much lately. Their rented house is always silent these days. Demosthenes has been home for almost an hour but hasn't made a noise. That boy is upset all the time, she notes. He has been sullen and distant since the camp at Terra Sancta. Maybe he is reaching puberty, she rationalises.

Perhaps, like me, he simply wants to go back home. That's it—the poor child misses his home. His country. His language. Of course, that's what it is.

Demosthenes and Konstandinos (he has grown a light moustache—thirteen now—I've got to remember to start calling him Dinos) are outside playing with their only toy, an aeroplane made out of an aluminum foil roll on which the boys have drawn windows and attached bits of cardboard in the shape of wings. Coke tops serve as engines. Demosthenes is still immersed in the technological brilliance of our long flight. Konstandinos doesn't seem too interested in imaginary hijacking and terrorist bombing missions. But he plays tolerantly along with Demosthenes all the same. My baby son has always had a wild imagination. Jumping off the balcony. How he survived that I shall never know.

She calls out to them to speak in Greek, but she can hear them continue to yap in English. Her boys have many a time explained that knowing Greek didn't help them in the playground, but that saying *Rack off, Daryl!* instead, in the right tone, did wonders for their social survival. Just then, Philadelphia appears suddenly, asking half-heartedly if she can help with anything, and is very pleased that nothing needs to be done. There are no placemats or a jug of water to be filled with ice and mint leaves cut off from the garden pots.

I don't even have a pot of basil.

Philadelphia sits on the floor, has her head buried in a book within seconds and steals glances now and then at the boys and at the disappearing sun outside.

Her Evagoras too, at last comes home. He seems irritable. Again. Standing in the narrow kitchen they talk about the rent that is due, the instalment for the airfares loan, the electricity bill, the need for Manchester, cookware and the general lack of money to buy anything.

'A happy rich man is happier than a happy poor man,' Philly calls out to them and goes back to her library book.

Tomorrow seems so far away. Everything seems wrong tonight. But when tomorrow comes, they will see what can be done. Before then, there was an entire peaceful night to spend with her family, knowing they are safe. Feeling thankful to be alive. And later, when everyone is fast asleep, her husband snoring brilliantly, she will hear the horses in the field next door and hear the crickets too, out on their nightly rounds. She tries to sleep, holding onto the certainty that at sunrise, when she opens the back door to let the morning air in, she will smell the freshness of the new morning, and then stare at the sun, blinding these peaceful fields of heaven.

23

My new names at my Australian schools included: Reffo, Fresh-off-the-boat, Greaseball, Wog, Dago, Fatwog, Fag, Faggot, Poof, Poofter, Dimwit, Dipstick, Demos, Dumb-dumb, Dumbo, Demon, Timbo, Themos, DemosPenis, Fatso, El Greco, Theo, Stupid Ethnic and Bulldog (did I really look like the dog breed with the smashed-in face?). All were spat at me like rubber bullets. And not always in the classroom or playground.

I had no idea why teachers used *NESB* a lot when my name came up. For several years I felt anxious when I heard this nickname used by them, their eyes rolling, to refer to me, whilst I was standing mere feet away from them. I wasn't sure what rule I had unwillingly transgressed.

I'm sure I have been called heaps of other things since school. Adjectives I can't bring myself to fully analyse. Kids are not the only ones capable of being cruel. As I myself was (and still can be) at times.

But school in Australia.

Why Declan Mitchell decided to call me *Dougie*, with what appeared to be genuine affection and a smile, I can scarcely remember. I had no idea who Dougie Walters was. I had to check the encyclopedia in the library. Declan Mitchell was a handsome Australian boy with golden locks like Shirley Temple and blue eyes and a smile straightened by braces. I decided I should be pleased that such a boy, a boy from the 'other side', chose to bestow upon me what appeared to be an honour. Most classmates did not even speak to me as I was different.

The first year of our arrival was like trying to breathe with your mouth open in the sea. For almost a year I went to school wearing t-shirts and blue corduroy shorts (big in the mid-1970s) as my parents could not afford to buy me a second-hand school uniform and those were in fact the only clothes I possessed. For most of my classmates, I may as well have been a Martian. Nobody knew where my island was, where I had come from.

At my third school, why hugely popular Declan Mitchell chose to be friendly towards me, in front of the class, nobody could rationally explain. Not even Miss Mitchell our teacher (no relation to Declan and the reason perhaps why everyone always called Declan Mitchell, Declan Mitchell and not Declan). And for him to give me a nickname inspired by an Aussie cricketing hero was really something I did not see coming. It really was a big deal to be treated almost like a friend.

But perhaps he was having a go at me? I wasn't familiar with the Australian custom of sledging then. Declan may have been the Smiling Assassin and was taking the piss because my accent was so far removed from Walter's over-the-top ocker one. But I doubt Declan was ever that intellectually agile.

I wonder, whatever happened to cheeky Declan Mitchell?

I hope he has not gone bald.

24

We had to keep moving. There seemed to be no long-term tenancies like back home where a family could rent the same house for life. My uncle had rented the same house since before I was born. Many of our neighbours in Nicosia had rented for generations. Australia was different.

Every week, Father would go through the *Greek Herald* to find a place to rent. He and Mother then had a boisterous conversation about any house he proposed we should move to, with our mother using her veto against the proposed property. Finally, one day Mother just shook her head and said to him, 'I can't do this. I'm leaving it up to you. It's your turn to make big decisions now. And anyway, I don't speak English.'

'It won't be forever. Just until I find a better job. We can't stay here as a family, so we have no other choice. I don't know what else I can do.'

The house Father chose was owned by an old Greek woman. As we did not own any furniture, we got our suitcases and our bags and caught a bus to the new house, near the city. The streets surrounding it did not have lawns. We had been spoiled by the lawns around the boarding house in Hunters Hill and our short-term rentals in Putney and Gladesville. The houses in this new urban neighbourhood were stuck together, as if they were fake.

Houses drawn on architectural paper and not real ones that could accommodate any living and breathing humans inside.

There was lots of noise on the busy Botany Road and huge green double-decker buses made a heck of a commotion every time they passed by. Stopped metres from the front door of this horrible little house. Father went to get the key from the old woman, who lived across the street while we sat on the front steps waiting for him. Konstandinos got bored waiting around and went to the narrow lane behind the house and jumped over the fence.

'It's got no yard,' he told us when he returned. 'Where the hell can I play?' he asked looking at Mother. She remained silent. This was a new aspect of our mother's personality. Back home, she would have immediately said something sharp to Konstandinos that would have shut him up at once.

'It's horrible enough from the front,' Philadelphia piped in. 'Yuck!' she made a face of disgust which she kept in place for at least the next ten years.

Mother was still silent. Stony-faced. I wanted to squeeze her hand and tell her things would get better, but I found myself frozen. Not wanting to risk making her cry. Or get angry with me.

Things did not improve when we entered. All of us were silent. Even my brother. Mother made a strange sound but did not speak. She looked as if she had been sobbing for days.

'It's all we can afford,' Father said, firmly.

Living so close by, the old landlady used to come around every other day to purportedly *inspect the house* and castigate our mother for anything she spotted that she didn't like.

'*Po, po, po*! Don't tell me you've been cooking sausages in my house?' was one of her favourite, exasperated criticisms.

'I don't *ever* cook sausages Kyria Efrosisni,' Mother answered, insulted.

'I don't know why I don't just throw you people out of my house. *To spitaki mou…*', she would always say at the end of her sentence.

'*Siga ton polielaio*,' (*As if it's a chandelier*) Konstandinos would mutter in derision.

We all agreed with my brother and tried not to snigger too obviously. The house was built almost right on the road, separated by just a few feet of concrete and by the steel spikes of a fence. Mother warned us repeatedly not to run or carelessly rush past the gateless fence in case we got caught *on those deathly hideous spikes*.

Inside, there was no natural light but lots of mould.

'It's *an attached, single-level worker's terrace*, apparently,' Philadelphia announced to all of us one Saturday morning as she read the broadsheet newspaper that had lots of photographs of houses for sale. The *terrace* had a narrow corridor and three rooms all next to each other before you got to a tiny living room and a little lean-to two steps below, with the kitchen. It had a stainless-steel sink, a stove and a narrow orange Formica bench about three feet long. Everything had to be stored in a yellow painted cupboard above the sink.

The peeling paint was green. It was all too much colour in a tiny area. Mother was often heard invoking the Madonna's name, when trying to open the tricky kitchen window. And sniffling into a beautiful lacy handkerchief she had brought from Cyprus that she finally got out of its wrapping.

'Is this all we are worthy of?' my sister asked frequently.

'It's a dump,' my brother said, and I loved him for having the courage to speak his mind. 'My feet get black from the filthy orange carpet,' he protested.

'I doubt the old biddy has ever had it cleaned,' my sister surmised.

'I reckon the carpet is as old as the house itself—the fucking dump,' my brother said before muttering an apology. Mother did not reprimand him.

Where was my actual mother? Was this new version of her a fake?

I hated my father for bringing us here.

Why didn't he leave us alone like he usually did? I preferred the life we had for the first eleven years of my life. Him visiting for a few days each year. That's all I could take of him. He had hardly said a word to me since we had arrived. Some days, we didn't even see him. He would leave for work before we'd had our breakfast and would come home late after we had already gone to bed, banging the torn screen door as he arrived. He wasn't gambling or drinking in a pub but working his two jobs. So none of us could ever complain. Except for the stink his rolled-up Drum cigarettes made when he'd have his after-dinner smoke.

No matter where we lived or what decisions our father took, he either chose to be absent or life circumstances gave him little choice but to be mostly absent.

Not caring if any of us woke up in the morning.

25

It seemed weird having a man living in the same house as us.

Father had thinning hair, smoked either a stinking pipe or rolled-up cigarettes, sometimes even before we woke up—we'd smell the residue of his smoking in the bathroom and narrow hallway in the morning, long after he'd left for work. He would leave his dirty work boots discarded in a different spot in the house each day. He had to have two pairs of work boots as he couldn't afford the expensive ones that didn't get your socks wet so he'd have a dry, back-up pair. He was working in construction as a labourer. All his years in the Middle East meant nothing to the foreman and his employers who simply disregarded his skills and experience. He had many grey bristles on his face and always wore dirty work clothes. His feet smelled.

He never complimented us. Or said an encouraging word. Several times I'd show him a drawing I had made, using the discarded newspapers as my paper, but he'd just give me an impatient look and say nothing. He reminded me of his mum, *Yiayia* Virgin, as he seemed to have taken her role-modelling about being non-effusive to heart. Even now, when she was so far away, and he didn't have the means to ever contemplate visiting her.

Every pay day evening, my parents would inevitably argue about the cost of the airline tickets from Greece to bring us all here. Fiscally desperate, and ridden with guilt once again, that he was not by our side when the coup and the invasion happened, our father had been convinced by some mercenary travel agent to pay him back in instalments with an extraordinary percentage of interest.

'I can't believe you were so foolish as to agree to those conditions,' our mother would remind him weekly.

'I got you all here safely, didn't I?' was Father's defence.

'Yes, you managed to do that. You brought us to this…,' our mother would say bitterly, indicating with her open palm the reality of our new life—an empty rented house.

Our father was moody. Did not want to be asked any questions, and never said much more to me than, 'Are you a good boy at school?' without showing the slightest interest in what my schooling may have entailed; I knew that he did not have any capability or interest in helping me with my homework as his English was limited to a few words and phrases he had picked up from other migrants at work. He'd repeat whatever he had retained from his informal lessons and make us three recoil in horror when we realised his workmates had taught him the inaccurate or inappropriate phrase they themselves had picked up incorrectly.

'What's the Greek word for *context*, Mother? Oh my god, what am I doing— asking you?' my sister would say, brutally reducing our mother to an infant who has not yet uttered her first word.

'Dad, the dictionary says, *symfrazomena*—you can't ask your boss, "How's it hangin' man?"—please tell me you haven't asked this of the foreman.'

'*Rezili*,' my brother said, walking away.

Philadelphia was my only hope when it came to helping me understand our new language but she had never been generous with her time back home, so I didn't expect her to now change. To suddenly become my homework tutor.

Our father had seemed a lot more exotic, younger, more handsome even, more successful, when he lived in a different country to me and I knew him only as a photographic version, such as those from his wedding photographs and the occasional photo he would send from his dessert posts. I knew it was wrong of me, but I preferred the version of him shown in his old studio photographs, professionally lit, with his hair still black and in a suit. Sadly, as a three-dimensional character sharing our daily lives in real time, he failed to impress me.

He'd clear his throat early in the morning and at night too, sometimes whilst having his dinner. In tangible life, he was obviously ordinary. Never showed any physical affection to his wife or to us. Some days I'd set myself a task—I'd challenge myself to make him smile, but our conversation would quickly run dry, and he'd turn his gaze away from me and back to the days-old Greek newspaper, leaving my mission aborted.

He remained absent even when he sat right next to us under the same roof.

Philadelphia was not exaggerating—his English truly was terrible.

Worse, he got angry easily, his temper escalating from *I'm barely tolerating you,* to *Get the fuck out of my face before I throw you against the wall.*

We didn't talk together as a family. Here, where for six hours at school there was no one to talk to. In our first two years in Australia, none of my classmates invited me over to their house to play or do homework together. I tried hard to read the newspaper, of course only after Philadelphia had finished with it. I could not understand most of the words, but I wrote heaps of new words down. One by one I would look them up in Philadelphia's hand-sized *Collins Dictionary* behind her back. My sister kept a vigilant proprietary guard over any of her possessions. I had no idea who this Mr Collins was, but I surmised he had to know lots about the English language.

'Get your own dictionary,' she'd tell me if she caught me.

'I would if I could afford it.'

Photographs accompanying an article helped me guess the content. I wanted to learn everything about Australia there was to know. I learned that the new weird-looking building near the Harbour that looked like giant seashells to me, took fourteen years to build. I looked forward to seeing it for real one day. We learned about it in school one morning and the teacher disappointed us by announcing that an excursion was organised for the older students in the grade above us, but not for us.

I learned the names of the Prime Ministers. Whitlam then Fraser. First, there was Mr Whitlam who had white hair, so I guessed he was pretty old. Mother loved seeing him on television even though she had not a clue as to what he was saying. But her eyes would light up whenever he was on the screen. 'What is he saying now?' she would constantly ask us, and we were anxious not to wound her by admitting we had not yet miraculously learned conversational English just because we had started school.

How could Mother think this was possible? If it were that easy, how come she had not learned any English? When we would complain about our father, and her own bitter recriminations about the cost of the aeroplane tickets that delivered us to our new life, Mother was quick to remind all three of us that without him we would still be living in tents in a camp alongside other displaced people. Terra Sancta was only an emergency measure during the school holidays when the war started. We would have been moved on to a tent city, she'd remind us, herself horrified.

'No running water, mud and dirt everywhere. I shudder to think what may have happened to us in a camp. To you three.'

I kept quiet as my secret made my face go crimson.

Mother did not notice.

It's way too late to cite safety now I wanted to admit to her.

26

At school one day, the teacher wrote the word NUCLEAR on the chalkboard and was very sombre. He mentioned calmly that our lives were at risk. I understood that the Soviet Union was thinking of killing us all and I despaired that no matter how far we had come, away from bombs, threats of war seemed to follow us around everywhere. Even to the end of the world, here in cricket-mad sunny Australia, with its mowed lawns and Holden cars.

Dinos (his schoolmates had tried calling him Kosta, and then Con) and Philly were changing and did not include me in their chats. They would set off for the bus to their high school and I would be envious they had each other as company. When the three of us would have a squabble or even a serious fight, raising our voices and calling each other names—I was habitually (and predictably) called 'Lotta' by Dinos—Mother would warn us that we three should treasure our time together. Instead of arguing with each other over silly things.

'What for?' Dinos would question Mother unabashed.

'Because when you're all grown up, things will be different between you.'

'We probably won't even see each other, might be living in different countries even' Philadelphia admitted, cryptically.

'Mark my words, you will look back on this period of your lives fondly. You'll miss each other, of that I'm sure. But it'll be too late,' she sermonised, wiping tears and sighing in that tone older Greek women used in the village.

At that, all three of us would roll our eyes in unison, dismissing what Mother was suggesting. Thinking the reverse, that we'd be glad when each of us had our own house and never had to exchange a word with one another.

'As if I'll miss this poor, fat bloke,' Dinos would scoff, pushing me back on the shoulder. All of us agreed we couldn't wait to get away from each other, but Mother hadn't won a nursing scholarship to Alexandria, Egypt in the 1950s for nothing. She had always been fiercely intelligent.

'You'll see,' she'd insist. 'One day you are all going to think about your poor Mother's words. Maybe even admit I was right. But it'll be too late. For me...'

Had Mother always been so self-pitying I wondered, or was it because she knew no one here in the suburbs of Australia?

Soon enough, Dinos no longer wanted to play any games anymore with me. I'd beg him to play hangman or race each other to the back fence and back but he'd just say, 'Leave me alone, you idiot!'

Philly spent most of her time in her room writing in her diary. I knew this because when I could, I used to sneak a read of her innermost thoughts, out of boredom. Somehow, she would nearly always find out. Did bloody Dinos tell? In exchange for chocolate? Mother would ration four squares for each of us every Thursday evening from a block of *Cadbury's*. It was our weekly treat.

Realising my transgression into her privacy, Philly would get filthy mad at me. At first, I'd claim total innocence which made my sister even madder and my already frazzled mother more frazzled, trying to placate the commotion that ensued.

If anyone had suffered the most out of this transatlantic move, it was our mother.

Her bouffant was gone. Her hair was streaked with tufts of grey. Her matronly suits were gone. She had put on a stone or more. She never wore her lipstick anymore. She would get hysterical easily whereas back home she always remained in control even when seething at something Uncle Pericles had said or done. Even when all three of us would be screaming, crimson at each other over some minor injustice. Her reputation as a good listener had been extinguished. Here in Australia, she'd still have her Nescafe but always alone, staring at the backyard through the kitchen window. She knew nobody who might share confidences with her discreetly or seek her counsel.

Worse for us, she started slapping us hard across the face, when she had never done that to us when we were kids. Her ring and bangles would hurt us and cause welts. She'd hit us even when we hadn't broken any of her rules and had eaten all our lentil pilaf. Back home, she had always been unflappable. She always knew what was happening in the world. Now, she got her news from the two-week-old Greek newspaper a co-worker of our father's passed down to him.

'Did you hear that...,' Mother would start telling us and one of us would cut her short.

'*Der* Mum! That was two weeks ago.'

27

· · · · · · · · · · · ·

Soon, Konstandinos, Kosta, Con, Dinos, officially became *Dean* at school when he started to shave. Philadelphia went from Delphi to Della, to Dell, to Philly and finally back to plain old *Phil.* She asked new friends to call her Philly, but many couldn't be bothered with two syllables and just called her Phil. Then everyone assumed she didn't like boys as a result of having a boy's name. Even when she had let her hair grow again into its beautiful mane, everyone called her Phil.

Me? Well Demosthenes was out of the question in Australia: way out. As was Thimos. We tried Theo, and Tom for a while, then Timmy and Timbo but finally settled on Demos or *Demon*, or *Cyp* depending on the situation and the heritage of the person addressing me. The teachers could never say my name right. Some kids kept calling me Dimwit or Dipstick or simply, Dim, thinking it was still funny the thousandth time I heard it. I refused to show how mortified I was each time.

Mother mostly still called me Demosthenes but weirdly she didn't mind calling our Konstandinos, Dean or Dinos with her Greek accent softening the D.

Our rented house didn't stay our house long enough for us to buy any furniture to put into it, to fill it up. It stayed cold and sparse. I wondered if all rented homes in Sydney were owned

142

by old Greek women. In all the houses we briefly stayed in, the landlady was a cantankerous old Greek woman who begrudged us our tenancy. There was never a lease document, so we were at their mercy.

'I can't live without that money. It's the only money I have. I am not a dole bludger or on compo like so many bloody Greeks. *'Thelo ta lefta mou tora sou leo'* (*I want my money now!*).'

Our latest septuagenarian oligarch was raving. Mother was trying to explain that she would absolutely have her money when Father got home from work—'*Kitaxtai, Kyria* Papadopoulou, when my husband gets home, like we do every fortnight, you shall have your money. We have never not paid you on a Thursday.'

'I will sit and wait for him then,' our elderly landlady announced.

'As you please,' Mother said in a benign tone, 'But, you see, sadly, we don't actually have any chairs to accommodate you comfortably for all that time. It'll be hours before my husband gets home from his second job. It might be best to wait in your beautiful car. What do you think?'

And with that, Mother demonstrated to all of us, that she had not yet lost her old diplomatic skills completely.

28

· · · · · · · · · · · · ·

We left Mrs Papadopoulou's house early the following year, after just a few months, still with very few things of our own. It made moving an easy process. Father went with Dean in one taxi and Mother, Phil and me in another.

Our mother could not take to the new Prime Minister who succeeded Whitlam— Malcolm Fraser. 'He seems unreliable. And as if he is doing us all a favour. Living a life of luxury, in that waterfront mansion with the uninterrupted Opera House views' she commented, whenever he appeared on the television.

'In Kirribilli,' Philadelphia said.

'I can't say that word without sounding rude,' Mother said in Greek, almost disappointed, alluding to the last two syllables. My brother snorted a laugh, as if he had indeed heard Mother saying the Cypriot colloquial word for *dick,* out loud.

We moved to Marrickville, where there were a few other kids of immigrants at school and even though they weren't the top faction in the school hierarchy they were a force to be reckoned with. Not that I went out of my way to be identified in the migrant group. You see, I still retained my *fresh-off-the-boat* status as the other pupils who were children of migrants were all born here—with the exception of a Vietnamese kid nobody could make any sense out of, who was literally fresh off a wretched boat.

144

People just assumed that all Greeks (it didn't matter to them that you were from Cyprus, which was an independent country, a republic) stuck together. That all migrants could do was form a ghetto of their own. The way the Yugos stuck together back then, the way the Germans did, the way Irish Catholics had.

The reality was, that no one ever gave me the option of consenting to belong to a group. Simply, my racial origin was determined externally. Others chose the box I was shut in. Contained. I had no say in it.

But yes, we migrant kids were a force to be reckoned with at Marrickville Public. Especially when Nick Eleftheropoulos and I (both round as basketballs) miraculously smashed the lunchtime handball competition, outplaying all others, including Liu, the skinny Chinese kid who everyone predicted to be the dead cert winner. Mr Daniels, the PE teacher who openly scowled at my foreignness and my weight, actually spoke to me then for the first time, in a nice way. I even liked his nickname—all the other male teachers, no matter how young or old, referred to him as 'Danno' with what seemed genuine affection. I craved someone male to call me by a positive nickname and regard me with affection.

I had had several graphic dreams about Mr Daniels, on account of his muscles and long, blond hair. I told myself my dreams were out of my control. I could never look this young teacher in the eye. I would force myself to avoid staring at his muscular legs when he was on playground duty and would purposefully walk in the opposite direction to wherever he was headed. I worried I'd be found out if I was caught staring. I stayed anxious the whole time I was at the school that I'd be humiliated in front of the other students and teachers as a pervert and be expelled from school. My father would throw me out on the street.

When we won, Mr Daniels couldn't believe I was the same *Timbo* he had called *a fat wog* and *a waste of space*. He looked like the archetypal Aussie surfer, down to the blond, curly eiderdown of golden hairs on his strong legs. He embodied everything the majority of his male pupils could never physically be, even if we were ever good at rugby league or cricket. Being good at those two sports made you an honorary fair dinkum Aussie. The genetic discrepancy between us, the so-called *wogs* and our tanned-to-perfection Aussie icon teacher, could never be rectified.

We didn't know then that many of our idols of worship had European origins themselves, hailing from Germany, Holland, Poland, Czechoslovakia and Hungary. In hindsight, I expect Mr Daniels probably had a Danish or Swedish dad whose surname was abbreviated to Daniels.

A girl called Shelly Pattinson started to show a bit of an interest in me about this period. We were in Year 6. After a few months in my new school, she got her friends Kim and Susan to convey a message. I was standing outside our portable classroom with Nick or Thanh or Con. Girls did not usually approach us. Susan, who always looked as if she had just finished crying but could squeeze out yet another tear given half a chance, looked at me and said, 'Shelly really digs you!'

I think it was Susan. I'm not exactly sure which one of Shelly's two bosom buddies actually relayed the cryptic message to me. Kim and Susan had a habit of finishing each other's sentences. It's weird what things we remember as if they happened yesterday but other events, some that may have occurred more recently, we cannot recollect with certitude.

What I was certain about was the fact that I was not ready for the subtleties of the Australian accent for I could not at that stage of my Australian-English proficiency, distinguish between the production of the 'g' sound and that of 'k.' In my new-arrival's ignorance of phonetics, I had understood Susan and Kim were saying 'dick' to me and so I surmised that they were swearing at me.

I belted the poor unsuspecting duo one and got sent to lunchtime detention. In charge that afternoon was my tormentor/object of desire—the blond Phys. Ed. teacher. He was becoming quite proud of my notoriety and when I tried to explain in my busted English, that I was there because of a girl, he winked at me and seemed very impressed.

Nick, Bill, Kosta and Con, all of Greek heritage but who spoke only a handful of Greek words, were also sent to detention. As punishment, for not explaining to me in Greek the innocence of Shelly's intimate, innocent, message. When Nick or Bill or Con protested that they couldn't have explained because you weren't allowed to speak in a foreign language at school, the principal (or was it the Boys' Master?) was not impressed. Miffed, he decided their protestations were *direct impertinence.* He extended the detention to a week for insolence. *Back-chatting,* he called it.

I didn't have the heart to look Shelly Pattinson in the face again and she too cooled her emotions towards me; cross-cultural love having been made impossible in late 1975 in the playground of Marrickville Public Senior campus (now apartments). The way things had played out was quite unfortunate because I really liked

Shelly, and standing ramrod straight behind her at assembly in the mornings made me so nervous, I wanted to throw up.

After the incident, Nick told me that liking girls made me a nerd and that he didn't want to hang around with me anymore. Bill and Kosta and Con, aggrieved over the unfair detention they too had to sit through, called me a *bloody idiot* and *a stupid wog* and no longer asked me to play handball. So, I spent lunchtimes walking around the schoolyard pretending to look for someone or something, forever moving, lest someone suspect my isolation.

A while later, having left both Marrickville and its Public School's Senior Campus behind, I received a letter from Shelly in which she wrote 'I favourite...' but I can't remember which was her favourite football team. Her grammatical error unsettled me greatly for my English had improved dramatically by then. I also didn't quite understand what the letter itself was intending to do. Was she simply being friendly? Had she sent letters to all our former classmates, now dispersed at a number of local high schools? Was she romantically interested in me? I could not write back for Shelly had not included her address. Perplexed as I was, and certainly not impressed by Shelly's grammar, the letter proved to me that the universe was signaling to me that Shelly and I had never been destined for each other. I wonder what I would've done had she had written, 'I favour...' or even, 'I barrack for...'.

29

· · · · · · · · · · · ·

We moved again.

This time, to the outer-western suburbs, about fifty kilometres from the city. A Greek woman Mother had met in church had recently moved to this suburb and reckoned housing was much cheaper there than in the suburbs closer to the city. Her husband had recently left her for a younger woman and our mother felt pleased to have made her first friend in Australia.

'We are becoming untouchables,' was all Philly said but I was too young to understand what she meant.

'Just when you think we couldn't be more ostracised, we are. A spiral descent into poverty. From such heights…'

'You can hardly call living in that hideous boarding house, full of miserable untouchables good for your social reputation, nor our other three rented houses,' Mother admonished.

'People don't need to know my exact street address. I could still have said, *I live in Hunters Hill.* Or bucolic Putney with its fields with horses grazing. Nobody needs to know more details about my actual déclassé home. So first, you and your idiotic husband decide to move us to a street next to the housing commission hellhole of Waterloo, to that dump, full of mould. With the insane old bat of a landlady. Then, the Greek immigrant-central Enmore-border-Marrickville in that narrow terrace with damp on every wall. Now... God', she said, her eyes full of tears, walking away, shaking her head.

'Where the fuck *is* this place anyway?' was all Dinos asked, red-faced with disgust. If we wanted to go anywhere from our new tiny home in what Dinos called the *Sydney Bronx*, we had no choice but to catch the brown-coloured train. Two and half hours later it would be at Central. In the past, the 500 series bus would be our means of getting to the city in no time. When we first moved to Waterloo, my father was too proud to ask strangers what number bus went there. So once, he made me walk all the way back from Grace Bros in Broadway to Waterloo, using a map as a guide.

I was carrying the first and only toy he ever bought me in Australia—a toy Qantas jumbo jet that taxied around my room, whizzing with its lights on but not taking off. Soon the batteries ran out. Mother said she didn't have any spare money to throw away on a stupid plane toy that never ever took off. I didn't have the nerve to protest and run the risk of being accused of back-chatting and be punished.

Angry with her, there were many cruel things I could have said to her.

How she chose to see only what was important to her reputation. But I kept quiet because I did not want to upset her even more. She had always been so busy in Nicosia trying to look after us on her own and to pre-empt what gossipy neighbours may say, given our father was not there, that she had been oblivious to what abuse I had been subjected to. Decades later, whenever I was treated badly, the same kind of anger would surface and knock me for six—just like my dad's temper, mine went from mild to berserk at the first sign of disrespect or dismissal.

There were no public buses operating in our new suburb and the private bus just ran from the train station to the next two suburbs and cost more than two cans of Fanta and a packet of Olos. Nobody dared to walk the streets after dark, especially around the shops and railway station. At 5.00 pm, the shop owners would pull down metal shutters and padlock their businesses. It was the kind of place where rough-looking, unkempt women wearing big t-shirts and tights, regularly swore aloud between taking puffs on ciggies. Young women who told the bank tellers off without censure. It was not the tellers' fault they had no funds in their saving account. I wondered how grown-ups were allowed to blame others and get away with it. You would be asked for *loose change* every time you stepped out of the newsagent or the bank next door. If you refused, an avalanche of filthy words would be sprayed in your direction.

Father spent less and less time at home with us. At weekends he would be found at Cyprus House in town, near Museum Station; at least that's what he would say to Mother when she'd accuse him of neglecting us and simply not loving us enough. When he did return to our small brick veneer villa home, it would be late at night and we'd be fast asleep, only we'd wake up because of the noise he'd make and because we could all hear our mother's helpless accusations and then her sobs. It was a small villa, cheaply built, offering less privacy than a flat.

By this stage, I wasn't talking much to Phil, Dinos or Mother. I spent more and more time inside my head, feeling paranoid other boys knew my secrets. School breaks were spent talking to imaginary friends and pretending to be something other than what mirrors and shop windowpanes showed me to be. I was overweight. Obese. I was the only boy in Year 7 with hairy legs and a moustache. My hair was oily despite washing it daily on the sly with Phil's green apple shampoo. *Greaseball* and *Greasywog* were not uncommon epithets thrown at me without invitation by various Garys, Terrys, Craigs, Robs and Sharons.

Not being able to speak to Father about what was happening to my body was nothing new. The distance between us was becoming wider than it had ever been.

Since being transplanted to Australia, the changes in my mother frightened me so I could not entertain confiding in her or expect any kind of help from her either. I had two useless parents whom I could not rely on for support. Within two and a half years of our arrival in Australia, our mother had become a woman I could hardly recognise anymore. Our roles had been reversed— we, her children, were now the parents and she, our parent, had morphed into our completely helpless child.

She couldn't write me a note excusing me from school nor complete a permission slip for a school excursion. She didn't attend Parent/Teacher nights and certainly did not know any of my teachers' names. In Nicosia, she knew all the teaching staff by name (and that of their mothers) and saw many of them outside of school at community functions and Ladies' Committee community initiatives. She had direct access to the headmaster or the headmistress and they would fuss over her involvement in the school.

Here, she didn't have any friends, and she no longer had an interest in what we wore. If she did actually speak to us, it was in order to chastise us for something we had done or had not done. Asking us about some official form that needed filling or telling us what to say in translation to a tradesman or a medical receptionist or to the bus conductor. We inadvertently became her parents and she our child, despite our age. Fleeing our island for Australia had flipped our status as children needing parental guidance, support and confidence-building. Our parents could never provide us with any of that, not even with basic financial security. This burden, this reversal of the adult/child role would have consequences on all of us, throughout our life. Would make us run away from genuinely wanting to take care of each other, or even get together for celebrations, out of fear one of us would become a burden. This fundamental transgression by our parents, this dysfunction, wrecked any chance we had of developing healthy family and personal relationships.

All I thought about as I patiently waited for the late train, as I diligently answered Comprehension Questions from the textbook in my *Special English* class and filled in the missing blanks with the correct word in a sentence, was of a better life. Areos didn't seem to be as real as it once was. Even though we were the same people who had lived in it only a handful of years ago, the memory of our house no longer resonated strongly enough to help me get through the day at school.

Areos Street was dead and buried. A relative had written to our mother to let her know that our house was demolished, and an apartment block now stood in its place all the way to the corner. I no longer remembered what colour the walls were painted, not even that of my bedroom. I couldn't recall if there was an arcade opposite our house or not. Old Nicosia was renowned for its small arcades full of tiny shops providing all kinds of services. Everything from a store selling doorknockers of every shape and style to shops selling tablecloths and Manchester.

When we had first left our home behind, everyone reassured us that it would be for a short period of time and things would get back to normal on our island. *You'll be back home in no time* everyone said. Including Mother. Nobody warned us of having to flee our new rented homes twice in three weeks. Nobody said, *Prepare yourself for the horrors of being homeless*. Or that we and our neighbours would find ourselves in emergency accommodation in a Boarding School's auditorium with hundreds of others. Or forewarned us about the smell of so many people in the one big room.

Nobody prepared me for what was done to me.

I never spoke about my time in the camp to any of my schoolmates. What could I have said? I was pretty sure by all the smiles I saw on my schoolmates' faces every day, the rambunctious joy they all seemed to have about them every day, that none of them would understand my past. My misery. It was clear that nobody among my carefree schoolmates had lived through the same experiences. Nobody could share my shameful secrets. Even if I could tell someone what had happened, what did happen could not be erased. Talking about a horrible experience does not soften its sting.

Not a single relative of Father's warned us that we would have to leave our island for good.

Nobody in the family had ever been to Australia. This big island country called Australia only existed in vague terms to us. It did not exist as an escape route possibility until our father discovered he could get a visa for us. It all happened so quickly. Father had remotely made a decision about the rest of our lives and did not even canvas our own opinions. Shut down his wife's suggestion to consider emigrating to the United Kingdom to join her cousins' families there.

Now, we were banished to the outer western suburbs of Sydney. Exiles from our island and isolated in our adopted country that had kindly taken us in. There were no aunts here, or cousins or uncles or neighbours, or people who weren't our relatives but whom our grandparents had known or who had gone to school with Mother and we would call uncle or aunty or cousin. We did not know anyone's family backstory.

We were simply *boatpeople*.

Wogs among strangers.

I felt as if I didn't even belong to my family.

Phil and Dinos did have blue eyes after all. Maybe I had another father, a real father, a good normal father, somewhere else. During those first few years, when my family lived together in our city rentals and finally in *Westie Land*, I never saw Mother and Father demonstrate any sort of romantic expression of affection towards one another. I hated them for that too. They had always been like that. I knew this was not normal.

To console myself, all I thought about when I despised my parents' behaviour, was the handful of times back home when all of us kids had been allowed to sit down with the grown-ups to enjoy the Cypriot version of afternoon tea (watermelon, halloumi cheese and crusty aniseed bread) on the marble-topped table Mother had had shipped from Greece. If it was too hot to gather on the rooftop terrace, we all of us sat beneath the shade of the fig tree from next door, the scent of jasmine, of Greek basil and thyme and other herbs in Mother's sliver of a vegetable patch almost overwhelming in the heat. I do not remember with certainty whether Father was ever among those gathered.

I wanted to go back to my recent past. Rewind chronology to before the stupid coup. The invasion. I knew where I stood then both at school and at home. And in the family. Now, here, everyone's role was different. Why did Father continue to be absent when he was now present?

I thought of Cousin Dimitris and how much he loved me, in his own good way, always with a smile and encouraging me. Listening to me go on and on about stupid things or about my dreams about the future. He listened to me quietly and seemed impressed with my silly dreams about drawing and painting. Always gave me hope that all I wanted in life would come true. I recalled our day excursions in his tiny sports cars to various beaches, thanks to a couple of photographs mother had brought with us to Australia. One particular trip I remember vividly was a trip to Salamis with its volcanic sand, so different to the golden sands of Kerynia where we spent our summer vacations.

Dimitris must have been in his early twenties at the time the photograph was taken, but there he is, a fatherly figure, trusted by our mother to look after us three and his own young brother too. Upon arrival, Dimitris showed us how to bury a whole watermelon in the sand and after supervising our swim and our thrilling jumping from the jetty into the water, all of us would dig-out the watermelon and, miracle of miracles, it would be chilled. The laughs we had with the juice of the fruit running down our chin, something that would have horrified our mother but did not seem to perturb Dimitris in the least—in fact, he seemed pleased when we felt liberated enough to act as children and always regarded us with a beautiful smile and lots of laughter. Made us feel secure. And loved.

Was Dimitris alive? There were all kinds of theories about the whereabouts of Cyprus's *disappeared* boys and men. Some people said the enemy had selected the most good-looking men and had forced them into marriage back on the Turkish mainland. In an attempt to make sure, even if they had the chance, that they could never leave and return to our island. Most logical people were certain the disappeared were executed. Buried in makeshift graves.

But no matter the truth, Dimitris was still alive to me.

I thought of the men who had touched me and who had hurt me in that half-finished house we stayed in for less than a fortnight. And of the peasant men in the camp who hurt me. I felt instantly ashamed. Repulsed. With myself.

When we had Personal Development class here in Australia, I was convinced that all the other students knew what I had done. I was crimson with shame and wanted to throw up. I didn't know which way to look when the teacher asked certain questions about sexuality. I tried desperately to mimic the other students' responses. Tried to act as dumbfounded and shocked as some of the other boys in the class seemed to be about what was considered *normal* sexual experience.

30

I daydreamed a lot, continued to paint canvases in my head, as I sat in the ESL class, filling in grammar drills and missing prepositions. I was getting fed up with being categorised as a *migrant* by the school authorities and needing to or not, was made to attend ESL classes. I truly felt I was only playing a numbers game to keep the second ESL teacher in work. I didn't begrudge her the job for she did it better than the first tenured teacher who would be keeping her job, insufficient student numbers or not.

But I was so sick of filling in blanks and reading naff British-produced texts that had nothing in them that was real about Australia, nothing that related to my life in outer-Western Sydney. No material in their content that could assist me in my desperate goal to be like everyone else here in our new country. Not to stick out so much. I wanted to learn all the weird expressions other students used daily making me feel like a moron not knowing quite what they meant. I wanted to attend a normal class all the time, along with everybody else. I didn't want to be contained in any ghetto, or be part of a labelled, *marginalised minority*. It was bad enough daily attempting to cope (and failing) with the memory of my prematurely active sexual past.

I wanted out of that boring *Special English* class. After all, I

158

had topped sixth class Maths at Marrickville Public, surprising the handsome PE teacher yet again on Speech Night. As MC, Mr Daniels shook my hand stiffly and presented me with my *Certificate of Merit* whilst I prayed that nobody noticed what was happening in my shorts as a result of his powerful grip. I felt an electric surge power through me as his strong hand grabbed mine. And once again, felt ashamed of myself, instead of being proud at my achievement. A pattern I repeated, again and again and again.

It was about this time too, at twelve and a bit, that hair started to sprout like a sturdy, blooming oakleaf hydrangea plant everywhere on my body. I started to feel irreversibly guilty about my body and daily felt utterly disgusted with myself and my past. Even more than the usual disgust I carried with me. Angry with my headspace for finding myself thinking about some of those men sometimes, in a weird way.

Did I bring on the sexual trespasses myself?

Did men recognise something in me that I had not been aware of as a boy?

Did I wear a sign on my forehead that signalled I was open to be sexually abused?

Was it all my responsibility?

Was I born that way?

I felt certain that my teachers, especially the male ones, knew, when they looked at me, that I carried a secret. Worse, that they knew exactly what the revolting secret was. To avoid any kind of intervention I started avoiding people's eyes. All through high school, it didn't matter how many school committees I willingly served on, how many school magazine articles I wrote or how many school dances I attended, my guilt, my paranoia and shame, stayed with me and started to consume me.

One day, not long before the end of the first school term in Year 8, I got home early on account of jigging Sport to find Mother crying. She wouldn't talk to me. She wouldn't tell me what the matter was. Hopeless, I made her a cup of tea, like I saw people doing on the television soap operas I watched but unlike the characters in the television series, my offered cup of peppermint tea did not miraculously heal my mother. I even tried making her a Nescafe with two teaspoons of condensed milk but still she remained silent.

When, three days later, there had been no physical sign whatsoever of Father (his work boots on the back verandah for instance, no banging screen door late at night) I realised exactly why Mother had been crying.

He has left us.

Again.

Acknowledging this, saying these words inside of me, I wanted to scream blue murder. I wanted to punch someone, wanted to ring scratch every neighbour's Kingswood and Monaro and Ford. I wanted to break Dean's LP of *Tattoo You*, smash Phil's Bonnie Tyler's *Lost in France* cassette, extricating the narrow brown tape from its reels until it was a long, intertwined mess. Stomp on the bloody thing. Each time I hear the chorus of that song, I'm back at that point, when the penny dropped that our father had abandoned us again.

My father's familial duty stage lasted just over three years.

I now hated him more than I hated Armando Merek. Armando

was the most muscular and handsome boy in my year at school. All the other boys in the school called him *Arman* or even just *The Man*. Nobody male dared to say the last syllable of Armando's name. His teeth were perfectly straight and white. He looked a little bit Greek. I never found out where his parents had come from but guessed he was of mixed blood of some kind on account of his skin. Armenian perhaps? Something else— Palestinian? Iranian? Fijian?

Everyone knew that his parents were filthy rich since a long Jaguar with dark tinted windows dropped Armando off at the school gates most mornings. Armando was not academically gifted and never seemed worried about assignments and essays. I knew unequivocally that I would never be as successful or popular in life as Armando. He would cruise through life having a blast and good things would always come to him. Everyone he met would like him and want to spend more time in his company, in his glow. He was tall, very handsome, and strong. Blessed with clear skin and a permanent winning smile. Never worried about life or questioned his place in it.

Nearly all the girls in our Year had a crush on Armando but he remained aloof, unattainable. Rumour had it he was dating an older woman outside of school and basically two-timing whichever girl was lucky enough to briefly hold hands with him during recess and lunch. I avoided sitting next to Armando in our one shared subject even when there were no other desks free. I was afraid I'd accidentally touch his forearm and even willingly lean in to smell his long dark curls.

A week after Father left, Phil, Dinos and I held a family meeting in Phil's room and decided we all now had to get jobs. We agreed our mother had suffered enough. We made a pact not to discuss our job aspirations with our aggrieved, silent mother, until after we had been successful and had to assure her of our whereabouts.

But our sad mother was one step ahead of us as usual. She had already gone through both Greek newspapers and scanned the employment ads. Within four days, Mother had found herself her first, low-paying, tax-free job, sewing tacky, polyester, floral dresses for a sleazy, older Greek businessman who never used deodorant. We could smell him as he alighted from his Ford LTD. He would arrive early on a Saturday morning and deliver huge plastic bags filled with gaudy frocks that needed stitching.

Mother, with our help reading the classifieds in the *Trading Post*, bought herself an old Singer machine. From then on, the two of them were inseparable. She set-up her working space in one corner of her narrow bedroom, getting us to move a dresser into the shed. She'd be at the sewing machine when we woke up and she'd be there when we went to sleep. She would always find time to cook something in-between, but we had to do the supermarket shopping ourselves on the way home from school. We had no idea our mother could sew despite her father's occupation for we had never seen her mend anything back home.

I was generally the one to run to the shops when an ingredient or item was needed in the villa because I was the youngest. Phil would claim that she had homework which was more important than Dinos's. Then Dinos would claim that he too had homework and that I should go because he was older than me and his homework was far more complex and important than mine. I had to do as I was told.

'You could do with the exercise, you fatso,' he would add just to rub salt into the gaping wound of my lacklustre self-esteem.

Father had left us no explanation letters. Over the summer break, not long after his disappearance, I was purposely shedding weight, getting good haircuts at the local hair salon from a guy with bleached hair and an earring worn on the right ear (he looked like a member of Duran Duran, but gone obviously wrong). He sold me expensive Delva shampoo and conditioner bottles that he reckoned would make my hair shiny and healthy.

When school started that year, I styled the dull Year 9 school uniform with touches of a rebel—the shirt tail left hanging out the back on one side, poking through underneath the grey school jumper; wearing non-uniform shorts at Sport; buying the phallic-shaped Pierre Cardin after-shave costing a month and a half of my wages at Chook City. My immediate aim then was to get a girlfriend for that was the ultimate proof that you were successful as a boy, that you weren't a *dag*, a *poofter*, a *fag* or a *loser*. Tangible proof that you were a real man.

I fought compulsively within myself to assuage my guilt for having lost my virginity at such a young age, albeit unwillingly. I intrinsically believed that I had brought it on myself, convinced it must have been my fault. So, I was prepared to do anything, undergo whatever change my peer group demanded of me so that I could be accepted by them. I had to prove to others, and to myself that I was a normal guy.

However, despite my good intentions, my first attempt to embrace heterosexuality and symbolically erase my sexual past was rebutted by a friend of the girl I told myself I fancied. I only liked her because she was pretty and had Greek heritage and was not a complete *veg head*. She also wore nice things at school dances and her hair was nice and neat. Symmetry had always been a thing with me. I did not feel right if things were out-of-place, messy, or not in functional order. If someone's left eyebrow was not an exact replica of their right, it would disturb me and I would start to stammer—even if the person whose face I was dissecting was a complete stranger I had caught a glimpse of on the bus or the train or in the supermarket.

I remember surreptitiously leaving a card with a note for Connie on her chair in History class. I was praying she'd sit at the same seat she always did on Tuesdays third period. That *Farting Fotini* didn't end up inadvertently receiving my invitation to never-ending love. Sure enough the message got through. At lunchtime, the friend of the object of my affection came over to where I used to sit, saying that she had been sent over by Connie.

'Come over to where we hang around,' she dared me and I followed her, my heart racing. I felt as if I were being led to the electric chair for execution, although this prospect then seemed to be less onerous and painful than how I felt walking behind Connie's friend. I was certain everyone watching us in the playground knew what was going on.

Please do not publicly expose my failure.

Please.

'Why do we have to go to where you hang around?' I finally protested, halfway there, feeling as if I were going to burst if I had just kept my grievances quietly bottled up.

'So, it doesn't look like we're coming over to your area of the playground, Einstein. People talk, y'know.'

'Oh,'—*How dare she* I thought. Even if she was Connie's best friend. Pretty or not, neither Connie, nor this arrogant, less attractive version of Connie who was granted best friend status, had ever won anything on *Speech Night* last December. They would never be prefects. They'd never see the inside of English Class 1. Yet, here she was, looking down on me. We were safely behind cover in front of the girls' toilet block, which was down some stairs and away from view of the playground, a level above.

'Look...' I sensed brutality but stayed put. Frozen. 'Connie says it's really nice of you, but she's not interested.'

'That's okay.' Bloody Hell it was.

'She doesn't want to go from an A to a B.'

I thought she was talking grades. The fact was, so far, I had never been awarded a B in high school!

'That's alright. I'll wait until she's ready to have another boyfriend.'

'No, no, you don't understand.'

'I don't?'

'Her last boyfriend was an A, and she doesn't want to go to the Bs. I mean, your nose is crooked and that...'

I was suddenly baptised a B. Sooner or later everyone gets one. My God. I, who spent an hour and a half to get ready for school in the morning; I, who managed to learn English in less than a year, who survived an all-Anglo assault in Hunters Hill and Boronia Park Public and Putney Public.

But justice for all, they say. Two weeks after the *End of The Connie Affair*, while stuffing a super-sized chook at Chook City, I fell in lust with Maria. She was a Super Chook City hostess who wore lipstick, was heaps prettier than Connie and thought I was definitely an A minus, at the very least.

And much later in life, I ran into Connie of the Bs.

'You got your nose fixed,' she pointed out with a knowing smile.

She was a TAA *hostie* (she said this as if she were having a go at herself, rolling her eyes) had bad acne scars and told me she had *men problems*. She told me all this in an Indian craft shop in the city where I was checking out incense sticks as a birthday gift for my sister. I was disappointed to see the princess of my high school dreams, the girl I had put on a veritable pedestal, was not that pretty as a grown-up. I would have been mortified had she married a strapping, six-foot-three WASP articulate architect or funds manager from Mosman. A man who may have kept her in the manner she had hoped would be her lot in life, when she had dismissively baptised me a B.

<h1 style="text-align:center">31</h1>

By the time third term of Year 9 had come around I had become infamous. Unintentionally that is. Tongues were wagging. Young girls screamed as I walked through the playground. I was a hit. But the older boys in Year 10 demonstrably hated me and called me a *fuckin' poofter dago*.

All this notoriety within the enclosed gates of our public high school simply because of my newly discovered dancing prowess. I took part in a lunchtime concert alongside the second-most popular girl in our year. Michaela McKenzie. People wanted to touch my John Travolta-inspired hairstyle. I wore retro outfits to two school dances: narrow 50s trousers Father had left behind and a silk shirt with a grandfather collar.

My infamy was brief. Lasted about three months. A group of senior boys bashed me as I left the last school dance of the year. Some of them were prefects. *Fuckin' show off wog pansy* was thrown at me as my crime. Some senior boys would shout out pejorative epithets at me as I minded my own business, walking from class to class or going from the canteen to the library. Right in front of the teachers, both male and female but the teachers pretended the abuse was not happening.

I didn't speak up.

That was my mistake.

But speak up to whom? The teachers? My mute mother?

To this day, every time I hear *Ring my bell* (the last song played at the dance before we all left) I am distressed. I wish I were a football player or an athlete. Or that I was taller. More muscular. That I could have fought back harder. Show the bullies with my fists that I was their equal. At a time when I was starting to acknowledge who I was I learned painfully it is not good to stick out in any way.

By the beginning of the new school year only the bullying, shoving and name-calling continued. The girl fans in the playground had moved onto another dude. I was a has-been at fifteen. I worked all day on the weekends at Chook City and tongue pashed Maria in my breaks. I was topping my classes (who else would come first in French in a Westie high school?).

Armando didn't seem so perfect anymore. Well, sort of didn't...

Maria made me feel as if there was nothing I could not achieve. With Maria, I won disco dancing competitions even when I had never actually gone through the process of learning to dance formally in a class. I just did it. Maria was pretty. Guys would ask her to dance when I'd be getting us a Kahlua and milk and she'd point to the friendship ring I'd given her and smile apologetically. I won many 12 inch-45s, which was really something, considering I didn't even own a stereo, not even Dinos had one.

I bought Maria gifts because she was a gift-seeking kind of a girl. I gave her a silver whistle (with borrowed money from Phil who had by that stage graduated from Chook City), which she blew all night as we danced at Pitt Street Gardens one sweaty night to the tune of a Donna Summer song ('Bad Girls'? 'Hot Stuff'?)

long before Donna had become a fundamentalist Christian born-again type.

I was trying so hard to be normal.

To be accepted.

Not just by the older Anglo guys at school but by everyone.

Sometimes though, even as I kissed Maria or when we were holding hands, it never felt quite real. It felt like we were play acting what we perceived we should be doing. Perhaps that was what all adults did in relationships anyway? Maybe part of being a grown-up was to simply follow a script society had constructed thousands of years ago? A script that was tried and tested over the generations and proven to be effective?

Was all of life just theatre?

I did not know how other boys my age felt about this—were they happy doing what the media, books and teachers of religious education told us was expected of a boy? I made feeble attempts to bring up the subject with a couple of other boys who I knew had girlfriends, but never managed to get to the crux of the matter as their responses were monosyllabic and made me wonder if merely by asking, I had blown my chances of being perceived as *normal*.

I was learning that teenage boys, and even guys a lot older, left a lot of important personal stuff unsaid to each other. I was unusual in wanting to voice aloud more details about personal stuff. Stuff that nobody else wanted to be honest about. *It's orright* was the stock reply to my questions about how their dating lives were going.

I was constantly tempted to broach the subject of my sexual past with Maria. After torturing myself with whether to share my secrets with her I chose not to burden her and risk tainting her with my shame. It is a heavy load to put shit like that on another person. Especially a person you presumably love. I do not know if it was my upbringing, my religion or just my own personal character to stay quiet about it.

Ever since I could remember, I have tried hard to avoid causing other people any kind of stress or worry. If I can avoid it. Instead, I withdraw into myself and shoulder my own burden. Brood. On my own. Back to hiding inside my figurative French armoires and under illusory dining tables.

What was there to be gained by any revelation? I made lists of advantages and disadvantages like Miss Phillips had taught us when we were preparing for a class debate. (Declan Mitchell used to call it a *massdebate*—making the entire class break out in a raucous chorus.) There were not many things listed under the advantages column. Telling Maria, just to make myself feel a little better, so that I had a witness to my pain, was way too selfish an advantage I decided.

What could Maria do anyway with such a burden? She was a teenager; she was not a psychiatrist. She was not responsible. She could not rewrite the script of my past—it was too late for anyone to rewrite my history. Or my fate. Too late. Even as a teenager, it felt like it was all too late for me to have a happy, carefree, good life.

The horse had bolted out of the gate and was now a wild brumby at risk of being legally shot by government rangers.

No. Logically, Maria did not need to know about my private pain. She was happy with the world. She loved life. She loved her parents, both of whom doted on her. All her extended family loved her. Even her female cousins who would try and outdo each other when it came to clothes and make-up. Maria trusted everybody. Even some of the more dodgy, creepy older managers at Chook City who were always openly flirting with her. She was full of dreams for the future, always beaming even when mopping the floor at work and everyone we met as a couple adored her.

Telling her would serve no practical purpose.

I kept the same outlook on my secret pain for dozens of years.

Needless to say, my own parents had never modelled for me a healthy approach to relationships and sexuality. I never asked Mother for advice about girls, and I had certainly never spoken to Father about anything personal, let alone anything sexual during the short time we had spent living under the same roof in Australia.

Moreover, it hadn't taken long for me after we had arrived in Sydney on that crisp night in September, to suspect my parents would never be accepted here, would never *make it* in Australia. Right from the moment we arrived, Mother turned to us when the passport official asked her a couple of questions. The look on his face, the disdain he showed when he realised our mother could not understand what another adult was saying to her, made my heart sink.

It was the first time I saw exasperation mixed with anger in my sister's face. Even a young child knows that language is an essential tool for social success. I could not help but resent my parents for their foreignness. They and Australia never mixed.

Starting over after forty in a new country was fraught with risks. They may have had a chance if they had been wealthy. Not speaking English then would not matter as much. Even if I could bring myself to ask their counsel on deeply personal matters, I knew their response, their advice, would not be at all relevant to life in Australia for a teenage boy in the late 1970s. Whatever they may have had to say to me, I had guessed, would not be topical to my life.

My parents' views were influenced by their experience of having lived for forty years or more on a small island in the Eastern Mediterranean Sea. Living a sheltered life, surrounded and loved by extended families, a huge circle of friends and acquaintances and neighbours, all of whom knew all their family backstories, rivalries, catastrophes, joys and disappointments. Everyone knew what everyone else's temperament was, what they were capable of, what their limits were; their strengths and weaknesses. Everyone knew what their grandfather, their grandmother and parents were like. 'He's not from a good *soi*,' people would explain in disapproval about any minor social transgression of someone who lived in the street. 'Ah, well if his *soi* is no good, what do you expect?'

Conversely, if somebody had achieved something others approved of, the women in the street would nod and reassure themselves that the high achiever or the woman who had done a good deed was of a good caste, '*Einai tis ratsas*,' they'd say and everyone would concur that individual achievement started with one's genetics and the correct role modelling by the person's forebears, five generations back.

Within a few years of our arrival, I kidded myself that my foreignness didn't really matter—Mr Fraser referenced the term *multiculturalism* in 1974 and Mr Whitlam and Mr Grassby implemented the policy. More relevant to us *import jobs*, John Travolta lit up the silver screen with his disco dancing and quickly became our hero. But even though a government can come up with a new social policy, it doesn't mean this policy changes long-held views overnight—the actual reality was, all of us *ethnics* were made to shorten our names, Anglicise our ethnicity, hide our mortadella sandwiches and try hard to assimilate. Keep quiet about our differences. We'd never confess that the date of Greek Easter each year varied and would be determined by a different calendar to the one that proclaimed the *normal* Australian Easter. *What the fuck is the Julian Calendar?* would've been my school peers' response had we dared to stand our ground and assert cultural norms Greek culture had abided by for thousands of years. When a schoolmate or workmate would ask, 'What didja get for Christmas?' all of us Greek kids would just go along with it and omit to mention that in Greek and Cypriot cultures, Santa delivered his gifts on New Year's Eve. And God forbid, he wasn't even called *Santa*, but Ayios Vasilis.

If we wanted to be tolerated, we had to assimilate. If we had the vaguest hope of mainstream success. Or of gaining acceptance.

Lots of politicians spoke of assimilation as the only choice migrants had in our new country. I inferred that big word to mean that no matter where you might have come from, in order for your dreams to come true in Australia, you had better do what everyone already here did—otherwise you would be on the out. You would remain on the periphery, stay an *ethnic* permanently. In an ethnic ghetto. Denied opportunities and exclusive membership of the lucky club called Australia.

Who would want that?

Our school principal had also used the term *assimilation* over and over again at assembly in the mornings, especially when admonishing those of us who spoke to other kids from the same backgrounds as ours in the playground in our first language, or parents' language if they themselves had been born in Australia. It was repeatedly made clear to us that it was *Un-Australian* to talk to our friends in a foreign language. Aussie kids (many whose parents and grandparents had come from Germany and Holland in earlier decades) threw raw eggs at us at school and then pretended to have seen nothing if a teacher bothered to investigate. Even some of the teachers used to pretend they weren't hiding a smile as they tried to sort things out.

There were no wog actors on *The Restless Years* (I only watched that series for the wonder of Peter Phelps's blond hair and his amazing tanzanite-blue eyes). By the time he was the leading son in *Sons and Daughters* I noticed his eyes a little less and his body a lot more and felt ashamed.

Nor did we ever see any actors who spoke with accents in leading roles. Sometimes they played baddies on *Cop Shop* and there was a Spanish doctor on *The Young Doctors,* but he played the cliché Latino lover with a thick accent. In real life, Tony Alvarez died young. The baddies were always played by immigrant actors. Chantal Contouri was the pantyhose strangler on *Number 96,* a show Philly sometimes let me watch with her surreptitiously.

At school, we had never studied any books written by any migrant writers. All the reporters on Channel 9 were Anglo. All the celebrated rugby league heroes were Anglo. In the handful of Australian movies we were shown at school, the theme was always Australia's past or, if it was set in the present, it would never feature a protagonist who was an immigrant.

I remember once seeing a film advertised that featured an actress with an obvious Yugoslav surname and I recall how excited that made me feel. Gave me hope I could be someone, in the creative industries. *If you see it, you can be it*, was not an adage taught to immigrant children in the late 1970s. In any case, that actress died in real life in a car crash before the movie was even released. So, the two creatives who had managed to get cast in major roles paid the price of dying young in real life—who wanted that kind of future?

I did not know if any artists were immigrants as there were no art galleries in the outer western suburbs of Sydney. I found only a book on Monet in our school library but didn't have much enthusiasm for his watercolours back then. I was attracted to bolder colours, more drama, more anger.

At home, our mother, isolated and often going days without speaking to anyone, was now someone we were embarrassed of. Some days she would attempt to make conversation with us, trying to talk to us when we returned home after school, or after Greek School and work. We had nothing to share with her as her world and our worlds were, by this stage, divergent. Daily, she would turn on the small transistor radio that was the only radio able to receive (albeit with constant static) the ethnic 2EA radio broadcast in Greek early in the morning and again just before the evening news. That would be her only engagement with the outside world.

The broken-Greek of the announcer's voice would wake us up in the morning, as would some forty-year-old bouzouki tune sung by Bithikotsis which made us cringe. 2EA was always promoting some community dance which basically meant a bunch of ageing Greeks would get together in some draughty hall on a Saturday night, eating meat-based dishes and listening to old tunes, always with three generations of their families. Large tables were compulsory, and the Greek newspapers would then publish some photos of the night in their next edition.

The photographs' captions would always specify the particular group featured by referring to them as, 'Mr Pappas's group from Kastellorizo' but never 'Mrs Pappas's group from Zakynthos'. It was always made clear the family belonged to the man. Even if Mother could have afforded the cost of the tickets, we could never go to one of these Greek family dos as we simply didn't have any male adults to accompany us. No large family to fill a table. And we were *Cypriots* to boot, considered not 100% legitimately Greek by many Greeks living in Australia.

After 1974 Cypriots would forever accuse the mainland Greeks of having abandoned us. The Greeks themselves would skip over the fact that our Motherland benefited from the slaughter of Cyprus as it led to the end of military junta in Greece.

We were a strange 'Greek' family in Australia.

As soon as you said you were Greek in Australia everyone assumed you had a huge family and that you were the apple of your father's eye. Always assuming you had a traditional, God-fearing, wife-loving father who adored you. Since Dimitris's disappearance, there had been no paternal figure in my life to make me feel secure. I did not have a fatherly assurance that if my marks were good enough and I ever matriculated to uni, I need not worry about buying expensive textbooks or paying the fees.

Nobody promised me a car if I made it to uni. There would

be no deposit put down on my behalf on a house or even a studio flat when I finished university or whenever I felt like it was time to buy my own place.

I intrinsically knew there would never be a paid wedding reception for me. No wedding dance during which friends and family would pin hundred-dollar bills onto my clothes as I danced around with my partner. I knew I was attracted to other males and everywhere I turned there was evidence that this was the worst possible thing I could be as a Greek son. A proclivity destined to lead me to either prison or being an outcast.

'He's worse than a murderer,' my father had said, pointing to Liberace on the Mike Walsh television program.

So that was my second deep secret I kept to myself.

The burden of both weighed me down each day and kept me on the periphery of life. Acting 24/7 like a different persona to who I truly was, became onerous. It turned each day into a battle day as my life could be destroyed by a wrong move at any moment if I made a misstep. All I needed to do was to stare at another man on the train a moment longer than was acceptable or make an innocent comment about how gorgeous a man on television or in a magazine was and I'd be banished.

It wasn't until I was in my twenties that homosexuality was made legal in my city. By that time, the damage was done. My internalised homophobia and self-oppression had taken hold of me. You can't instantly wipe clear more than two decades of self-loathing, created by your perception of what society thinks of you, being verbatim referred to as a *filthy pervert* by relatives, schoolmates, employers, police commissioners, priests and radio disc jockeys; this pejorative estimation of others cannot be got rid of as quickly as deleting something you've written using a word-processing application. There was no software available to help you wipe everything that caused you harm from your mind's hard drive. Or move it all easily to the trash folder. Then empty the trash folder and have no detritus from that point on in your mind's metaphorical bin.

Sadly, legal marriage for my kind was not approved until decades later still, by which time I was in late middle-age and no longer a great catch—not even for men of my own age. Gay culture always had and has its own system of worthiness, mostly involving youth, a gym body, disposable income and dick size. I had failed to meet all the prerequisites.

I could not compete. Worse, *the oppressed make the worst oppressors*, a wise Mapuche man from Chile once told me.

32

· · · · · · · · · · · ·

Everyone just assumed that being Greek, I'd have a strict but loving father around. I struggled to even hint to the other kids at school that Father did not live with us. Being honest and telling even schoolmates the truth was not an option.

I already had heaps to contend with, enough failings for others to point out gleefully and put me down for; I was ostracised enough without pushing myself into more pigeonholes from which, I imagined, there was no escape.

Oh, all the lies I have told, just to save face. And not unnecessarily upset others.

The harsh reality was that my family was just our mother and my two siblings. Not a big enough cohort to impress the newspaper photographer from *The Greek Herald* at any community dance. It was just us—the members of our nuclear family. Nobody else from our 'village' of Lefkosia was here. All the other refugees from Cyprus had come from villages and not Nicosia itself. Father's third cousin, Agamemnonas, who had settled here as a young man and who had officially invited Father to Australia, had not shown any interest in us except for the occasional phone call when Father was still around.

Our Mother was terribly unhappy.

As a teenager, when you have to be careful not to say or do

anything that might further upset your mother, it means there is no space for you to unburden your own unbearable feelings. So, you learn to hide them, you keep them to yourself. Just like a smart dog takes its cue on how it must behave from its master, so does a child. We look to our parents for guidance. And we then choose the path of least resistance. If one or both of our parents are not capable of providing the appropriate role modelling for us, we learn bad tricks, we behave in a way that then bites us on our own proverbial tail.

Sadly, by the time we're an adult, we can no longer be taught new tricks.

Mother used to take a Bex daily and claimed it was to keep her going with her sewing. Her desolate loneliness made us feel guilty if we had had a good day at school. Or if somebody had said something that made us laugh. We stopped confiding in her anything that made us happy in our lives. We did not want to rub our teenage joy in her face. Or conversely our own dilemmas. Our grievances with how the world was treating us.

Even if she knew what torment there was at school for me, what could she actually do? She could not politely discuss any issue with my teachers or the headmaster or even ring up the school administration ladies to complain or ask for advice on how to stop me from being picked on and racially abused daily.

She sat. Silently at her sewing machine. Sewing those garish patterns. For a pittance. The three of us made sure we paid the electricity bill and the gas and the telephone. Mother would ration herself one brief telephone call to relatives back in Cyprus each month and still shudder when she checked the Telecom phone bill when it arrived, gingerly screwing-up her face for the cost of her brief indulgence in reaching out to family still in Cyprus.

When a fellow churchgoer who lived nearby developed a crush on the greasy boss of theirs, things started to sour between them, as Kyria Toula, was convinced Mother was trying to steal Mr Tsippas from her. She too soon stopped coming around for an occasional afternoon Greek coffee and a *paximadi*. Without having done anything for which she could be blamed, our mother lost her only friend in Australia. She then relied more and more on the *Greek Variety Show* and her stalwart companion 2EA for company, for information about the world, for entertainment. These two sources of information were Mother's only contact with the outside world.

The truth was, Mother had lost it.

She self-diagnosed ailments that had never plagued her before. She had migraines. She refused to eat some days as her stomach was upset. She ate too much. She got diabetes. She had hypertension. Back problems. Angina. She never left her Singer nor her tiny transistor silent for too long. Sometimes she even listened to programmes in another language, broadcast before her own, just so there was some noise in the house.

Father's presence had long been erased.

All traces of him, like his Old Spice after shave bottle in the bathroom drawer, had disappeared. I think for all of us, but mostly for our mother, he once again became a romantic pantheon of disappointment. She kept the grease-covered clothes he used to wear when he would tinker with his battered EH Holden, which he took with him when he left. They were folded neatly in the laundry outside, and the bag they rested in still hanging on the doorknob. The bag made a funny rustling sound each time we opened and closed the door as if to remind us that he was still present, watching us.

We blamed him for everything that was wrong with our lives. We used his abandonment to explain all our bad behaviour. He took with him our security, our sense of belonging, our dreams for the future. Just like he did when he had left us when I was a toddler. Growing up without a male presence is not helpful to a child who needs a grown-up version of himself as a guide.

I used to desperately look for him everywhere in the big house back then, thinking he was simply hiding in one of the out-of-bounds rooms. Or inside the giant French armoires that I myself used to hide in when visitors came. I'd put my cheek to the cool marble floor and whisper to him that I knew he was hiding beneath it. Begging him to come back to us because I needed him. We all needed him. I knew perfectly well that beneath the marble squares from Pendeli there was the ground floor of the house my mother had inherited from her mother. I stubbornly refused then to believe he was thousands of kilometres away and that only an aeroplane, once again, could bring us together.

Unfortunately, flying overseas to anywhere from Australia was only for the wealthy. We did not have the means for a bus ride to Canberra to see a major art exhibition from overseas. Let alone the money to fly to Cyprus, which necessitated a long-haul flight to a major port in the Middle East or London and then an additional flight, not to the abandoned ghost-airport of Nicosia but to the new Larnaca Airport. I knew Father would never indulge in flying regularly, on a whim. I could hear him saying that *only fools throw hard-earned money away like that.* Perhaps that was a favourite line spoken by another relative? I can imagine his tetchy mother saying a line like that. Or was it a line I had heard in a television series spoken by a no-nonsense type of character? I do not know as memory plays weird tricks.

Who can recall the past with one hundred per cent veracity?

What genius could remember with exactitude who actually uttered a particular phrase that has stuck in our minds for decades? And who did *not* say something we have held onto as an epigram on how to live our lives? I cannot be sure if something happened in 1977 or 1981, in 1990 or 1995. Unless there is a diary entry showing me that an event took place on a particular day, I cannot be certain with exactitude of anything. To complicate accuracy, at times I wrote about something important that happened under the wrong date in my journal, as I had used up the space for the actual day already.

I rationalised Father leaving us a second time by settling on the belief that he was a sick man. Emotionally sick. Mentally battered. That for whatever reason, he wasn't as strong as a father must be, was weaker than other fathers in the world. Average fathers who worked hard and who took pleasure in spending time with their children and their wife. Although, admitting even to myself that my own father was weak made *me* feel weak. As a teenager, I desperately wanted to be strong.

I knew a boy had to be strong or he was not respected. Would be humiliated for his weakness. I wanted to be successful in my interactions with others. With other men in the world. I wanted other males to accept me as an equal. I was already behind the eight ball as I did not play cricket or rugby league or even soccer or rugby. I had no status as an Australian male—no validity.

I knew, deep down, I was fighting a losing battle. I had never been shown how a successful man of the world behaved. My father had never demonstrated this. To a boy, the most important grown-up in his life is his father. Consciously or sub-consciously, we take in our father's patterns of behaviour, process both the good and the bad in him and seek to replicate these in our life.

Without a role model, or an uncle, an older cousin, an available parent, I was left struggling to understand my own emotions when someone I found attractive gave me that sick-in-the-stomach-feeling that made me feel both ashamed and excited all in one.

Shame is not an aphrodisiac.

Nor does it build your self-esteem.

33

Dinos coped with our absent father by making jokes.

When he was fond of a joke he would recycle it. Endlessly. Boring all of us to tears. Philly never found these jokes funny. I occasionally rolled my eyes and made a little laughing snort. But my sister did not. She had a habit of coming across as seriously aggressive. When the ticket conductor on the bus would say, 'Thanks, luv,' to her if she gave him the exact fare, she would roll her eyes and mutter something about not being anyone's 'luv'.

She was impatient with us all. She complained most days about how far we lived from the city. We all had to traverse the same distance, so she was preaching to the converted and her complaints actually made us all feel even worse for our plight. And made us like her less too. She hadn't changed much with the years; that is, changed in her behaviour towards Dinos and me. She still treated us as if she didn't really belong with us, that we weren't good enough for her. She stuck to sitting in her room. Reading. For hours staring out of the window, at the horseshoe cluster of villas that surrounded our small one.

I knew this because I took to watering the garden that I had planted. I had drawn a design of all the plants and trees I would plant and then set about bringing my drawing to life, symmetry always front and centre in my execution. Watching plants and quick-growing trees like wattles grow made me feel more secure. Gave me a sense that I was in control of my life. If I stood at a right angle, outside her window, despite her curtain being drawn, the afternoon light would reveal my sister's pose, as if she were on the stage. She too was miserable, and I wondered what her plans were on how to escape our misery.

But Dinos's jokes. He kept repeating the same ones with slight variations but neither Phil nor I found them particularly funny.

'How many hospitals haven't you been in?' he'd ask us, and we would both look at him askance. 'None,' he'd holler and slap us on the back. I used to duck but poor Phil always copped it.

'Brother, you are soooooooo amusing!' my sister would tease.

That particular joke was on account of Mother who had been in and out of hospitals since we came to Australia. On each occasion, taking with her old photographs from the time she was young in the fifties. She looked like a Hollywood movie star then. I wondered where her abandoned clothes had gone to? Which relative or neighbour had helped themselves to her outfits? Her jewellery? These days, her wardrobe was predictable and banal. She wore simple black cotton dresses she made for herself when she didn't have to work day and night to meet a Saturday deadline. Then, her creepy boss would arrive in a van to collect the finished dresses.

Sometimes, Mother would tell women she met occasionally at the new church she started attending after Father had left us, that her husband was one of the sixteen hundred or more Cypriots who were listed as *missing* after the war, presumed to have been killed. Like Dimitris and our two other cousins. I was angry at her lie but said nothing. I understood she was desperate to be accepted socially, to gain approval, as I battled with the same desperate need.

Dinos too was becoming another version of himself. I wanted my siblings to stay the same so I could feel some sense of continuity. I did not want our lives back home on our island to be erased. My brother grew his hair long at the back and had it permed. He chose not to shave every day and never listened to a Greek record.

'Don't call me *Dinos*, ya wog,' he'd holler at me and hit me on the head with his heavy hand if I forgot to call him Dean. I forgot most days. He drove a used Holden coupe, a Monaro. Phil and I weren't allowed to touch his car, even if we had wanted to. Phil even had a licence, a whole year before Dinos got his but he wouldn't let her borrow his car even when there was a train strike, and she had to get to work somehow.

'I wouldn't be caught dead in that thing anyway,' Phil would seriously tease. At the time I thought she was only stirring him but in hindsight I now see she meant it.

You see, Dinos's car was what we used to call back then *a wog chariot*, with its fat mag wheels and a horn that had a melody that was too embarrassing for words. It had a double carburetor that made too much noise when Dinos would start it and give it a good rev in the morning, pulling out the choke. Neighbours, who did not ever speak to us or greet our mother when they passed by, would loudly swear at him from behind closed doors and give him the one-finger salute from their window.

When he drove me to a school dance once, all the Aussie blokes were impressed and kept asking me questions about the engine of my brother's car. I was lost for words trying to find the right words to appease them. I could not. All I was interested in by then was looking after our small garden and working on my charcoal drawings that I stashed in folios stacked against the wall behind our shared bedroom door.

I had told no one but at fifteen, I decided I wanted to become an artist. Drawing was the only continuation from my early life on our small island, my only constant.

Dinos's burnt orange chariot never caught my imagination. Neither did his mullet that seemed to be very popular in our suburb with young men who wore a flannel shirt both to go to work and when they *dressed-up* to go out.

It was a sight to see Mother, sitting self-consciously in the bucket-seat on the passenger side in my brother's car going to church on a Sunday. Dean, begrudgingly driving her, when all he wanted to do on a Sunday morning was sleep in until two, which he would do when he came back from the church, twenty minutes away by car. Mother always got a lift back from some old codger who was forever trying to fix one of us up with his neighbours' overweight daughter, 'She owns two houses in Kingsgrove *re vlaka*! Okay, she's thirty-five but what does age matter when you get two houses, not just one, all paid off, eh?' Or his third cousin on his mother's side, 'Alright, she's not the prettiest girl you've seen but she keeps her mother's house spotless', or in Phil's case, with some poor bloke who had been a fisherman or a peasant shepherd near Volos and who was barely literate in either Greek or English.

'*Ela Filadelfia mou*, he doesn't speak English, no, not a word, but he's really tall and his grandfather's family *einai me to nami sou leo.*'

Dean didn't see anything wrong in not going to university like Phil had. There was no way he could get a teacher's scholarship like my smart sister had scored. His school results were terrible, and he jigged school most days by the time he was in Year 10. Instead, he got a job in a restaurant, a Greek restaurant in the city, where he learned to cook. He had never so much as boiled an egg at home, let alone present us all with a complete meal. Not that Mother would have let him anywhere near her cookware.

Phil was teaching by then but only casually. Truth was, there were no full-time teaching jobs available she could apply for. She was put on a waiting list for vacancies that stretched to almost a decade. My dream of emulating my sister and following the same route to university was cut short as the teaching scholarships were withdrawn from offer the year after Phil started her studies in English and French. She was lucky.

Phil chose to study French at university because she believed the marketing spin that Paris was the most romantic city in the world, but also so she could trace the family tree which had links to the Lusignan dynasty that had ruled Cyprus for nearly three centuries. My sister claimed that her research would have to be done in French, and she did not want to be another foreigner speaking a handful of mangled French words to some poor unsuspecting French archivist or *to a gorgeous male librarian*. Phil was always wanting to be qualified to do something before she ever attempted it. If I had asked her to help with the winter pruning for instance, she'd protest that she wasn't qualified to cut rose bushes.

'I'd willingly lend a hand dear brother, but I am afraid we'd have to first buy the right kind of hatchet.' I'd protest saying it didn't matter, any kind of secateurs could do the job, but she'd shrug her shoulders apologetically and leave me to it.

Mother was proud of Phil's French endeavours because it was her side of the family that apparently had House of Lusignan progenitors. Father's roots were traced back to the Venetians. Cyprus was a bit like an old woollen jumper that gets passed down from brother to brother, from generation to generation. One, even if it is frayed at the sleeves, that nobody in the family dares to finally chuck out.

Mother had never forgotten that she had had French lessons (but not a private tutor like her brother Pericles who, by the way, had never once written to us since we had left Cyprus). Mother had attended a girls' class just a block down from Faneromeni, at *L'Academie Francaise*.

'I once went to French lessons, you know,' she'd tell Phil à *propos* nothing, when we had all heard this a thousand times before.

'Yes, I know, not far from Areos and near the sandstone, bougainvillea-covered Ayios Savvas church,' Phil would snap back, shutting her Colette novel and storming off to her room.

Mother would look at me, once again hard done by, put in her place by her own aspirational daughter and I'd blow my fringe off my face wondering what I had to do to get away as quickly and as scot-free as my sister.

'Areos, Faneromeni, do you remember them, Thimo *mou*?' she'd ask me, and I'd go red because I knew Mother was more than likely to burst into tears at any moment. If I dared say the wrong thing. Or, if I said the right thing but in a way that might push her over the edge all the same. I could not win either way, so

I struggled to find the words to respond to my fragile mother's question.

I did remember.

Lots of stuff.

I lived with unpleasant memories of the past every day and had to psyche myself in order to keep going. Rationalising all kinds of excuses for my parents' consummate failure to keep me safe. My only choice was to keep moving forward. Keep fighting to believe I had a good future ahead of me. Trying with all my might to forget the past. Suppress the shame I felt. The anger.

Devoid of attention from my siblings I turned to doing the gardens of two Greek ladies that Mother had met at church. The original agreement was for me to mow what little lawn was left (naked concrete which could be hosed down clean each morning and afternoon was popular with the Greeks in the 70s and 80s) but soon enough, I had them buying pots they filled with holy basil and letting me plant climbing rose bushes, hydrangeas, geraniums and nasturtiums and with a bit of spiel about drainage, even a jacaranda tree. But Kyria Pavlides drew the line at the wattle trees I loved.

'*Vre*, it looks like a cemetery tree. *Ohi*! Unequivocally no, *paidi mou*.'

Their protestations aside, soon, both Kyria Pavlides's and Kyria Konstantinoprokopoulou's houses were framed in wonderful potted colour. Their sons teased me saying I was *a poor bloke* spending my time looking after bloody green things instead of saving my wages at Woolworths to buy a car or *get a chick*.

I honestly never felt as if I were wasting my time. I simply was becoming accustomed to the reality that a huge volume of experience separated me from other boys my age, whose birthdays came and went just like mine did, but who looked more masculine than me. Boys my age who were much stronger than I was physically. Whose bodies were more tightly muscled than mine. Boys who simply, were confident young men. Youths, who knew all about the realities, the pragmatics, of life. Boys who never doubted themselves, who had been raised with a sense of security, who assumed the whole entire world and its riches belonged to them.

No matter how I coveted their entitlement, I was aware I had none.

34

. . . .

Just after her twenty-first birthday, Phil started seeing a guy. A much older guy, who looked as if he had anaemia. They had had only a few surreptitious dates, behind our mother's back when he bought her an electric blue BMW coupe, in lieu of an engagement present, and told her that the ring would have to wait.

'He's rather old for you, isn't he?' was all that Mother could bring herself to say when presented to Phil's fiancé the first time.

'If he can't even give you a fuckin' ring, what sort of a bloke is he?' Dinos asked.

'So, he's rich...' I surmised, leaving for the garden, but not before Phil fixed me with one of her icy looks. And sure enough she followed me out.

'Do you think I want to spend the rest of my life teaching grots?'

'Well, I sorta guessed you just *lurve* Westie kids,' I joked.

'Very funny Timbo. Very amusing.'

I bent down to pull out a bunch of weeds which were strangling my dahlia seedlings. Phil looked around as if she couldn't quite believe she was where she found herself standing. We could hear angry raised voices in a foreign language emanating from the villa opposite. This was a daily occurrence in our complex. A veritable house of Babylon. A myriad of tongues all raised. All spoken in fury. Screams and angry words that shouted the same in all languages.

'I just don't want to spend the rest of my life around *here*, that's all.'

'It's not so bad,' I said, feeling insulted. The small garden had started to come of age in the last year, and was already providing the villa with some shade from the 40-plus degrees we got in blocks of a week or two in summer.

'Thimo *mou*, there's a whole world out there you don't even know about.'

Oh yes, I did.

I had been places.

More correctly, had been *taken* to places she could only shudder thinking about. I had been left in a mess of sperm, spit and sometimes urine. I had not chosen to go there. How dare she patronise me as if I were some naïve, spoilt brat who had been sheltered by the harsh reality of life? Guarded from the bad behaviour of adults? How dare she tell me that there were unimaginable places I had no idea about? How had she suffered exactly? She had had her own room forever, even since moving here to this small villa. Dinos and I continued sharing a room big enough only for a toy poodle pup. Had my sister, my big brother, hell, my mother, ever bothered to ask me about my shame? About my lost childhood? About the facts of my life? My dreams?

'Oh, Thimo *mou*, you should see his place at Darling Point. Stunning,' she added, as if she had already lived there all her life and had only just now come to realise how wonderful it was. And how dreadful our tarnished suburb was.

'Better than the houses we used to check out on our walk around Hunter's Hill, when we first arrived. Do you remember?'

'Don't you believe in love?' I pleaded, squashing snails unsparingly with a seashell I had nicked from Austinmer Beach. It was the closest beach to us, ninety-minutes away, down that spectacular Bulli embankment. Dinos used to make us all scream with utter fear as he drove so erratically down the massive bends, descending the hill in his wog chariot which did not have power steering or ABS brakes.

'Not really,' she answered wistfully, and she didn't have to tell me anything more. So that was it. She was a pragmatist, and I had my head up in the clouds. People were always telling me to stop dreaming.

Your imagination is going to get you into a whole lot of trouble, my boy.

When had Mother started telling me this as a general warning about life?

'So, when are you getting married?' If she wanted me to be pragmatic, then that was what she was going to get from me: practical questions untainted by sadness or romantic disappointment. Not questions tinged by my fear of abandonment by anyone I loved.

'Late July.'

'That soon?'

My birthday was in July. How dare she move in on my month? Everybody would be busy preparing, planning for her event. Everyone would be preoccupied. Innocently overlooking my special day. It somehow didn't seem fair to be born third and last.

I ached for someone to fuss over me. Shower me with attention.

In a good way. Not in a stultifying Greek way.

By this stage Maria was a distant dream.

'The guy's a total sleazebag,' said Dinos, unexpectedly walking past us, his black muscle AC/DC T-shirt so tight, his stubborn chest hairs were sprouting through it. Phil turned to face his back, started, as if to say something cutting back at him, but Dinos was already in his car, revving it at full throttle, drowning out anything *smart-aleck Phil* (as Dinos called her) may have had to say.

And so, without much ado, Phil had landed the sleazebag, not to mention the Beamer. Dinos had his restaurant job, Mother her sewing and I had just started studying *le Français* and other languages for my Year 10 School Certificate. School was two hours away on the train each way. Then a bus ride for another twenty minutes.

I had refused to change schools yet again. I could not face it. I had changed primary schools four times in two years and each time felt as if I were drowning. Instead, I cursed the train system for always allocating red rattlers to service our area. They were not air-conditioned liked the double-decker trains on other rail lines and made a hell of a racket. In summer, when passengers were sweating and putting up with the rampant humidity, the opened windows made you feel as if you were free falling without a parachute from the sky.

For downtime I had my shears and pulling out weeds for comfort. Planting a petunia bed in a straight line like a machine and watching the seedlings bloom. In due course, their giant purple flowers made me feel as if my life was worth something.

That all the pain I had survived made me a worthy person and that everything would eventually be all right. I sought to find comfort in anything positive like a seedling actually sprouting colourful flowers. Doing exactly what it was intended to do by Nature.

I longed for any kind of solace but did not seek this from other people. I did not know how to be friends with other guys without risking my physical safety. This might explain why I found it hard to have mates. No one my age could possibly offer me solace or companionship. For how could they? Nobody had lived through my life and my experiences, so they had zero chance of being able to offer any kind of meaningful help. It was the Maria-syndrome all over. There was no possibility of asking for solace from anyone as my past belonged just to me.

Instead, I looked for solace in aesthetics. In any kind of symmetry I could control. In my art. In beautiful things Nature could offer me and that I could draw. As long as I tended my seedlings, my plants, the trees I planted, the lawn, I would feel I was doing okay. Only a prickly pear grew out of neglect, on the side of a road. I loathed prickly pears ever since our father stopped the car he had borrowed one day, during one of his blinding visits to our island, and got out to cut some fruit. Cursing as the thorns took their revenge on him for stealing. I remember I felt justified that Nature had made him pay for his pilfering of someone else's property

We too had grown with his neglect, and I wondered if I were ever to mature into the full version of myself whether I'd hurt anyone who dared to love me.

35

I don't know how, or at what point I had stopped channeling an amalgam of John Travolta and Miss McKenzie from *The Restless Years* with my extreme blow-dried Elvis-inspired bouffant and retreated into a silent world. I think it must have been around sixteen and a bit. I don't know if it is significant, but it was just about ten months after Maria and I broke up.

Everything in my life seemed to end badly. People always left. Abandoned me. Forgot I existed. Every situation or relationship, even if it had started off as something glorious and positive, ended up smashed in emotional smithereens. Take the example of me being the only boy in the top English class. This fact should have demonstrated to me the possibility of the triumph of diligence over adversity. Unexpectedly, it instead led to my social downfall as all the other boys in my year thought I was too smart for my own good, a teacher's pet. Somehow, being good in English class made me less masculine. Using grammar correctly and reading heaps of *boring* books of literature apparently, at least according to my male peers, was for girls. For *poofters*.

So something positive, like doing well in English, despite my handicap of learning the language a good decade after all my fellow students had, left me without a group of mates to hang around with during breaks at school. Just like in primary school.

Forcing me to sit mostly by myself, or with three or four other social outcasts that even I found weird. *The Freaks. The Weirdos.*

Later, in adult life, I found that even if I had been very kind to a friend or a colleague or someone I managed, bending over backwards to always be there for them, support them, nurture them, mentor them, listen to them, that sooner or later, they would turn on me and show zero gratitude. Leaving me stunned, wondering if I had the words *ABUSE ME* written on my forehead. Their callous behaviour transporting me back in an instant to childhood, making me feel powerless, and just like I felt as a child: completely without agency. The philosophical dictum that I had read about, that I tried to apply in all exchanges with others, that it is not what you do in life but how you do it, was not a mantra others lived by.

We freaks used to sit by the main road fence. Far away from whatever the normal students were doing in the main playground. As if we were lepers banished from the colony of the healthy. Away from the canteen and the peripheral eyesight of teachers on playground duty. Ready to run out onto the road to escape any attack by people who had dismissed us as worthless and who regarded us as easy prey to pick on to demonstrate their power at their whim.

I never quite felt comfortable in this group of outcasts (a recent arrival from Cambodia with an unpronounceable name, a large Italian boy with a very high-pitched voice, a Chinese boy with glasses whom nobody understood but who always came first in all the Science subjects, and a very peculiar short, thick-set Welsh boy who always abruptly said the wrong thing to everyone and who always seemed as if he was about to hurt someone and evidently, take pleasure in it).

None of us were ever picked to be on a sports team. It was up to the PE teacher to basically offload us as extras to one team or the other. As an afterthought. Or just tell us to go sit on the sidelines. In the full sun.

My Art teacher made me see a psychologist at the end of Year 10 and I did as she directed but I was only allowed a handful of visits. I told her some things about what had happened to me in Cyprus, but not the whole truth as I could not put into words what had happened. Spoke about my father choosing to be absent for most of my life. About my poor sick mother who had lost herself in transit to Australia and could not complain about her loss to the airline as she did not have the proficiency. About desperately wanting to become someone worthwhile in the world.

She wanted me to keep on seeing her as a fee-paying client but that was out of the question. She suggested I take medication, but I could not afford it nor could I ask my mother to do all that sewing just so I could pay for the anti-depressants. My wages were needed for household bills and for transport.

I felt defeated. That there was no way out. I retreated mostly into an internal world I had created. Like in a painting, where everything was in its place, just as I had placed it, and nothing could alter its perfect position except me. *Nothing stays the same forever* by Hush became my anthem as it was true—life was always evolving, changing. Nothing stayed as you wanted it in your own, insular, carefully arranged world. Throw in another person either by accident or design or happenstance or desire and everything was in instant disarray. Others always ruined things by something they did or through ill-advised words they spoke, inadvertently shattering your fragile, personal palace.

I wasn't interested in anything besides my furtive drawings which I was careful not to show to Dinos. On many occasions, sifting through my folios, carefully and privately stacked against the wall behind our bedroom door, he would simply scoff, 'What's all this crap then *re*?' A drawing could be relied on to stay the same. Unless someone intentionally destroyed it. I was in control of all my drawings and paintings. Nobody could interfere with them.

I'd given Phil a charcoal drawing of her sitting at her desk reading Germaine Greer and she said she would frame it, but I begged her not to do so until after she had moved to the Eastern Suburbs. To terrorise Darling Point natives with her consummate driving skills learnt on the *take-no-prisoners* roads of the outer Western suburbs. Think *Robocop* marries *Mad Max* to get an idea. I didn't know where Darling Point was exactly, as we had always lived southwest of the city since leaving the boarding house in Hunters Hill and our rented houses in Putney. But, I knew instinctively that there'd be a lot of other BMWs and Mercs there for sure and was relieved when one Sunday morning Phil had assured us all she was *fully and comprehensively insured* before driving Mother to church.

Mother, of course, was not impressed with the BMW coupe.

'That blinding blue is a bit showy, surely, isn't it Philadelphia?' was all she had said to Phil before fastening her seat belt. After all, Mother was used to German luxury cars, as in Cyprus all the taxis were Mercedes-Benz and Mother, who had never obtained a licence, and without a husband who could drive her anywhere, had kept most of the taxi companies of the island financially afloat with her trips to villages and to appointments and meetings for her charity work.

Phil could only shrug, again helplessly unable to impress Mother, despite her own spectacular social ascension and Mother's immense and unadulterated social downfall. You could say whatever you wanted about Mother, but she knew the meaning of superficiality through and through and could have spelled *nouveau riche* backwards, even if her own French lessons had been learned decades ago.

As Phil spent less and less time at home, I knew that I was soon going to lose my eldest sibling for good. Another member of our family was about to leave us. This was the girl who had been my hero. When I was little, if she didn't have breakfast, I wouldn't have breakfast. If she liked pink, then pink became my favourite colour.

'Whadjyawannadrivethatpieceofshitforanyway?' Dinos asked Phil when Phil complained she did not like the smell of diesel emanating from her status symbol. Our Dean reckoned his Monaro would beat the Beamer hands down in a street race and that nothing could match the quality of sound of the sub-woofer he had installed in his supercharged mean machine. Not even the latest sound system of German luxury engineering. Whereas Phil had started buying three-dollar classical music tapes from Coles Variety in town to play in the BMW, on Dinos's stereo, AC/DC and 'Lick My Lolly,' an old Supernaut track, ruled supreme.

Dinos was not into what he dismissed as *poofter music*, which was basically any song that did not include an electric guitar solo.

I heard Dinos backing out of the driveway and presumably gone. He stuck his head out of his car, hollering, the engine running, waving me over as I watered some pots.

'I forgot to tell ya, ya poofter, Maria and her brother came to the *restrant*, on Sat'dy night.' The word restaurant only had two syllables for Dinos. The rest of the vowels having been left behind in the ocean, halfway between Cyprus and Sydney.

'Didya hear what I said, you ole poof?' he asked, just to make sure.

I looked at him. He sat there in his car, his head sticking out, smiling the smile of an idiot, but an idiot who has no idea he's an idiot and therefore an idiot who is charming and still a little bit cool. I was forced to say something incoherent, to mumble something in order for him to wipe that idiotic grin off his handsome face, lest somebody walk by and notice, not for the first time, I had a complete moron for a brother.

'So?' I retorted, tossing a handful of soil where it wasn't needed.

'I knew you were still keen, told Davo just last night.'

'Don't be so sure Deano. She's now got some other bloke anyway.'

'Will ya switch that flaming car off or piss off and drive?' shouted one of our impossibly handsome Maori neighbours. Dinos made an internationally recognised sign with his forefinger in the direction of our neighbour and kept revving his engine to show people in the complex he was not scared of anyone, even a tall and hefty muscled Maori.

'So what? Even if she's got some other poor sucker. She can giv''im the flick.'

'Yeah, just like that, eh Deano?'

'She's a spunk *re*. Real cute!'

'I thought you weren't into Greek chicks Deano?'

'Some of them are alright mate! I'd fuckin' give 'er one.'

'Gee, I'm sure she'll thank you for that stupendous compliment.' Dinos looked a little lost and his brow frowned.

'*Stupendous*. That's S. T. U. P.' I started to spell.

'I thought you called me fuckin' *stupid* for a minute. What kind of bloke uses a word like *stupend*ous for fuck's sake? What the hell does it mean anyways?' he asked.

'It means...never mind'.

'What's got into ya, little Timbo mate?'

'Nothing. I couldn't give a...'

He wasn't letting me off that easily.

'I told her you were still studying hard to get into paintin' at uni an' all that and she seemed real impressed mate.'

'I bet she was. And by the way the degree is called *Fine Arts*.'

'Same shit,' is all my brother said, shaking his head. Making me feel he was tolerating me simply because we were connected genetically. Barely tolerating me. Begrudgingly.

Suddenly I hated bloody gardening. Gardening was for old folks. What the hell was I, a teenager, doing spending my time in the garden? A garden without a fence that neighbours' children and pets trampled on without a care every day.

Handling the soil in the heavy bags I carted all the way up the street from Flemings made me itchy. I never wore gloves as

Dinos would have had a field day calling me *an old woman* or something worse. I had once calmly explained to him that potting mixture contained living organisms which could kill you if your body had an allergic reaction to it. It was written right there on the plastic packet in black and white, just below *instructions and directions for usage.* Just a tiny scratch or tear in your skin, a sneeze or a breath taken in when too close to it, or when there was any wind blowing could lead to your torturous and painful death. My brother reckoned that that was *bullshit.*

Gardening meant that you also had to avoid the flies which tried to get into your mouth or up your nostril, fight off all sorts of insects that wanted to have a taste of your blood. Especially in the heat of summer in our suburb which was always at least ten degrees hotter than in the city. Insects frustrated me with their persistence—if I were an insect and someone had shooed me away two or three times, I'd get the hint and leave them in peace. Was that my fundamental problem? I wasn't pernicious enough to be a man. Did I give in to despondency quicker than I ought to? Was I simply a bad warrior?

I did not engage with my brother as I knew Maria wouldn't be impressed if she were to see me in my frayed, dirty overalls. She was obsessed with the latest fashion. Maria, just like my sister Phil—who aspired to never have to set foot in this suburb again—had loved the luxurious things in life which I knew for sure I couldn't afford.

'You look like a proper poof in that getup,' Dinos would often say—as he passed by me either on the way to somewhere fun or having just come back from more exciting pursuits than gardening.

Maria had wanted us to get engaged as soon as we had finished high school and get married within a year. She kept telling me this. Every time I saw her, even at our age. Her father owned a huge house on the hill in Undercliffe that was big enough for twenty people to live in and never bump into each other. We would, of course, have had to live with her mother and father and her single sister Evdokia until she too got married. Their father had DA plans already approved. He planned to knock the old house down when Evdokia finally got engaged and then build two enormous duplexes so the family could stay together. He'd order marble all the way from the Motherland and not care about the freight cost.

Maria's father was born in Kingsgrove and spoke hardly any Greek, but he acted as if he was an expert in the language. I'd be embarrassed when he tried to speak Greek to me as it was a bastardised version my mother would find execrable.

But even before I turned sixteen, I knew in my heart that I only wanted to be with Maria because it was *the right thing to do*. Everyone treated me differently when she and I were together. Even people who were real bastards usually, like the tetchy station master at Bardwell Park station, seemed to mellow a little, would treat me more as a mate when Maria and I were together. Made me feel as if I were part of a brotherhood which would look after me and which would be there to support me. The world encouraged my loving Maria, but not my heart.

At nights, I thought not of kissing Maria but her handsome, tall brother, Lambros. And the shame would consume me, making for a restless, sleepless night.

'Bro, I dunno why you're gettin' upset by it,' Dinos said, now leaning against the bonnet of his car, his feet an inch or two away from my face. If I didn't know him better, I would have been fooled into believing he was genuinely concerned about my emotional well-being. He had gotten out of the driver's seat and his face looked almost concerned for me.

'I've been talkin' to you for a bit, but you were away with the pixies. I thought you might've had a stroke or somethin' bro'...'

'Look I don't mean to snap, it's just...' I started to explain.

'Just that you still wanna get into her pants *re*? I get it *re*!'

'Can't you think of anything else except sex?'

'It's better than pullin' meself silly every night,' was all my beloved older brother said, whacking me on the back, banging the car door hard, then driving off. His slap was so hard it pushed me face down, onto freshly cut lawn and the dreaded contaminated soil. Leaving me to wonder if my beauty queen ex-girlfriend Maria would have been impressed then, seeing me covered in muck like that.

36

· · · · · · · · · · · ·

Dinos was like that. He'd say and do what he wanted openly and directly, to your face, without fear or compromise. If someone upset him, he would have no qualms in saying right away, *You're pissing me off somethin' bad mate.* He never stewed, like I did. He was sure of himself. If there was something he wanted he would go for it. It wasn't long before Dinos won. Without too much effort. Like he always did. I too ended up calling him Dean pretty much all the time now. I'd slip now and again, and he'd call me a *fat wog.* Phil's fiancé's name, Konstandinos had also been shortened to Dinos. So, in order to distinguish them, Phil and I observed the rule of referring to her Dinos, as *Dino,* when he wasn't present, which was ungrammatical, erroneously dropping the *s.* We made up for our trespass when we addressed him directly as *Dino,* just like Greek grammar demanded. Our Dinos was distinguished from that time on as Dean.

Mother was the only one among us to suffer confusion as a result of this renaming of her middle son by a non-Greek name. A lot of us immigrant children had to reinvent ourselves in the seventies as we grew into young adults and attempted to join the workforce on an equal footing. We had to try hard to be seen and one day, hopefully be accepted, as Australian. I had gone through a number of incarnations myself and had finally been given the moniker of Theo by Year 10. That was half-way between being Greek and an Aussie. I was in a permanent state of becoming. My figurative, never-ending Odyssey.

Aussies were allowed to have a first name of more than two syllables, but any name with more than two syllables was a challenge for the local lazy tongues to bother with and quickly found itself abbreviated, approximated or altogether discarded. Regardless of the fact that the person had been given that name at birth or at their baptism, or whether they willingly agreed to its abbreviation by others or not.

Sebastian was shortened to Seb. My untouchables gang member Massimiliano tried getting others to call him Massimo, but he had no luck. Max was what people chose to call him by. So, Max it stayed. Mother enjoyed calling me *Theo* more and more, as the same four letters, given an emphasis on the second syllable, meant *God* in Greek. Girls like Maria's sister, who had been baptised Evdokia, would suddenly ask you to call them Vicky. Eugenia morphed into Jenny. Guys of Greek origin whose name appeared as Athanassios on their birth certificate had Dane printed on their business card as their first name. Periandros and Pericles both became Perry. Vassilios became Bill. Or Will. Maria's easy-on-the-eye brother Lambros morphed into Liam by the time he turned eighteen.

Sadly, Mother could not for the life of her, say *Dean* properly. In the same way she always added a voiced vowel 'e' at the end of Marrickville (Mar/ick/villi). Even so, the way she said 'Dinos', especially her tone, was Greek enough for us to know she meant our Dinos.

Phil's Dinos was never referred to as just mere *Dinos* by our mother. She would always put the personal article in front of his name. I am guessing as a way of making her communication with Dinos number 2 less personal, when talking about him you understand; face to face with D2 she stuck to using the plural form of address. We knew, despite our fast-diminishing Greek, that she'd never address our own Dinos in the Greek formal plural version of 'you.'

Phil stopped casual teaching to the envy of her fellow teachers. It was bad enough for teachers where Phil taught, that she drove a new BMW coupe to school (testing the grots' ring scratching tendencies in the process). After all, Phil's status as an on-call casual was bottom of the bottom rank for teachers. But then to get married and not have to teach, as well as live in Darling Point, well, it was too much for her work colleagues. 'Don't forget I'm a refugee' and 'Please call me Philadelphia' became Phil's favourite go-to lines when she felt she was at risk of alienating others. She didn't get it that saying stuff like that only made envious people dislike her even more.

'They're all so bitter,' Phil would explain to us all, when she found out her invitation to a school function, like the end-of-year school formal or a staff get-together to celebrate some staff milestone socially, somehow never arrived.

'They'd all like to think they're leftist ideologues but all they care about is accumulating more and more money and saving for that holiday home in Batemans Bay. Always whining about their Balmain mortgage when they've got two full-time salaries coming in! Greedy much? And what about their parents' houses? All that tax-free inheritance in a few years' time will make them instantly wealthy. What have I got to look forward to? What *I* will inherit when mum dies is a personal loan. To bury her!' Sometimes she would say the last sentence angrily, at other times, her eyes full of tears, her face red.

Dinos would promise Mother to have Philadelphia home by midnight, but I stayed up late a few times, just to see if this promise would be kept. It wasn't.

'We've lost her too,' Mother would lament as we sat around watching *The Sullivans*. Mother approved of the family matriarch Grace as she *wasn't made-up like a whore*. And she loved her devoted husband, Dave. She was devastated when Dave cheated on Grace with Maggie.

'*Efiye...*', Mother would say during a commercial break.

'Thank God for that,' Dean would say, relieved. 'Only jokin', he'd add, when I would look at him, incredulous at his callousness.

'Your turn next Dino-*mou*,' Mother would forewarn.

'Keep dreamin' mate,' was all Dean had to say on the subject. His idea of commitment extended only to finishing off a twelve-pack of beer with one of his Monaro-loving mates. Similarly unemployed or under-employed young guys of immigrant heritage who wore the same dark, checked shirts and who all went to the same barber. From behind, they looked like replicas of each other.

'Do you think Father might make it to Philadelphia's wedding?' I asked out loud of no one in particular.

'He might,' answered Mother. Dean stopped in his tracks, abandoning a plate of Mother's *keftedes*. Suddenly, the meatballs could wait. I sensed trouble, as food was never left untouched by Dean, even if he wasn't hungry.

'What's that supposed to mean?' he dared Mother. He looked at Mother, as challenging as a Pamplona bull. But our mother was not perturbed. After all, she had given birth to him. Had boiled eucalyptus leaves in the middle of the night, which she had to beg others to drive twenty miles out of Nicosia to find, all just so she could help Dean breathe.

'He might,' she repeated, and it sank in that she had actually meant it the first time and wasn't just innocently hypothesising to give us hope. 'Yes, there's a good chance he might make it,' she repeated emphatically now.

'He knows about it?'

Mother went back to her sewing, and it needled us both that much more.

'We haven't heard from 'im for years but,' was all that Dean could say, smugly thinking he was logically putting an end to some perverse fantasy our mother was hallucinating in.

'What, you think we've been surviving on these?' she asked, surveying her pile of half-sown floral dresses with a grimace on her face as if she were going to vomit. Her tone showed her clear self-contempt for what she had become, revealed her despondent mental state, her humiliation at having lost her former self. She was on the bottom rung of society now, destitute, alone and unable to communicate in the language of the country.

She had lost everything: her relatives, her house, her prized china, her green metal mortar and pestle, her place in society, her family's renowned reputation. She had to face these grim facts daily and yet continue to act out as if her new loathed persona did not bother her. And she tried to go on. For us.

For our sake. To give us a sense of normality. A feeble façade of having a home.

She looked with disgust around the tiny brick veneer villa, which was nothing more than a narrow flat, shaking her head from side to side. As she surveyed the small open plan area it was obvious to us, she was thoroughly unimpressed.

'Dean my boy, you hardly make enough for your car repayments and your petrol.'

Dean stormed out, but not before his face had gone crimson with anger.

'One day you'll understand,' she shouted, turning to me, even though I was still sitting there, prepared to understand right there and then. 'You'll all understand. Life is not like a soap opera where people are only good or bad. It's more like a comic book where people do unexpected things. Life *is* stranger than fiction. Everyone knows your father's never been one to stay in a place too long,' she explained. 'It's not in his nature. We have all got to learn to love people for who they are. I mean, who of any of us is beyond reproach?' Mother rattled off her monologue as if she had been preparing it for decades.

I wanted to protest, lodge a formal complaint with UNESCO, assert that other fathers too seemed to have peripatetic lives in terms of their job requiring them to go interstate occasionally or to travel overnight around the state now and then. But, that they, nevertheless, returned to their families at the end of the working day. More importantly, being home, being with their family, was where they craved to be. But my own reductive bilingualism meant I wasn't sure how to say all this in Greek without sounding accusatory and by this, making my depressed, dispossessed and abandoned mother feel even worse.

I had become the parent, we all of us had to, without wanting to. I was trying to look after my mother. She was now someone who needed my assistance to complete the simplest social transaction like paying the checkout chick or requesting a withdrawal from the bank teller.

'I suppose it was his early training,' Mother threw in, to make things even more complicated.

'What early training exactly?' I asked, feeling confident of the fact that Father had no formal qualifications whatsoever, that all he knew he had learned *on the job*.

'Chasing goats. They don't let you rest for even a minute. Eat everything in sight, including your shoe if you doze off in the fields.'

I was caught halfway between amusement and genuine suspicion that Mother's sense of humour was pissing me right off.

'You're not serious Ma.'

'About what Theo *mou*?'

'Dad and the goats.'

'Of course, I am. He told me. Your father's family may have been peasants, yes, but in those days, they had the most sought-after long-haired goats in Famagusta.'

'Yeah sure...' I said dismissively somehow wishing that my father's family had been renowned for something a bit more altruistic, creative, charitable even. Mother shrugged as if to say, *what do I care if you don't believe me?*

It dawned on me then that Mother had spent a considerable

amount of time living with Father before any of us were born. That their time together had been legitimate. That they had lived their lives, their love and intimacy in a language they both understood. Until our arrival in Australia, they had had the support of an enormous extended family who, when push came to shove, were mostly fond of my mother, despite what they perceived as *her city airs*.

'Do you know where he is?' I asked, seriously contemplating that one day soon I would see him fixing something in the back yard with silver-coloured masking tape. Metal, wood or plastic, his go-to fix was to use masking tape. And lots of it. The reality was I craved my father's presence. Just to see the blue of his eyes, even feel his rugged palms playfully smack the back of my head. I even craved his unique smell of metal mixed with car oil. I even missed his bad moods.

'Not exactly. He never stands still enough for his cowlick to sit properly.'

'Well, aren't you gonna tell us where he is?' I shouted. 'We have a right to know.'

'Last time I spoke to him...' I didn't let her finish.

'You mean all this time we thought he had left you, he had abandoned all of us, you've been talking to him?'

'He *has* left me,' she pointed out tears in her eyes, getting up, leaving her sewing unattended long enough to cross herself three times, invoking God, the Virgin Mary and the Holy Spirit under her breath in a rehearsed, automated mumble practised by Greeks the world over. You heard this same mumble from commuters sitting on a bus in Cyprus or Greece, if the bus drove past a church or monastery.

'Once you're married and you have kids, you can never leave somebody,' she muttered, stitching her ostentatious material.

'I can't believe you!' I shouted, hating her, wishing she were dead.

'Theo-*mou*, shoosh up. Don't scream in my ears, *paidi mou*. Ah, he's sulking now.' I was looking out the window watching clouds race a marathon of late summer afternoon relays.

'I wish you didn't see things in black and white. And you kid yourself you are going to become a painter. An artist! Ha! There are other colours, in-between, my boy,' she advised, picking up a putrid orange and green fabric which didn't see things as plainly as I did.

'I just do the garden around here, and the shopping,' I said bitterly. Not so much because of her colour-blind joke against me but more because Father was still able to wrap Mother around his little finger. Evidently, she continued to love him despite the demonstrated fact he was not man enough to stand by her side, and together try and make a better life for all of us in Australia.

He ran away. Like he always did. And yet, he still managed to keep her hanging on. He was like a disease you get for life and no matter how many antibiotics you take, what treatment you take up, the disease stays active. Father was like a low-grade tumour killing us slowly.

To me, it was clear he was a selfish, immature manipulator who only cared for himself. Mother had been trapped by the Mediterranean dictum of allowing your narcissist husband to do whatever he wanted, as long as he had married you in a church and had given you children. That was all that was required of these types of men. You could count it as a certainty that they had played no active role in planning or paying for any aspect of their wedding. That they had no input or given a second thought to the reality that life had to inherently change when two people got married and had children.

No. All these men had to do, the world over, is to get married. That is all that was asked of them by their family. By their own mothers. Then, these men were free to sleep around, stay out late, gamble, drink, even have children with other women, some of whom they may marry at some stage, some not.

Without ever having to account for where they had been, what they had done and with whom. There were no dire consequences for their actions. Many of these types of men replicated the disaster of their first marriage with a second, younger wife and then even a third. I had overheard talk of this social phenomenon often enough way back, when our neighbours in Areos St would confide in Mother over their Nescafes or at gatherings, confessing their philandering husbands' transgressions. Not realising I was hiding behind an armchair, or inside an armoire, as they drank their coffee and had their fortunes told.

'He left you, remember?' I called out. 'He left us all. Couldn't give a fuck about us. He's a total, selfish, spoiled prick,' I blurted out, and despite my anger still feeling like a traitor to my gender. In that moment, I ran away, just like my father, bolting out the front door, the screen door giving its usual bang.

Mother's sewing machine continued its low hum, and she didn't come running after me.

37

Things kept changing.

Before we knew it, Phil wasn't just *our Phil* anymore. She was getting married. Suddenly, she had a son aged twelve from Dinos's first marriage. The three of them would all live together after the wedding. The particulars of Dinos's life hidden behind the veneer of respectability and Greek formality were revealed slowly and in an unpleasant manner. Painfully too for Phil.

In just a few weeks after their engagement, her fiancé was unmasked as a man who had lied about pretty much everything he had convinced our sister of about his backstory. He had another two children, daughters, in Greece, living with their mother, to whom Dinos paid child support. The girls attended an expensive private school and Dinos was compelled to contribute to the fees. His own mother was dependent on him too as her pension was negligible.

The unit in Darling Point was only leased.

Phil's BMW was imported minus the usual obligatory fiscal duties and really on paper still belonged to Emmanuel Motors of Randwick, owned by some hairy guy from the same village in the Peloponnese as Dinos. Dinos had made some kind of suss deal for tax purposes as in reality, he was pretty much broke, his monthly wage not even covering his basic outlays.

'Mafiosi *mayte*,' our Dean declared wisely, convinced Dinos was up to no good.

'*Skase vre paidi mou*,' Mother would admonish. Telling Dean to shut-up as she always did if she had to protect one of her own—Phil, in this case. Our sister, with each visit, told us less and less about her new routine and we took this to mean things were not ameliorating. She started looking thinner than she ever had. I started reading up on bulimia nervosa and its cousin anorexia deciding that Phil, being Phil, would not suffer from the latter but rather the former. In the end, whatever it was, wasn't nice. It was a medical condition that killed women. So, foolishly, in a vain attempt to play doctor, I started baking wholemeal, sugar-free, soya bean everything. Progressing to carob dessert this and lactose-free that.

'What are you trying to do? Get on *The Greek Variety Show*?' Phil would tease.

'They won't have 'im on the telly, he's too fat, eh!' Dean would add, just in case I contemplated sending in my recipe to Harry Michaels for the cooking segment.

I found Dean's reference to my weight unfair. After all, it had been years since the photographer taking the fifth-grade photo had removed me from the front row and in my place put three other pupils.

If you're overweight, people leave you alone. You become mostly invisible.

Men don't like young boys who are morbidly obese. If I were ever to tell Dean the truth about my experiences, he'd probably not accept it. My brother would not believe me. Might never ever again speak to me. Blaming me for allowing it to happen. I could just predict him saying, 'What kind of a man lets something like that take place?' I loved my brother enough to know his good aspects and his twisted, outer-suburban Alpha-male brain.

'He's got fat on the brain but,' Dean would add, just in case he was misunderstood the first time.

Even though I didn't like it when he was sledging me, I loved it when my brother shit-stirred Phil's Dinos. I wanted desperately to sledge Dinos too and even tell him off, but I just wasn't that way inclined, it wasn't in my personality. Everyone thought I was quiet and respectful. I was quiet because I was frightened, anxious and never felt I was entitled to speak up. Moreover, I didn't know *how* to sledge.

'Con, mayte, d'you think you've got enough dice hangin' in the car?' was Dean's constant rebuke to Dinos, each time our sister visited us with her fiancé. Despite the consular position, the BMW 5 Series (he had also arranged for himself to have a BMW through his compatriot) and the Darling Point apartment without water views, Dinos/Con/Konstandinos was a legit *wog* at heart; he stayed up all night to watch soccer videos sent to him from Greece, much to Phil's chagrin. Although, in her defence, she steadfastly refused to have any furry dice in her own car.

'There are limits,' she used to say. 'Compromise in a relationship is one thing but social death another.' Phil would never have been caught, dead or alive, driving a car with a pair of brightly-coloured dice—not even Dean liked that idea, and the dice would have accessorised his over-the-top purring Monaro nicely.

Mother, who had never approved of Dinos as a suitable, worthy husband for our Phil, started noticing that Konstandinos's socks never matched his too tight, narrow suits, or that his tie was never tied properly in a Windsor knot. He smoked too, like a chain gang, and his English was as appalling as that of some of Don Lane's international singing guests.

What I personally objected to was that he kept trying to fix me up with various Dinas and Fotinis and, of course, the ubiquitous Marias and Helens, all to no avail. I, Demosthenes, DemosPenis, Dimwit, Dipstick, Theo, call me what you like, had no intention of becoming a ghetto Greek with a wife who wore too much make-up during the day. Who thought painting meant painting the lounge room in the Maroubra semi we were destined to live in, decorated as the latest luxury home catalogue dictated. No Siree, an Orthodox marriage arranged by relatives was not for me.

I was fairly sure I was never going to get married.

I simply knew I could not pretend. That it wasn't fair to either party. I did not share the Greek cultural trait of *marrying for sensible reasons* and not for love. How often had I heard the line *Get married then do whatever you want*, from my own mother?

'You'll never a find a girl who'll put up with you,' was an often-repeated line of Mother's. She would say this, sometimes in passing, out of nowhere, as we sat drinking Turkish coffee and having *paximadia* or *koulouria* of an afternoon. The coffee hadn't been imported from Turkey. God forbid.

'I wouldn't want anyone who would just *put up* with me,' I'd say back defensively, challenging her with a plain *koulouri*.

'Get me a sesame one,' Mother would demand and I couldn't

refuse, couldn't begrudge her request since it was her terrible wages which had bought them; even though it was me who had done the shopping on the way back from school, getting off the train, walking to the deli, then walking all the way back, waiting for the next train, often arriving home after dark in winter.

Phil's Dinos kept calling Mother *Mother*, but it never rang true and she, conveniently, never heeded his call when he did so.

'Get yr own,' Dean would scold our future brother-in-law, leaving the room in a huff.

But our mother was not so hot-headed. She was learning to be (or had she always been?) an impressive diplomat. I recalled her Nescafe counselling sessions once again. She knew Mr Kalamata Olives needed her approval so she started giving him little positive encouraging smiles in return for the little *favours* Dinos would do for her. Like bring her imported Cypriot newspapers, a Guy de Maupassant novel in translation, a Marinella or Parios record. She'd casually suggest it would be charitable of him to make a donation to the church she attended or buy two blocks of raffle tickets for the church's Charity. Little things, nothing major. I mean, it wasn't as if she would cajole him into buying New Year Eve's Ball tickets for the whole family to the Castellorizian Club in Kingsford where all the wealthy Greeks gathered to welcome in the New Year. So, in short, Dinos was slickly duped into believing he was being accepted as a member of the family.

Behind his back, when Dinos was not present it was an entirely different version of Mother who would lament her precious daughter's fate. 'A married man, for my only daughter,' she complained frequently as we watched *Cop Shop*. She sometimes forgot herself and lamented Phil's choice of groom even in front of Phil herself, who nevertheless remained impassive.

'*O theos na mas voithisei*,' Mother would mumble, doing her full four stations of the cross, asking me again if John Orcsik were Greek. The fact Mother had noticed I would look away when the actor was on screen, made me blush, suspecting my mother knew a lot more about me than even I did. Orcsik had played a gay character in *Number 96* and his naked hairy chest was often on display in that show. I had never forgotten how disturbed I felt the first time I saw him with his shirt off.

'Do you like my new dress baby brother?' my sister would ask me, trying to sway the topic of conversation away from her husband-to-be. Even though I could tell the dress or outfit was evidently expensive, I thought her choice of clothes to be a bit too old for her, for a girl in her twenties. I assumed Dinos made her dress like a *Black and White Ball* matron in her fifties so when they appeared in public together, he could camouflage some of their immense age difference. Older men like Dinos were so entitled they didn't realise that if they stood next to a much younger partner, their own age was brought sharply into focus. And actually, made them look older than they were. So, in fact, having a young trophy wife, who they thought would improve their social capital, actually diminished it.

'It's okay, but your complexion needs a bit more colour, I reckon.'

'What, you want me to look like Maria Venuti on stage?' My sister was smug in the knowledge that she looked nothing like the buxom entertainer. She knew her outfits were worth more than the entire contents of our modest, synthetic-carpeted lounge room.

'Seems to me,' Dean would interrupt, 'that your artistic brother wants you to look more like Al Grassby.'

Phil, struggling to keep her composure, would then bite into another *koulouri*, move her mouth around it as if there was something distasteful with it, even though it was the same kind of *koulouria* she had been eating happily for years. Finally, she would drop the remainder of the offending *koulouri* onto the saucer, sighing in disgust.

'Aren't ya gonna have it?' Dean would then ask, and before Phil had time enough to answer, the sweet biscuit was in Dean's mouth, obliterated in a second.

38

Archangel Michael's opulent church was packed.

We knew just a handful of people. Mother was aggrieved the lucky couple had decided to have the service held there. None of us had had any say in the preparations for Dinos's theatrical extravaganza of a wedding.

'I am expecting a veritable Fellini freak show,' Mother warned us on the way to Rose Bay in Dean's car. Mother would have preferred a quiet, intimate ceremony at her local church in an attempt to finally validate her normalcy among her fellow churchgoers. But it was not to be. As if intentionally conspiring to usurp Mother's wishes, Dinos made sure everyone whose hand he had ever shook, everyone who owed him a favour, anybody he had had nefarious business arrangements with—hell, every yeeros shop assistant in the Sydney Metropolitan area and everyone who was related or known to anyone from his Peloponnese village would be in attendance to witness his Australian nuptials to his younger bride.

Getting dressed earlier in the morning, Mother had cried, openly and unashamedly in front of Dean and me. This wasn't unusual, since she had made sobbing her own sport from the day we had arrived in the lush avenues of Hunters Hill.

Putting on my hired suit, in my shared room, I had also cried, but I guess for different reasons. I cried knowing that things would never be the same again, no matter what happened. Things always changed. Everyone tells me at every turn that *change is the way of the world*. But I do not have to like it. I wanted a static, secure life. Worse, I worried terribly for my sister. I had a premonition that she had already learned that what glitters is not always gold. Not even gold-plated.

Father remained absent.

That was our family's only constant reality. He was with us for a couple of years when we first arrived in Australia. Then he suddenly went AWOL without any explanation. I had read many novels, and absent parenting was never promulgated as an appropriate parenting strategy in any of them, even the ones in translation from other little-known exotic cultures that seemed a lot more accepting than Western culture.

Mother had been a VIP in Cyprus, a respected woman, who would be the first one to offer a hand to anyone needing help. Now she was an invisible, abandoned middle-aged immigrant housewife who could not speak the language of the country she lived in. She only looked forward to going to church on Sundays and seeing her Greek-speaking GP once a month, who prescribed more and more drugs for her.

On my sister's wedding day, I also cried knowing that I would never experience being married. That I would never be a proud groom with a beautiful partner standing next to me, both of us dressed impeccably. I regretted the fact that I would never go on a honeymoon or be able to have my own biological children with the person I loved most. If such a person ever materialised and actually stuck around beyond the infatuation stage. It seemed wrong to me that two people who deeply loved each other, were not allowed by the law to marry. I cried as the occasion made clear to me the fact that we had been torn apart from the rest of our large, extended family. If Phil were getting married in Nicosia, say at Ledra Palace or at The Hilton by the pool, we would have had hundreds of relatives to share the occasion with us—many of our older cousins had got married already and had children. Our father's family was constantly expanding, whereas ours was shrinking. I lamented the way things had turned out, circumstances not of our own doing, which now prevented our many cousins and aunts and uncles, nephews and nieces, great uncles and great aunts from sharing this special day in my sister's life. Hell, we couldn't afford even an international telephone call to Cyprus at Christmas.

What can possibly compensate us for the erasure of possibilities when my parents were compelled to flee our island? For the life opportunities we didn't get the option to even consider? For the missed chance to create lifelong memories in the language, landscape and society we already knew?

So much was taken from me: all the melodies of Greek songs I've never heard, the poems and Greek authors I haven't read, the traditional dishes and pastries I've never tasted or been shown how to prepare. The Cypriot idioms I've never learned, the lovers whose physiognomy and speaking voices are simulacrums of mine whom I've never met; the ecstasy they could have endowed me with and the self-esteem desperately sought—now withheld.

We missed out on the family get-togethers, the weddings, baptisms, funerals, New Year's Eve celebrations we could not attend in the company of dozens of cousins, with my aunts and uncles and great uncles and nephews and nieces and schoolmates. The picturesque Troodos Mountain villages perched on hilltops and crevasses or built in dramatic valleys I never visited. The aquamarine crystal waters of Famagusta beaches I shall never again swim in.

The innocence of a childhood I never got to enjoy.

All this and more, and worse, that was unceremoniously taken from me, denied me. I never gave my consent let alone my informed consent to any such transformative transgressions against my fundamental rights as a Cypriot citizen.

Who will compensate me for all that was not ever mine to experience? What can placate this immeasurable blatant loss? A loss of home, of self, I did not cause. Always a good boy. Obedient to my mother, my aunts, my teachers, old ladies, perfect strangers. What international court of justice can I appeal to? How can I ever rid my conscience of these multiple traumas? How can anyone, even someone who may fall madly in love with me in the future, someone who has grown up with a sense of parental safety, with a healthy sense of self, of belonging to the society they live in, with security, wealth and the taken-for-granted confidence that the world will look after them, ever understand me? Let alone help me to ease this donkey load of pain and grievance I carry around, weighed down with supplies for a very long walking journey, always fretting and fearful I'm going to be hungry and petrified. Afraid at every turn that I shall be annihilated and nobody will be able to save me.

I didn't know whom to blame. The Turkish government? The Greek Junta? Was Makarios singularly responsible for the blighted fate of our island? Did he miscalculate how smart he was, playing both the Americans and the Russians while the Cold War reigned and then as payback being cut off by both? Was he such a megalomaniac that he made decisions not for the best outcome for the Cypriot people but rather in order for him to remain in power? Did he not open the door to the invasion by declaring in his UN Speech that all of Cyprus's guarantors should take whatever action necessary to restore the democracy of Cyprus after what he referred to as the 'Greek invasion'?

Weirdly, lots of people we initially thought were heroes turned out to be nothing more than self-serving ego-maniacs. Toxic leaders who believe they deserve more abundance than anyone else. Entitled. Who mistakenly assume they are smarter than Einstein. I was too young to judge Makarios with any factual forensic analysis. For all of his ambitions, his tight grip on the leash of power, he died three years after the invasion, aged just sixty-three. But Cyprus remained occupied. I read that Turkey had re-settled thousands of mainland Turks in the occupied part of our island. Once new settlers had had children in their new land, it would be hard to budge them. I doubted whether Greek Cypriots outnumbered the Turkish Cypriots anymore by four to one. I wondered if leaders like Makarios, the Junta generals, Kissinger and Nixon, were all wily, lackadaisical, inept, negligent narcissists. Were all politicians the same the world over? Stirring up populism rhetoric to serve their own ambitions notwithstanding the damage this caused to the same people they purportedly were trying to *look after*?

Makarios gained his fame initially as a fervent supporter of *Enosis*. Then he did a one-eighty turnaround and promulgated independence and somehow convinced the people of our island to follow his new goal for our small country. Perhaps the Cypriots saw how easily the young King was manipulated out of power in Greece and were too aware of the austerity the generals of the Junta had brought on the lives of our Greek brothers and sisters? Rightly chose to forego joining such a regime. So Makarios in fact, spared our island years from living under a treacherous military regime.

Nobody ever starved in Cyprus like they had in Greece during the Civil War. Makarios had his religious attire and funny hat to make us all feel we were in trusted hands—in God's hands. Greece just had cold-blooded generals in charge—who in their right mind would want those cruel men as their leaders?

Similarly, our father may have realised how difficult it was to raise children, not from afar as he had been used to for more than a decade, but up close, and present, day after day after day. He simply did not have the emotional balls to deal with it. It was too much of a burden. If Aunt Hara were still alive and I dared to say something like that to her face about her brother, I'm sure she would have smacked me right across my face. How I missed my aunt with her rhyming verses learned by heart from generations and generations before her. Aunt Hara would be beaming with pure delight now, if she were stood beside us in the church pew. Undoubtedly, she'd have a pertinent comment to make about the groom. About his age, his awkward asymmetrical face. The bird nose. His hangers-on.

But Aunt Hara was now only a figment of memory and imagination. She did not exist. She had never been to Australia; in fact, had never travelled outside Cyprus. She would have been visibly shocked to see our poor excuse of a home in the much-maligned outer western suburbs of Sydney. Would curse all those in authority she held responsible for our plight and would invoke the *Mati* onto them and their entire clan. We would not be celebrating my sister's marriage together with the dozens of Nicosia women who loved our mother. Or with other women whom we'd call *aunty* but who were totally unrelated to us by blood or marriage. Simply, they had been around Mother's family for so long, for so many generations, that they had been elevated to family status and the useful moniker of aunt was given to them to demonstrate their status. We'd call their children *cousin* and their husbands *uncle*. None of them were going to be in attendance in this new church today either.

In our father's village, the marriage of a man's only daughter would be a seven-day affair, with busloads of family and acquaintances arriving from all over Cyprus, some even bringing their own kid-goat as an offering. Goat meat was held in high regard on our island and celebrated much more than lamb. A concert stage would be built in the fields surrounding the patriarchal home, lanterns and fairy lights would be wired, a band hired. Local women would be working for months ahead of the ceremony, making lace and the sheets which would warmly embrace the couple on their all-important wedding night. A make-up artist would put up a schedule for all the female relatives to observe. Everyone would try their best to be happy, even the widowed aunties who had not had sex in twenty-five years and who were still dressed in black.

When we would go to such affairs, Phil and Mother would be the last to be made up as they were classified as city-folk visitors.

We would all sit at the long, white-dressed hired tables close to the *pista* with Cousin Dimitris and Uncle Pericles and Petros and Aliki. Petros would make Phil sing a Beatles song between toasts. Kid goat, pork and lamb would be barbecued in their entirety.

In the mud *fourno* lemon potatoes would be baking alongside hares and *kleftiko*. Aunt Paraskevi would make her renowned *koupes* using pine nuts which she would carefully roast first. She made a living from making these for any celebrations held in her neighbourhood. Aunt Pezouna would make trays and trays of *pastitsio*—she had won seventeen competitions for her dish. The older aunties would be making dessert offerings by hand: *shiamisshi, pittes, daktila, tsinopittes,* party-sized *tahinopittes, eliopittes, halloumopittes, tiropittes* and *flaounes*. All would be made in their dozens and *loukoumades* too, *amigdala*, and of course, the omnipresent *kourapiedes*.

No lady's house was legitimate unless the hostess presented her *kourapiedes*. God help her reputation if her parcels of shortbread were stale or no good. Or if they didn't have the appropriate quantity of almonds in them. Or God forbid, if another nut was used.

The *bomboniere* would be given to every single soul who stepped inside the church. If Phil were getting married back home, Mother would have insisted that the almond-paste biscuit that's also included in the wrapped tulle be prepared by her good friends at *Noufaros*, once the best cake store in Nicosia. Mother had not been asked to make any contribution or decision relating to her daughter's wedding and despite pretending this was not a big deal, she was humiliated at having been completely sidelined.

In Father's village, throughout the seven days of the wedding celebration, people of all ages and genders would be in high spirits. It was an occasion where people were encouraged to flirt. Some did so discreetly and others more brazenly. Shamelessly. For instance, some of the older men would get tipsy very quickly and start being sleazy, in a drunk but happy way. Some would even start reciting *tsiatista* about the beauty of some woman, present, imagined or long-gone. Teenagers would sneak off and kiss a brand-new lover; others, a little older, would use the occasion to announce their own upcoming engagement date or nuptials. The next day, it would be the same all over again, and the same the following night and the nights which followed right up until the following Sunday.

But that was Cyprus. That was then.

Years have passed since we were part of an extended family, a community. Where Mother and Father had an extended support system at their disposal. Mother always knew whom to telephone if one of Father's relatives was in strife or needed a job or assistance or was applying for the public service. She would always reach just the right person who was able and willing to do a favour for *Kyria Konstandia's daughter.*

And now, this was our first family wedding in Australia, and almost five years had passed since any of us had been to a village wedding. Looking up, from all those childhood memories, I caught sight of Dean, surprisingly all teary-eyed, and I leaned across to him, for this was my big chance to show him that we weren't that different after all, he and I. My brother's usual bravado was all for show.

'*Re, klais*? Don't tell me our Dean, our cool dude's upset? I mean, *mayte*, you're actually showing an emotional response in public, and nobody's even touched the Monaro!' I teased him, but at the same time was concerned at seeing my brother in tears.

'Yeah, yeah your bro' is cryin' *mayte*,' he admitted, and I thought he wasn't such a bad macho shit-stir after all.

'I'm cryin' 'cos this bloody service is takin' two friggin' hours!' he barked at me. We had to stop chatting though because Mother iced us with one of her looks and as if that wasn't enough, she had had her hair all teased up in the same way she had it when we were kids and a sense of *déjá vu* embraced us. Reminding us instantly of childhood, when there was no doubt in our minds that Mother's authority had to be respected and obeyed, without question. Her authority was supreme on any subject.

'My fuckin' shoes are killin' me,' Dean said, directing his complaint towards Mother who couldn't resist a chance at a jibe and who, quick as a flash, shot back, 'You should try wearing shoes more often *Konstandino mou.*'

I wished at that moment that *Yiayia* Konstandia had allowed her only daughter to take up that nursing scholarship in Alexandria way back then. Mother would have made a formidable sister-in-charge. She would have been imperious in her treatment of her nurses, ensuring their uniform and grooming were impeccable and that they treated patients with dignity. But the nurses, fearful of her most of the time, would, at the same time, not hesitate to seek solace in her arms when something went pear-shaped in their personal lives. For our mother would do anything for people she knew, even if she wasn't particularly fond of them.

Mother might have then met a man who would willingly choose to be the kind of father who delighted in being present for his family. Admittedly, our father got into debt to rescue us from Turkish peril, but then chose to dump us in the wasteland of outer suburbia and then washed his hands of us. He chose to disappear.

He was reportedly smitten by my mother the moment he saw her at a community picnic. I knew for certain that my sister was not smitten with her groom.

Phil was now walking around and around in circles doing Isaiah's Dance with her almost-to-be husband whose face exuded a mixture of surprise and drunkenness. He too walked Isaiah's Dance, the fragile wedding wreath slipping off his egg-shaped head twice, only to be steadied by his best man, a man whom we hadn't even met once. He seemed as inept as our future brother-in-law, following the couple two steps behind, shuffling around and around, as the two priests shrieked and tried to outdo each other with what they thought were their wonderful liturgical singing voices.

'They look like hairy monkeys, except they're uglier,' was Dean's sacrilegious summary of the assembled reverent brothers, resplendent in their gold robes.

'It takes one to know one,' I said, knowing that Dean's face would react with one of his *Must you be so predictable little brother* smirks. Yep, he smirked back.

'Theo *mayte*, are you gonna cop it on your broken nose or what, when we get out of here?' he growled, and I remembered he weighed twice my weight and had ten times my muscle tone. And that my nose was broken enough already.

We were just the three of us in our pew, down the front of the church. Father failed to materialise, despite Mother's deluded expectations he would make it. He was absent in the same way he had always been—we could not depend on him *being there for us.* Ever. I wasn't sure if he had sent our mother any money for this special occasion or whether she had maxed out her Bankcard. She wore a beautiful new dress that was obviously not obtained from the back of her boss's van.

I looked around and I saw plenty of pudgy, heavily made-up matrons standing beside their grey partners in outdated suits. Men with lemon juice on their dark, stained hair and suddenly felt that our family was a sham. If a father can't be present at his own daughter's wedding, what use was he? Watching your sister being given away by a middle-aged man whose surname you're not sure of, in front of hundreds of people, all seemingly coupled or at least escorted by someone whom they could claim to be their own flesh and blood, was not a comforting sight.

Ola pan hamena, Mother was fond of saying in elegiac tones. Normally, I wanted to challenge her nihilism. But at that moment in time, I had no evidence I could present to prove my point.

I too shared her depression.

It would be decades before I could bring myself to say it out loud to a doctor that I suffered from depression and not some kind of generic Mediterranean melancholy.

'Your turn next, Dean.' I said half in jest, half serious, dreading the prospect, as then I would be left all on my own to take care of our mother. To try and help her emotionally to come to terms with her lost dreams when my own dreams had not yet been embarked on.

'Me, get married? Keep dreamin' mate,' my brother responded, his lips hardly moving.

'Shh!' This time it was a woman behind us, who prodded us in the back with her *bastouni* and whom we had never seen before. Dali would have loved her face.

'Shove off, *yiayia*,' was Dean's response to her but she didn't look as if she had understood Dean's idiom. She just half-closed her right eye, both her eyes twitching in disgust, and Dean and I started laughing. Just at the exact moment that Dinos's wreath finally fell from the top of his egghead and fortuitously landed on the pillow the page boy was carrying. The flower girl started crying, throwing her bouquet onto the floor and her mum rushed up to appease her. The best man awkwardly tried to pick up the errant wreath and carefully manipulate it back onto the crown of my soon to be brother-in-law. Alas, his actions were not executed deftly enough and there he was, breaking out of character, smiling, exposing three gold teeth just as a tuft of gelled hair broke loose from Dinos's padded down scalp and stuck up, making him look like an exotic punk cockatoo.

'*Panayia mou*,' was all Mother could say, invoking the Madonna's name, in quiet desperation.

39

Mother was becoming more anxious than ever.

She was now stuck in the less than salubrious outer western suburbs of Sydney with two recalcitrant, wifeless males at home, whilst an unmentionable third roving male remained AWOL. Missing in action like Dimitris and our two other cousins whose whereabouts remained unknown still. Debriefing after the wedding, she insisted our father had actually attended incognito.

'He was there at the wedding, late but he came,' she claimed, feeding her delusion her husband had not abandoned her. Neither Dean nor I believed her claim. Why should we have? We never saw our father at the wedding, not with our own eyes, and hadn't seen him for years. Still, momentarily we entertained the possibility that our mother was right—perhaps he *was* there but Dean and I did simply not recognise him? As far as we boys were concerned, he was dead, a half-known acquaintance from our past. A man who kept disappearing.

A grown-up who could not cope with having a grown-up life. With daily having to make decisions and take on responsibilities. It was much easier to disappear and occasionally send some money to his struggling wife. As compensation for his guilt. For his inability to shoulder the vagaries of daily family life and raising children.

'When you're older you'll understand,' Mother would say and

we boys shook our heads, openly sniggering because that cliché seemed to be her answer to everything.

After our sister's wedding, Dean started spending less and less time at home. He was always nagging me to get a girlfriend but he himself always complained what a headache all his girlfriends were. There were a series of girls, mostly carbon copies of each other with whom my brother became infatuated for a couple of Saturdays, or a month or two. Then his attraction to them fizzled out. Real life would mar their attempts to keep it casual. Or insecurity would raise its ugly head, and the girl would demand that they go steady. Hearing that, Dean ran a mile. Or rather, drove away fast. Very fast in the Monaro.

I kept dreaming of my life as an adult, working quietly alone, in the small front garden. Dreaming of visiting all the museums of Italy and France. And in Spain—I wanted to visit not just the Prado but the cathedral in Old Toledo.

Dreaming of being loved.

Of being loved without the threat of pain.

Or abandonment.

Daydreaming of having the financial capability to visit Cyprus again. To take my loved one to my country of birth. To take in the intoxicating scent of our Greek jasmine. To be given the opportunity to pick wild freesias on the side of a country lane, their perfume infiltrating not just our nostrils but the inside cabin of our car.

Dreaming of winning major art prizes which would help to give me the wherewithal to live from my earnings and from commissions that may come my way. Of being respected. Fully recognisant that I had never experienced what gaining respect might feel like. If I were honest, I did not respect myself or my efforts to erase some memories from my headspace—it just wasn't possible no matter how many positive thoughts and mantras I applied to doing so.

I felt the only way out of my claustrophobia from our narrow villa would be having a space of my own, large enough to enable me to paint large canvasses. Like those of David Hockney. Or Pollock. The latter's abstract oeuvre made my heart skip a beat. I had read so many books, borrowed from the library in Bathurst St in the city about Jackson Pollock that I thought I already lived in the USA.

I'd sit on the rattler train to the city and close my eyes and imagine I was riding the subway. I had my ordered and successful life in a New York loft, in a Soho warehouse, already sorted—at least in my reverie. I also had a large studio in the meatpacking district where it was cheap to lease an old warehouse space. I would eat two pastrami sandwiches on rye filled with layers and layers of pastrami for lunch—I had read New Yorkers made the sandwich a work of art and a sandwich for lunch was a substantial meal for their delicatessens were generous with the fillings and the amount of butter, unlike here, where you just got a slice.

I would own an old stone house in Abruzzo, living there for six months each year with a partner who would love and respect me and be proud of me and encourage my creative endeavours. Who would be supportive and who, with love and sustained kindness, would help me heal my emotional wounds. Even a smidgen of healing would be good for me.

But the reality was, I had not yet been able to breach the

emotional gap which exists between two people. I dared not. I was inexperienced but already aware I was attracted to heterosexual men. Men who fitted the prototype of man I felt was more manly than my own pathetic version. Taller men. Men who were muscular. Unafraid. Educated men with perfectly shaped noses. Men from well-to-do, established families who became brokers and played rugby and who never had to worry about financial security.

In other versions of the miracle of love I sought, I imagined being Rupert Brooke's companion.

I dreamt of living anywhere else than the attached homette we lived in, in the outer-western suburbs. A suburb filled with misery, multi-generational unemployment and poverty, cheap-drug addiction and overt anger. Going to the local shops meant confronting (and dealing with) these realities no matter what time of the day it may be.

I tried to be likeable.

I once or twice tentatively reached out to see if I could be loved.

I disappointed others.

I did not know how to cross that immeasurable space that exists between all living creatures. There were no rule books about establishing a male-to-male relationship in the school library or even the big Bathurst Street library in the city. To help me navigate and cross that chasm successfully. No matter what preparation I'd put in before the actual navigation, I was destined to fail. To lose.

I was illegal.

My kind was illegal. I could find myself in gaol for loving someone physically. For being loved physically. Any step towards bridging the empty chasm of being untouched by a lover could land me in trouble. Any attempt fraught with risk. If I stared a second longer at a handsome man on the train I could be punched, told off, humiliated in public. If I were in a changing-room I had to keep my eyes downcast lest I caught a glimpse of a beautiful body and admired it a moment too long.

I worried I'd be caught out at every interaction that involved a good-looking confident male. If I lingered in a public convenience or in a park, the man who would be checking me out could easily be an undercover policeman whose goal was to entrap my *perverted* kind. The Police Commissioner was always quoted referring to homosexual men as perverts.

Even friendships with other males remained problematic for me as I was already aware I had a habit of idolising certain kinds of men who may innocently assume we were just mates and nothing more. So, instead of seeking to make friends, I redirected all my attention and energy into my creative efforts and scoured the newspapers and noticeboards for possible art competitions.

After a school excursion there, I discovered Sydney University's quadrangle and under one of the arches in the centre, noticed a huge noticeboard. Huge I say, for a boy who had never seen a university noticeboard in our troubled suburb where anything posted on the small square public noticeboard outside the post office would be ripped off, or have obscene phrases scrawled on it.

It was that noticeboard that changed my life. That made me believe I could be someone. A flyer promoting a contest. I scrawled the telephone number and address down on my hand. On the train back home, I made sure nobody could see my inked hand. I had to take Polaroids of my two entries and send them via post. I made sure Dean did not see me arranging the canvases on the floor on a sheet of white paper and using my brother's camera, carefully take four shots, two of each work. Anymore and Dean would know I had used his camera and he'd be asking me questions.

When the letter arrived informing me, just after my seventeenth birthday, that I'd had two small canvases accepted in a group exhibition at the Sheds on City Road, I was jubilant. The acceptance was the first time in my life I'd had my creative effort validated by my new country's gatekeepers and I felt elated. I took it as a symbolic sign that I was on the right track.

My monthly trips to the Art Gallery in town still took over two hours on the train, even when I was lucky enough to be in a newer silver carriage. My long hair did not seem to amuse other boys my age. Teenage boys always seemed to travel in packs in our suburb, and always terrified me as I walked past them outside the Post Office where they used to hang out with their bikes and chicks and dealers.

Why doncha fix your fuckin' nose you freak, was something I'd learned to ignore. For I knew I could never win a fight. Needless to say, the eight Telecom public phones outside the post office were always vandalised and sprayed with graffiti. Only one was in working order.

'Like a war zone,' Mother would often say as we drove past in the Monaro.

40

A fortnight after our sister's ceremony in the posh church we received a postcard from Phil and Dinos (*love, Phil and Dinos*) from Bali.

'Can't wait to get there meself,' Dean said in response to the sun-drenched beach depicted on the postcard.

'Looks a bit like Famagusta,' Mother said.

'You and your stupid country,' Dean shot back 'Can't ya get it through your head that you're not there anymore? You're here! Jesus!'

'Don't take the Lord's name in vain *Ntino mou.*'

'I'll do what I like.'

When this kind of bitter dialogue broke out between the two of them, I'd quietly leave them to sort it out. Nothing I could have said would have made the Turkish-occupied, illegally partitioned island of Cyprus come geographically closer to Australia in my mother's eyes. Conversely, nothing I could say, any argument I could present, could ever convince Dean that no matter what he thought of the past, it was all that our mother had. I kept wishing that Dean might realise this himself, without me having to tell him. He was the older brother, after all, not me. I shouldn't have to tell him or anyone else, obvious truths evident to anyone with half a brain.

I feared talking about *the past,* this vague period now gone, would be an intangible concept our Dean would fail to grasp. He had some good qualities, like everyone does, but he was certainly not wise. I wished to avoid sounding weak in front of my headstrong older brother. I did not wish to risk coming across like some kind of wimpy, mushy younger brother trying to explain to him, the older young man, things about life.

If I were him, I'd be pissed off too, if my younger brother tried to tell me about the world. Many a time he had been accusatory towards me, saying dismissively: *What the fuck would you know— you weren't even twelve when we left for fuck's sake!*

So, mornings and nights would come and go, and Mother and Dean would continue fighting about our lives here, in our suburban inferno. Arguing about what may have been. I recalled the island of my birth in images which were still potent. There was a recurrent image, a hazy vision of blue, of a crystal-clear sea lit by a soft shining sun. Always the scent of Greek jasmine and wild freesias filling the space.

Another, of open, lush greens fields with red dirt, like that we see in photographs of Alice Springs, but not barren empty fields. Instead, fields filled with vegetables and lemon trees, protected from the wind on either side of the allotment by tall, narrow, elegant cypress trees. These would sway and move as elegantly as a giraffe's neck and appear to disapprove of us humans. Looking down at all of us, as we helped our uncles and aunties gather their produce by hand.

In winter, Cousin Panikkos would take us to a taverna, in Paidoulas, a high-altitude village near Troodos. Wealthy foreign tourists stayed in Platres and skied the pistes and slopes of Troodos, keeping the economy going for all the nearby tiny villages. Cousin Panikkos was never curious enough to explore the smaller villages and stuck to us all eating at the same restaurant each visit.

The memory strong still, of the wonders our city-eyes took in the snow-covered landscape as his boxy new Skoda managed to grip the slimy asphalt of the narrow swirling road inches from crevasses. Panikkos pressed the horn of his new car constantly to alert any possible drivers coming from the opposite direction, as the road was so extremely narrow that even if a donkey suddenly appeared, we would risk parachuting into the chasm below.

'Can we one day stop in Kakopetria? Or drive to Kalopanayiotis maybe?' Philadelphia would ask but Cousin Panikkos was a man on a mission.

'Why would we do that when we know they have good food where we usually eat?' Given he was the only adult male in the car, we assumed he knew what he was talking about.

All around us, serenity, stillness and beauty.

I have never seen snow here. But I know we have lots of it in the south of the state. And we even have a region called *The Victorian Alps*. Australia has everything. Beaches, deserts, mountains, wine regions, tropical forests and bush in abundance. For those who are not damaged emotionally. For those wealthy enough to have the opportunity to travel, to take advantage of the plethora of geographical landscapes this island continent has on offer.

Mother had rescued several photographs of Phil and Dean and me and our cousins Petros and Aliki playing snow games on Troodos. There was another, of our mother in her twenties, sitting inside our uncle's 1963 Ford which from a distance looked like a plane with all its swirling panels. Mother is seen cajoling a baby version of my little cousin Alekkos and in another shot, leaning against the wide panels of the car, proudly holding onto her brother's arm. I recall my mother and my uncle would often stand by the car chatting and laughing together, watching us kids play. Or, if we had made an emergency stop during a road trip, and we had a piss out in the open, I would look up and see the two of them bent over picking wild *matsikorida* or freesias in a field.

Uncle Pericles was forever lighting a cigarette, and Mother would often be disapproving of him. That was their relationship. But they loved each other. That much was clear. It was just the two of them. Uncle would always run to our mother when life became tough for him to handle on his own. For example, when one of his marriages or affairs ended. Or, when he ran out of money paying spousal support to several women. Mother would always counsel him to sell his BMW motorbike and just keep his Honda bike, but never denied him a helping hand.

You could find many things to criticise in our uncle's life choices but his fight to keep his children by his side, when this was not a common occurrence back then, was admirable and was often commented favourably upon by Mother. Even perfect strangers found this admirable, before casting aspersions on our uncle by alleging that he had won custody simply because of the reputation of his surname.

I would think about our discarded island and all these unreliable images would resurface in my mind. Like an oft-repeated sitcom where you thought you knew the punchline of every joke but watching it again after some years, you find yourself confused when a favourite punchline is finally delivered, and the words are not what you had assumed them to be all this time. Memory does play tricks on us, on our recall and this jars as we would like to think we are entirely reliable narrators and bearers of the truth of the past.

But the images that haunted me were not something I had seen on a television show. These snap-frozen images, these scenes of the past were from within my own private headspace. Sometimes, I would question whether these same vivid scenes had any veracity to them. Were they ever played out in the way I recalled or were they simply figments of my sun-stroked Australian imagination? If I convinced myself they didn't happen, would I then feel better? Would I be healed? Would I forget? And be a normal teenager? Without having to carry this burden with me, day in day out? Making even great moments of joy laden with grief?

Had we ever built a snowman with our cousins, or had I just seen this in a promotional trailer for a film or in an advertisement for cigarettes at *The Theatre Royal*?

'You'll get sunburnt if you stay out there much longer,' Mother would shout in colloquial Greek, from inside the house, and all our unemployed neighbours who couldn't understand why Mother wore so much black, would give me a derisory look that I read to say, *why don't you teach her English mate?*

That was a subject we dared not mention any longer. Not even Dean who was much braver when it came to back chatting or challenging Mother. Assimilation had not been possible for our mother to achieve. She had had enough culture in her four decades of life in Cyprus, she was fond of saying, she did not need any more.

'Ethnic dances and food served on paper plates at outdoor festivals, that's multiculturalism for you here,' she'd criticise often enough.

Unlike Dean, I didn't want to offend our mother in the way he did by always speaking English and coming home late and sullen most nights. I thought she had been hurt enough, and of course I knew who was to blame.

He had better watch out, I would tell myself, picturing myself laying punches and kicks on my father's convulsing body, all the time crying inside for not having been given the chance to know him except superficially. For forgetting how his voice sounded, for not remembering any of the tunes he used to whistle, for not having learned how to talk to him. For not knowing how to play backgammon with him, for not having a clue how to get through to him. For never hearing him make a lame dad joke.

I kept wondering whether he may, one day, reappear at our front door without warning, shocking us to the core, like a horrific car smash one comes across unexpectedly on a quiet country road. Or roadkill dismembered by scavengers.

Before her three-star Bali honeymoon had even ended, our Phil was on the phone in tears.

'The bastard hit me.' She was furious.

'You mean really clobbered you or just playfully gave you one?' Dean asked, forensically, like a trained detective, grabbing the receiver off from me.

'What did you do, Philadelphia?' asked Mother, grabbing the receiver and shooing us away like Aunt Hara used to do with her inquisitive chickens when she'd try and give us a bath in the barn.

'I didn't *do* anything Mother, thank you very much for your support,' Phil responded.

'Well, that's all right then,' Mother said before passing the receiver back to Dean.

'I just thanked the waiter who brought us our drinks and apparently, I smiled at him *invitingly*...I think that was the word he used. I mean, what kind of a rock did this guy crawl out from under? I thought he was sophisticated, but he might as well be an illiterate shepherd. I hate it here. It's so humid. My hair's gone all fuzzy. Just hate it,' said Phil all in a rush before going silent.

'Well, come home then,' I called out, over Dean's hand, hoping she'd hear me on her holiday island in Indonesia.

'Theo, *o vlakas*, says come home,' Dean murmured calmly, and I could tell he was livid. 'And for once I agree with our fatso brother.'

'It's not as easy as that, boys,' she replied, 'I'm married now.'

'If that bastard touches you again, I'll choke him to death. Better still, I'll fix his brakes. Fuckin' bastard.'

'Dean, I didn't realise what he was like. He smokes constantly. He drinks whiskey as if it were chilled water, swallowing a tumbler all at once.'

'*Kori*, we all knew he drank,' Dean said, infuriated that nobody else had previously noticed this.

'I only used to spend four, five hours with him at a time before. Now, we're together twenty-four hours a day. Not a word to Ma about his drinking.'

'As if,' Dean sniggered conspiratorially and even though Phil was not feeling as if she were in paradise at that moment, I was certain she would have had a little smile on her upset face. Our Dean was forever *as if*-ing people; and with that Phil just hung up. She was gone. Like a *Wayang* puppet no longer being reflected on the wall, her voice disappeared.

'Shit, eh?' was all Dean said, his face serious, before reaching for his car keys and disappearing. Leaving behind him a whiff of monoxide, petrol.

Unexpectedly, Phil was losing her grip on her dream—the dream of escaping both our economic reality living in our small villa in our far-flung impoverished suburb and our depressed, emotionally-needy mother.

41

· · · · · · · · · · · ·

Dream escapes seemed to always come at a cost.

Phil had insisted she and Dinos go to Europe for a honeymoon, but he vetoed that wish by claiming if his ex-wife found out he was in Europe and did not make the effort to catch up with his daughters there would've been hell to pay. So, Bali it was. For Phil, Bali was the turning point; was there a way back after your new husband bashed you?

Our father's escapes over many decades probably cost him too. Perhaps he had days when he hated himself? For abandoning us on two different islands on either hemisphere of the globe. Maybe, just maybe, he was remorseful at his inability to stand by his family and take the mantle as the (responsible) head of the family.

He was no trusted patriarch. Like Makarios III, when forensically analysed, he was probably no hero after all. Just a narcissist obsessed with his own ambitions, own needs and wants. In the case of our father, evidently, he cared not for the needs of his wife or children. Our father was just like our former ethnarch, whose photograph our mother had had framed in a garish over-the-top gilt frame. Both men were master manipulators and in our father's case, we were no longer his loyal supporters. I suspected our Makarios, a man of the cloth we were all brought up to view as our saviour, had let us down by focusing on his own personal ambitions to hold on to power, even if it meant our nascent nation would be torn apart.

Here, in the peaceful landscape we called Australia, overhearing classmates at school talking about the weekend, how their dad drove them someplace, how he had fixed something or made something for them or told a funny joke, unnerved me. I had not had any such interaction or experiences with my own father, so once again, I felt ostracised from my peers. From daily life. I could not participate as my classmates did; I did not have any meaningful shared experiences we could compare.

Perhaps Father truly was *a weak man* as Mother often referred to him. I at first thought she was bitter about her own abandonment by him, but as the years unfolded, I recognised she was openly categorising him as weak, as a way for us to temper, assuage our resentment of him. Mother was hoping assigning victimhood to her husband would somehow excuse his parental failures in our estimation. Even though I had never had a partner, I intrinsically knew it was wrong to make disparaging remarks about your partner in the company of others; cast aspersions on the character, the masculinity of the man you purportedly loved, and do so in front of his children.

The fact was, though, he *did* leave his village as soon as he was able to when he was a teenager and moved to the capital in search of employment and adventure. That was not conjecture on my part as I was not around at the time, obviously; it was not a myth but historical fact. I am guessing his MO for survival was set in place early on in his life. Long before our mother had come along. Decades before my siblings and I were born.

Wherever he was, whatever he was doing, however it was he spent his days, I wondered whether he might still carry with him the art of our palms. Our traced childhood palms, drawn on the blue aerogramme paper, which had to be folded carefully, exactly as the arrows directed, so that it became a letter and an envelope in one. I lost count how many times each of us kids had diligently traced our palm over all the years he was away overseas. Our very own art efforts were solely for his benefit, sent to him at his request, sometimes embellished with a few words.

What did he do with all those drawings?

Did he put his flat palm against our drawn palm each time he received them?

Did he use them to estimate how big we had grown or to check how much bigger his palm may be, against our own?

Did he stare at the outline we had traced, imagining how tall we had gotten? If our voices had changed?

Did he regret making the decision to work permanently overseas?

I knew how hard it was to get a decent job on our island and how much harder it was to keep one, but surely all those years of work experience in tough conditions in so many Middle Eastern countries would have meant something to prospective local employers?

Why did he not make more of an effort to find employment on our island after a couple of years of gaining international experience? Undoubtedly, he had proven he could literally take the heat and do his job with successful demonstrated work experience in several desert countries and in isolated locations. Daily work life for him would have been no bed of roses.

Perhaps I am overthinking it? Admittedly, I've been accused of thinking more than doing by several people. Almost-friends who lost interest in me quick enough.

It may be that my father was so busy during the day exerting himself in physical toil, that he didn't have time, an ounce of energy to spare. I expect he was more concerned with survival, getting some deep sleep so he could face the next day of physical labour in the oil plant he worked at, and the day after that.

I doubt anyone's brain can have the luxury of quiet reflection after working in temperatures of forty or more and crashing onto a cot in a shared dormitory with dozens of other immigrant men. God knows what kind of food they were served. What bathroom facilities they had in the sleeping quarters. Perhaps he simply dreamt of Greek food rather than processing how his absence emotionally may impact his growing children for the rest of their lives?

Reeling still from Phil's horrible news, I doubted that our father would have kept those aerogramme letters from us as treasured mementoes. There was no way I could be convinced that he kept them all, in the chronological order they had been sent, in a treasured-memory wooden box. A box he had spotted in one of the open-air markets he used to tell us about:

'They have everything you could possibly want...' he'd say enthusiastically, but then immediately he'd be sullen. His ellipsis always worried me, as my imagination saw him getting into all sorts of situations with the sellers. With other customers who were spending time, surveying the goods on offer, meandering around the stalls. I did not trust that my father always behaved like a gentleman.

I had witnessed his quick temper with sales staff and service providers on the odd occasion I tagged along. And his stubbornness. Like that time, we walked home all the way from Grace Bros.

No. I was unequivocal in surmising there was no intricately carved special box he kept our drawings of our traced palms in, as a tangible memento of our growing up. As a physical reminder of his decision to abandon us, to earn a decent wage, albeit so far away from us. Supposedly for our own sake. I had never seen him being affectionate with anyone, not even his own mother. He didn't embrace *Yiayia* Parthena when they saw each other. She too had never openly shown affection to any of us, never hugging us with ardent enthusiasm. We kissed her hand upon arrival for our visits. We may or may not have got a pat on the head as reciprocation.

No, I was certain our palm art had long ago been discarded. It was what my father did in life. Discard. Survive. Move on. It was his ability to extricate himself from all kinds of emotional attachments that allowed him to survive. When I forensically analysed my father's behaviour and actions over the years I was alive (I could not be aware of his history for the decades he was alive and I was not yet born), it was crystal clear that our father had not exhibited any signs of sentimentality in any way.

I recall an anecdote of when his wedding band was lost, somewhere in the Libyan desert where he was stationed. He couldn't tell Mother how it happened or where exactly it had extricated itself from his wedding finger. He didn't even notice for days, he said, that he no longer wore an eighteen-carat band of gold. He most certainly did not rush to the nearest jewellery store to order another before his next flying visit home to see us, so as not to upset his wife. And yet, how many times had he regaled us with stories of how cheap real gold jewellery was in all the Middle East? And of what good quality the workmanship was. And how competitive all the jewellers were, knowing the jewellery store three doors down was prepared to offer a customer a much better price.

Upon discovering the loss of the signifier of their nuptial bond, Mother was simply left muttering something under her breath—did she swear? Finally fed up with him after more than a decade in absentia. Or was what she mumbled under her breath one of her usual routines? Her desperate invocations to God or the Madonna or the Holy Spirit? Or to Saint Barbara? I cannot recall. We would often hear her murmur, *Panayia mou* when she was struggling to remain calm or *Voithise me Ayia mou Varvara*.

That night, the night we received Phil's unsettling telephone call, I painted an ugly picture of bile, a putrid green. Green like the splattered guts of a caterpillar who had gorged heavily on newly planted busy lizzies. In the background I laid down the colours of Greece, blue and white. Green and blue clashed and that's how I started to see Phil and her Dinos; as two conflicting colours trying to do battle for dominance for position on an unsuspecting white sheet of canvas. A canvas that was too costly to chuck away and too thin to withstand another layer of paint.

In the immediate days after the telephone call, the three of us were trying to think of the right things to say to Phil when she got back from her ten days in heaven-hell so she could see we had her back. Dean soon withdrew from strategising together with me and Mother as he found out that he would be losing his job. The restaurant he had been working in was closing down as the

Chinese restaurant next door had pilfered all the lunchtime trade with their $3.90 all-you-can-eat buffet.

Among his friends, Dean was not the only one unemployed. Most of his mates, swarthy types with short/long mullets like his, of various Euro-ethnic denominations and combinations, many with unpronounceable first names—and *not all Christian*, Mother often admonished—were also without a job. They'd spend the day gathered around the bonnet of their cars, in someone's front yard or carport. These congregations had a religious fervour to them. As if they were gathered there to worship some supreme all-knowing, all-seeing spiritual motor vehicle *Being*.

Fiddling around with the engines, spark plugs, drinking beer from a can, playing music on their cars' stereos, they would call each other *poof* a lot. Luckily, they had some kind of rotating roster, which meant they were only at our place once a fortnight, or every third week. After Mother had returned from church, she would take them out a plate of *paximadia* or *kourapiedes* and ask innocently why they never played any Greek music on their car tape deck.

42

Year 11 continued like a dull dream for me.

I seemed less and less inclined to sit around in the library waiting for some special reserve article to be made available so I could prepare my essay on the causes of the Second World War or my assignments on *Brave New World* vs Orwell's *1984*— both novels had scared the daylights out of me. Just like the Nostradamus documentary did a year earlier. School did not feed my spirit in any way. Just brought my loneliness more into focus.

It all seemed ridiculous.

I started to feel unequivocally upset when everyone around me seemed to have a girlfriend or a boyfriend. I could not imagine exposing my chest with my fifty-cent size birthmark to anyone who might have professed their teenage love to me. Luckily in high school, if we were in the Skins team we could keep our singlet on. In one of the primary schools I had briefly attended, it was compulsory to be bare-chested and the humiliation and dread of being singled out for being fat, a migrant and having a birthmark made me ill and landed me the nickname of *Malteser*. To add to the cache of pejorative epithets flung at me daily.

I devised all kinds of schemes to avoid attending PE. Thankfully, we moved house so often, it would take a while before the pupils at each new school found out about my deformity. My t-shirt stayed on even on forty-degree days of which there were many in our suburb. During school breaks, I would envy the couples who would sit together in a half-discreet corner of the playground or huddle under the staircases, nuzzling each other's neck, talking intensely.

Armando had no such discretion and kissed his girlfriend of the day openly, even in front of teachers. He got away too with unbuttoning his shirts, completely showing off his tan and strong chest. How do the Armandos of the world get away with everything? I was prepared to bet that even if he were accused of murder, Armando would be exonerated. All he would have to do is flash a pearly smile at the jury and all of them, male and female, young or old, would pardon him without the need for any ardent deliberation.

I was on my own.

It was my curse.

Weirdly, it made me feel safe.

If you are on your own no one can hurt you. But not being close to anyone at school made breaks unbearable. Once Year 11 started, I was allowed the privilege of the relative quiet of the senior playground. At recess or lunch breaks I gave up the *outcasts* group as some of the guys in the group were just too weird for words. It depressed me, sitting there listening to talk of sports by young men who had never played any sport. Or having to listen to endless geek talk about computer science developments and how big companies already had these enormous computers that could do incredible human-like duties.

I wanted to be around happy people. I wanted to distract

myself from my own personal misery. I wanted to live free of fear. Being made ashamed of my heritage, my emerging sexuality, all that drama, so early on in life does not lead to building confidence. I found, that even when everything seemed to be going okay, say I got an A+ on an assignment, or if one of my art works was chosen to be exhibited in the principal's office waiting room for a month, I was always anxious, wondering when the next disaster might strike. When next I'd be disappointed.

I was certain that in the interim period between receiving the notification for the chosen artwork and the opening of the exhibition, I would receive further correspondence advising me that for this reason or that, my canvases were culled. And sure enough, the universe took on my negativity and another letter arrived advising me that due to funding being withdrawn the exhibition would be postponed indefinitely. That I should make arrangements to collect my small canvases from the reception on City Road.

Just once I wanted to experience joy at having been chosen. Having my talent validated by the relevant stakeholders. Use this external approval by adults who knew their stuff to learn to love myself even a smidgeon.

When we did group work and we would stop for lunch, I would clearly see that I was an extra, the bothersome odd number out, unable to fit in easily. I started feeling sorry for myself and helping myself to seconds and thirds at a time, when just getting food on the table was hard enough for Mother. My weight started to balloon, and I avoided any social gathering that included more than one person.

Arriving home from her aborted honeymoon, Phil came straight over, the boot of the Beamer loaded with grocery bags. Perhaps Phil hoped these luxuries could distract Mother for at least a little while. Provide opportunities for conversation to deflect from her reality. She was in Saint Philadelphia-mode that day, as when she found out about Dean having lost his job, she volunteered to ask around for something suitable. Dinos had always had visions of our Dean working, for less than the minimum wage, behind the counter of various greasy chicken shops whose owners he was acquainted with or indebted to. Dean, of course, wouldn't hear of working in a fish n' chips milk bar or anywhere without a proper kitchen.

'I never went to Tech for nothun'' he'd say in defence, 'Two whole years, two nights a week, that wasn't for nothun' mate,' he'd tell us all and Phil would arch her eyebrows helplessly, grab her expensive gold key ring, planning to escape a life that wasn't hers any more as soon as she had finished her Nescafe.

'What *are* you going to do, Philadelphia?' Mother asked once all the decoy groceries lines of convo had been exhausted.

'I don't know yet. I'm hoping he'll change.'

'Theo wanted your room so he can spread out his art things, but it is always there for you.'

'Thanks, I appreciate it. Maybe Dinos won't do it again. He was a little drunk when...'

'He's *always* a little drunk *mayte*,' Dean said, surprised as to how his intelligent, well-read sister hadn't picked up on this during the months Dinos was courting her.

'He slurs his words even at Sunday lunch,' I added just in case.

'It's just his accent, Dean,' Phil explained but none of us

believed her. 'Let's just enjoy our Droste chocolate,' Phil said and offered us all a milk chocolate pastille.

'The Dutch...' Mother started to say, then left her sentence unfinished.

43

Almost every evening after the first few weeks of the honeymoon, Phil called. Sometimes pleading helplessness but always steadfast that she was not yet at the point of giving up her Eastern Suburbs lifestyle. When visiting us on Sundays, Phil and Dinos never showed any displays of growing affection or fondness. I started to question all these misconceived notions of marriage I had held onto from the time I was a kid.

All the marriages I had known weren't in the least bit romantic. My uncle had had a few wives. My parents' marriage was certainly unconventional in many ways. None of the marriages I knew of followed the prototype of the marriages presented on television and at the movies. It got me thinking that if those representations weren't at all relevant to real-life marriages, what then should I deduce about other lifestyle relationships the entertainment industry promulgated as unappealing?

I knew there would be no marriage for me. But what was there in its place? I had seen *Death in Venice* recently and it had depressed me and made me feel ashamed for having same-sex pangs of attraction. The message of the film seemed to be that loving another male would only lead me to self-destruction and public ridicule. And death. It was painful to watch Dirk Bogarde's character humiliating himself out of a desperate need to be loved, make-up running and hair dye across his ruined face.

This path will only lead to destruction was the message that stayed with me long after I had seen the film classic at the cinema in town just next to the Cyprus club on Elizabeth Street.

Dean had, since the wedding, adopted the death stare with Dinos. Our brother-in-law could certainly register that my brother's stare hinted at physical violence.

What was it with us males and violence? Another gay filmmaker, Pasolini, seemed to be into sexual violence as a means of being turned on—I had walked out of the cinema near Central (was that cinema called Encore Cinema? I can't remember) showing one of his films. Again, I can't remember if it was *Salo* or another one of his films about sexual power and control, as I was repulsed and simultaneously frightened that my life would be one of a deviant. I did not wish to be any such thing. I wanted to be loved and respected and have other people praise me for my goodwill and the way I lived my life.

Dean's simmering anger would gather force the moment our sister and her new groom parked the car at the top of the street as the three spots in the visitors' parking area were permanently occupied by residents' second cars. Only the very brave had the guts to stand up to these perpetual offenders. Anyone who prized their property or their own personal safety and that of their family and pets, knew better than to stoke the fire of laying blame for parking transgressions. There was no reasonableness or community-spirit in housing complexes in the outer-western suburbs of Sydney back then.

Dinos, typically unaware of anything but his own gratification, would go to put an arm around our shoulder, as if to demonstrate physically that we were a family, that we were brothers, but Dean would extricate himself like white bait from a fishing rod, saying 'Ease off will ya?' to a bewildered Dinos, whose English wasn't advanced enough to cope with that kind of vernacular.

'*Na ftiaxo kafe*?' Mother would perfunctorily ask, and go off to the kitchen before anyone had answered yes or no.

'*Nai mitera*,' Dinos might say after her, a moment too late, in a falsely reverential tone, and Dean would get edgy and whisper under his breath, rightfully, that our mother, was definitely not old enough to be Dinos's mother.

Frequently, Phil would explain to us all that in the absence of his own mother, and on account of herself being so much younger than him, Dinos needed a maternal figure in his life. Because he was a Greek from *the old school*, the kind who thought women were a joke until he needed one for various reasons and functions; then, he would crawl and beg and flatter and cajole until his needs were fulfilled.

Then he'd be an arsehole again to them.

Were all men like that?

44

. . . .

Six months after Phil's wedding things changed again.

We were running out of money. Phil's wedding had cost us all our savings. Mother had insisted on paying for certain things, even when she had not been asked her opinion on anything. She had insisted on paying for the wedding dress, for the *bomboniere*, for the priests, the church, the wedding cars. I knew we had no money left as Mother stopped shuffling household bills in my face asking me to go to the post office to pay or to ring up and sort out some kind of part payment plan. That had been my experience since I was twelve. She did not have the skills to handle the bills on her own as she still had not learnt any English.

How could she learn anything being stuck in a tiny villa in the outer southwestern suburbs? Via magic transference? Our seen-better days local library did not offer any free community English classes and there was no way Mother would take two trains and a bus to get to the city centre or could afford to pay for a class. Still, it would drive me bonkers when I would be trying to study for my Year 11 final exams at the kitchen table, Dean's television permanently on and Mother's radio blaring in Greek and other languages and she would start talking to me about paying bills. Asking me how were we going to pay for these and to work out when each bill's due date was, and when would I be able to sort it

267

out? I was a schoolboy. I was not her husband.

One day, our electricity was cut. Mother realised when her iron, on twenty-four seven for her to iron the stitched hems she had sown, no longer emitted a red signal. We had also so many other *final warning* bills overdue. It was clear what I needed to do. There was only one thing to do.

Nobody in administration asked me why I had to leave school. Our part-time counsellor was not around the day I saw the Year 11 Master who was evidently disinterested in my private family dramas. He seemed surprised I had lasted to Year 11 as heaps of my Year 10 ethnic classmates had left school at sixteen. From memory only about a third of us had continued to senior school.

Dean thought about selling his Monaro. But the idea of doing so was tormenting him. He was unsuccessful in finding another job at another restaurant, despite various interviews.

'I am not going to accept less than the minimum wage, not for anyone,' he'd protest after his day and petrol were wasted travelling to and from another no-go interview.

Soon enough, I got a night job sorting packages. The building was a bit of a walk up from Central. I worked alongside all different types of immigrants of varying ages, skin hues and accents. All of us, disparate, desperate, marked with disappointment. All of us simply working to make ends meet. To survive. All of us in our own way, failures in the eyes of the world and in our own estimation too. Working the graveyard shift nobody else wanted. All of us immigrants who had failed to bring to life the myth of the successful migrant. I thanked the Universe that I was still a teenager and not an adult in my thirties, forties or fifties like my workmates. There was still hope for me that the future might bring better days. An easier way of life.

Dean still wiled away most of his time with his mates, commiserating about whose life was tougher. Arguing over whose economic circumstances were worse. He scored a Thursday night and all-day Saturday job in a spare parts shop in Lurnea. I would get in early in the mornings from my night job and try and do some work on my paintings as the light was so harsh later where we lived. Not that I believed I would ever get anywhere with my painting. He'd be having his breakfast and asking me if there were *any hot chicks* working alongside me.

The heat in summer was unbearable. There was always too much noise in the horse-shoe complex.

The blocks of land all around us, the scorched monotonous landscape of eucalypt trees was slowly disappearing as more and more of them were cut down. More and more houses and villas were built all around our complex. From early in the morning, to the time I arrived back, there would be construction noise that lasted until three or four in the afternoon. No grace period during the day when I would try and get some sleep. Then, when the noise stopped, I too would be gone. Back on the train system.

Exhausted.

Depressed.

Sleeping through the hottest part of the day. Mother kept pining for an air-conditioner that would cost six months' wages for me.

She continued to fade away. I blamed the diabetes, but it was her spirit that was disappearing. She was ashamed of her circumstances.

I did not blame her. She would look at us boys, as if she were going to tell us something very important she had suddenly remembered, but then not say a word. I wondered what kept her from throwing herself in front of the train at the railway crossing.

Bittersweet memories of the old country surely weren't enough to have kept her going? As she stitched another garish ten-dollar dress. As she slept alone in her bed at night. As she crossed herself at church, a living widow. Most days, Mother's only social contact would be with the boys who delivered the milk, jumping off their father's unrefrigerated open van, making a racket, or with the baker who delivered the sliced bread in his minivan. Our mother's life made the female characters in Chekhov's plays seem like cheerful party girls.

No word from him. Soon it would be time to celebrate yet another Christmas without him.

Phil kept up her now fortnightly visits with her husband, looking a million bucks in beautiful dresses and shoes but with bruises and dark rings under her eyes which even her expensive make-up would not conceal. She dismissed our concerns, always with an excuse that she had bumped into something. She steadfastly refused to go to the police when we confronted her that we weren't buying her excuses anymore about misadventures, accidents and her *terrible co-ordination.*

Dean continued glaring at Dinos. During meals, both kept drinking their respective poisons quietly, VB for the former and straight whiskey for the latter. Mother spoke to no one and did not let anyone into her kitchen. In the summer heat, she was always red-faced and sweating and busy, even if the meal involved pasta with a bit of grated halloumi, dried mint (there were always two bunches of mint drying on the clothesline) and ketchup. That was our most usual evening meal. Mother was excited when she could afford to add a stock cube to the pasta.

That first Christmas after she was married, Phil bought us all expensive but unsuitable Christmas presents. A linen shirt I did not have a place to wear to and car seat covers for Dean he found *too girly*. Dinos tried to kiss us as he wished us *Hronia Polla,* but we successfully avoided his unwelcome slobber and ducked in time.

'I'm no fuckin' poofter,' Dean muttered.

Our sister who had always chosen her words so carefully, who, as we were growing up, only spoke to us to say something cutting or ironic or to make a rhetorical comment, had now become a chatterbox. She literally could not stop talking. Even before she had parked the car, up near the brick wall of the letterboxes, she would be calling out something to us and look surprised at our blank stares because we obviously could not hear a single thing she had said.

She may have been afraid that if she allowed even a slight pause in the conversation, subjects she wished to avoid could be introduced by others, and once introduced into our conversation, she could then not avoid. She had paid for most of the food we were going to eat that particular Christmas and so none of us told her to shut up. Although, if she had just shut up, even for a few seconds, it might have done her some good.

'And do you still do your little *pictures*?' she asked me as we stood on the tiny back verandah, surveying the constantly disappearing green fields beyond our attached homette.

'Always will. If I have time that is,' I responded almost as a dare. Somehow give her courage at a time when I felt as if I were drowning.

All we could see now were blinding reflective roofs and fences in the new housing estates that seem to be built in mere weeks all around our complex.

So many people settled in Sydney. Every week more and more people were settling in our big city. Even here, fifty-odd kilometres from anywhere, people were buying little boxy houses with no backyards, off the plan. So many people kept coming. When might it stop? How many more broken immigrant dreams would it take before the doors to Sydney were closed? For the sake of everyone's sanity? The roads stayed the same. There were no more schools being built. Liverpool Hospital was the only big hospital for sixty kilometres.

Decent jobs were scarce if you were a recent migrant, or if your qualifications from your country were not easily recognised (if ever) here. Even those with the determination and time and money and patience to be able to do additional study soon found out their English proficiency, whilst at the top of the pack in their own country, would need years of study to reach functionality at a professional level in Australia. Meanwhile the rent, mortgage, food, transport, petrol, utilities had to be paid—nobody paid for you to start a new life in Australia. Nobody gave us so much as a free toaster, let alone anything of substance to help us kickstart afresh in this Great Southern Land with it sunburnt skies.

There were no tax breaks towards compensating you for the financial cost of rebuilding a brand-new life from scratch in Australia. Only those with family money, brought over from their abandoned country of birth, could afford the luxury of time needed to invest in rebuilding their life. Setting years aside to work hard towards regaining first, a professional accreditation then hopefully a professional role. Without simultaneously having to worry about paying for basic survival in less than salubrious accommodation. In miserable suburbs, old and newly established, so far away from any city amenities.

Dean sits on the edge of the concrete verandah, dangling his legs this way and that, as if he were nine. He sits like this for hours, sometimes rolling cigarettes just like our father did. He is silent.

I feel there is nothing more that can be said between the three of us. Each of us now has our own troubles. Our own versions of living hell. The gaps between each of us, now un-crossable, just like the gaps between the felled trees we had tried to jump over on one of our father's fleeting visits to the forest back when we were little.

'So, was it drawing? Or was it painting?' my sister asks.

Wasn't it obvious to her I had to now prioritise surviving? She wasn't stupid.

'Both. But at the moment...nah, I'm too busy looking for better-paying jobs,' I answer. Hoping she did not give me the rote speech of hanging onto your childhood dreams even when you don't have enough time to sleep. Or enough money to pay all the household bills that are due. When you have eaten nothing much more than plain burghul pilaf for three days in a row, without even a dollop of yoghurt to disguise some of its earthy taste. We got so excited if we found a recalcitrant chicken stock cube at the bottom of the herbs container to give our grain meal some flavour.

We look at each other with resignation. We are all disappointed with our new life in Australia. Let down with our own limitations and ability to be happy. Mother saves us from having to discuss anything meaningfully, by calling out that the egg-lemon soup, with the chicken Phil has brought, would be ready shortly and that we all ought to wash our hands and come to the table, adorned with a crochet tablecloth from Cyprus Mother used only on special occasions.

At the postal warehouse, I work alongside former doctors and nurses from China, Hungary and Uruguay. Architects from Spain and Yugoslavia. Electrical engineers from India and Malta and Chile. Side-by-side with other school dropouts like me who had left school years ago but who could not find meaningful employment without even their HSC. All of us wanting more hours from our boss. All of us stuck in a position that would never lead to a promotion.

But even so, more and more immigrants like us wanted to live here. Were scouted for by Australian government diplomats in embassies all over the world. Australia needed new settlers on an ongoing basis to keep the national economy ticking over. Less than one in five new immigrants settled in regional areas, so our cities were bulging at the seams. There was never enough established housing available to accommodate the hundreds of thousands of new residents arriving each year. That was why suburbs like ours, once farmlands, were now being sacrificed to construction; weirdly, the new housing estates had backyards smaller than the yards of attached terraces in inner-city Waterloo, St Peters and Redfern.

I wanted to forewarn any aspirants, before they spent their

money on paying for visa applications and aeroplane tickets, that there was no guarantee at all the immigrant dream of a better life in Australia would materialise. *All that glitters is not gold*, or a variation of it, surely is a proverb in any language. Only the clear blue skies were a dead cert. And perhaps that was enough for some to sacrifice family, friends, lifestyle, culture and personal history. Just so their children could breathe fresh air.

We never saw an immigrant actor on the local television shows except when a swarthy-looking actor played the criminal in minor roles. None of the principals at school were of an ethnic background. We never saw a policeman with Asian physiognomy. Nobody famous was an immigrant. Except for the occasional athlete or footballer. If you had an accent, even a slight one, Australia banished you to secondary roles only.

'It's just simmering,' Mother calls out to us loudly, continuing to watch over her prized soup even though the lid is on the saucepan, and nobody had asked her to provide an update on its cooking time.

'Found a full-time job yet Dean?' Phil then asks Dean, turning to him. Evidently, I had not provided her with much information about my daily reality she could mine as a distraction. At our sister's questioning, Dean seems even more uncomfortable in his collared shirt, for he has agreed to Mother's desperate plea for him to dress up today for the occasion and forego his black AC/DC t-shirt.

'Sorta. I'm helping out a mate who's got a spare parts business down Liverpool way. Outskirts of Liverpool, but it's a growing area and not much public transport so everyone has to have at least one car in the family. He reckons he might do well as not many can afford a new car. In time, he might put me on, full-time,' he says still swinging his legs as if preset by a timer and unable to stop at will.

'Sounds...um... promising. You know, get in at the start,' Phil manages to reply, openly shuddering. She had worked briefly as a casual teacher in the barren social wasteland that was Liverpool and its no-go-zone satellite suburbs. Had spectacularly loathed every minute of it.

I want to scream:

It's all shit, everything's gone to ruin. All our lives are fucked. We're the perfect Australian Tragedy. The reverse of the cliché migrant success story. The Greek tragedies were mild in comparison to what goes on in this house, in your bloody Eastern Suburbs apartment Phil. In our poor mother's head. In my loneliness.

But it's Christmas after all and I don't want to upset anyone's mood, don't want to derange anyone, even though God knows I'm feeling deranged to the nth degree. Just as I am about to lose it, Mother calls us all inside *at once*.

'Hope you washed your hands *Ntino mou.*' Mother says to my brother affectionately, dishing out her masterpiece, Phil playing waitress and assisting with plates and expertly wiping up any drops escaping from the ladle.

'*Mbravo Mitera,*' Dinos says falsely, tasting the soup and we all give him a look. What would he know about Cypriot egg-lemon soup? The Greeks don't favour it for major holidays. They have this other soup with lots of yucky guts and entrails.

'*Elate vre paidia,* smile,' Dinos says to us and at that point none of us are sure if he has realised his married days are numbered.

'Ma, come on, you've dished out enough plates,' says Dean, and he's right, as usual, everyone's already got an extra one for the bones of the poultry.

'There's one more needed,' she says, setting out another placemat on our already crowded table, but thankfully the bowl is empty. That at least is an indication of her partial acceptance. '*Yia ton Patera sas*' she says, looking as if she is about to sob, crossing herself three times, putting down on the table her own steaming soup bowl with dexterous fragility.

'Him, again,' Dean says aggrieved, standing up, his chair scraping the floor, leaving the table.

'Dean, come back here!' Phil calls after him, but the screen door has already banged and in a few seconds, Dean's revving his mean machine hard.

'Do you have to do that on Christmas Day, you bloody wog?' calls out the guy who beats his kids up regularly, from next door. Dean yells something disgusting in reply to being reproached by our neighbor but thankfully we can't hear his exact expletive. Mother sits still throughout all this, eating her soup too quickly, given the fact it's still piping hot. It must be forty-three degrees outside. The rest of us have ours, slowly, reluctantly. Only Dinos is keeping up appearances, showing any honest zeal. Soon, Mother, having finished hers, reaches across and takes Dean's.

'No need to waste this,' she explains to us, and we feel obliged to ask for seconds too.

45

Later, when Phil and her skinny, emaciated brute have left and Mother has retired to her room crying, listening loudly to her cassette of 'Hymns of Our Lady The Virgin', I sat in my room quietly sweating. Wondering whether Father had someone who could make him egg-lemon soup today? Wherever he was. Whether someone he loved had wished him *Kala Hristougenna*.

Whether he had thought of us at all on this celebrated day, however fleetingly, as he stumbled out of his bed in the morning? Or, whether he had already found himself another version of our mother? Had had more children, as many heterosexual men seem to do, quickly and easily after leaving their first family. Did he in fact now have a second family? How *could* he? A new nuclear family which preoccupied his time? A younger wife and young children from whom, given time, he would also escape? That seemed to be his way. Abandoning a lifestyle he soon grew tired of, disliking its responsibilities that were inherent in having a family.

It seemed to be the way of many men the world over who can't handle having to deal with a full-time job, with a wife and children to support, day in day out. Men who wake up one day and feel they have had enough of playing *the man's role*. A role they have been conditioned to accept; one they have been brought up to adhere to. By society, their parents, school, the media.

How hard was it in practical terms to escape this narrative for men who couldn't perform this role satisfactorily? The world is full of men who simply cannot cope. Flailing in taboo silence. Deep within themselves, they know they have failed but that does not make them stay with their family. In fact, this sense of failure, confronted daily, is one of the things they want to run away from; they no longer care that they have just finished renovations or that they are due for long-service leave in a couple of years. These men are average suburban men you see at the local mall. Men, some handsome, some not, who are dreading the Christmas break, the arrival of the expected in-laws and other members of the extended family most of whom they loathe and want to punch if they could.

Men who feel as if they can't even breathe, trying to deal with it all, trying to placate an anxiety attack in public discreetly. Running to the nearest bathroom or sitting with the windows wound up in their car, or at their desk at work, unable to move. Men whose sunburned skin is peeling off, men who feel as though their true self has, along the way, been lost, has been decimated by the responsibilities integral to signifying as *a family man*.

Men whose lost dreams taunt them daily. Men of all ages who are beyond help. Men who are filled with despair, a despair within their glands, their muscles, their millions of cells, that over the years, like cancer, spreads insidiously to their organs too, through their entire lymphatic system. In short, throughout their body. Making them feel as though their core of manhood, the core of their individualism has been eaten away.

So, choosing to fight, to rebel against this sense of powerlessness, their innate survival mechanism kicks in. It kicks in without them first thinking through a solid plan as such. Mechanically, they pick up a worn toothbrush, check to see their credit card is in their wallet and simply take off. Telling their wife they're going over to a mate's for the afternoon to have a couple of beers with the boys or down to the servo for a packet of smokes.

These last words, these banal words are exchanged with the woman who has given them children, the same woman to whom they had promised eternal love. They leave the family home they have struggled to pay the mortgage for, leaving behind this same woman, leaving behind their own children. And, for the rest of their lives, these abandoned women and children wonder whether their husband or father is dead or alive. Whether he is happier or more miserable than ever. If he ever thinks of them, regretting his decision to abandon them. Whether he shall ever return. If life might ever revert to the way things were before.

Will he ever come back to us?

46

· · · · · · · · · · · · ·

I buy an old Mazda Capella RX-2 in burnt orange from a young woman who is upgrading to the space-age looking Astina with its hidden front lights. I still work five nights a week at Strawberry Hills. I spend my free time at the university, pretending I am like all the other confident, Milky Bar-kind of guys there. Young guys from established families with money and weekenders in the Southern Highlands.

Eastern Suburbs and North Shore boys who do not choose to have a wog for a mate. Young men who have been prefects and school captains at schools not open, not accessible to refugees. These young men have new cars, pretty girlfriends who've been with them since high school. Enjoy the luxury of living a cloistered life with sporting facilities, tutorials and meals pre-prepared for them at one of the on-campus residential colleges which of course are not subsidised but are fee-paying. By their parents who can afford to pay.

I walk through these luscious grounds and catch a glimpse of a world that has not welcomed me, a world which shall remain closed to the likes of me even when I am older. Even if I manage to do well in the university preparatory course I've enrolled in and get accepted into a degree.

Even if I ever get to start a degree at some stage, how will I afford the set textbooks I'd need to buy? I will still have nothing and accept I will start from nothing. Without any access to family money to fall back on or to use to propel myself into the world of business. My parents will not give me a helping hand by gifting me or even lending me a deposit on a small flat. They cannot. As Phil feared, I will probably have to take out a bank loan to bury my mother. I do not have the prerequisite social background for introductions to people with power and influence who might recommend me for a cushy job. I shall always rely on newspaper advertisements to find work and not recommendations and not family contacts. Even my name would make some employers discard my application.

I am also damaged as a man. I am a eunuch. Nobody is proud of me, nobody longs for me to get home, nobody craves to touch me and kiss me and make me a part of them.

At dusk, as I walk through the grounds of the colleges taking a shortcut, I know I am invisible. I hear laughter, and the clinking of glasses, plates being washed, pop music. At the Women's College they always seem to be having drunken pyjama parties on the huge balcony verandah. I hazard a guess these do not comprise females-only celebrations.

I use the bathroom in the small changing room adjacent to a college oval one afternoon. When I open the cubicle door three rugby union players are there. I run out of the locker room. They are naked. Starkers. It is too confronting. Their beauty. Their amazing bodies. Their confidence. Their camaraderie.

I've never known what it's like to be surrounded by pure male affection.

I am becoming a stalker on the university campus.

If a security guard accosts me and questions my being on University grounds, I have a foolproof excuse. I have a meeting with the administrator of a University competition. One of my charcoal drawings, *The Archer*, will be exhibited in a uni space next month to showpiece local artists' and students' works. I saw a flyer advertising the competition for under-25s stuck at the Performing Arts Bookshop noticeboard in Elizabeth Street. I spend a lot of my free time in there browsing. I used my workmate Dragan's Surry Hills address to pretend I am a local so that I am deemed eligible to enter the art prize. I hope that this time there is no cancellation.

All the selected artists were invited to a getting-to-know-you session and the curator introduced us all. There were no other immigrants present. I felt as if I had to apologise for this to people who weren't in the least interested in hearing my explanation. Nobody knew where Cyprus was, or that it was an independent sovereign country. Everyone kept telling me they wanted to visit the Greek Islands. Weirdly, my slight Greek accent and stammer both raised their ugly heads as I introduced myself. The accent comes out unexpectedly as a surprise even to me.

Then I go into freefall of anxiety. When I hear myself speak with a nervous stutter and my vowels coming out not quite right, not elongated enough I become agitated, and my speech impediment worsens. My hard consonants like c and p sometimes escape from my lips too softly.

This tends to happen whenever I need to speak up in front of a group of more than two. All my Chinese, Malay, Filipino and Islander workmates at the sorting office are always pushing me to talk to the Union Rep because they think my English is the best amongst them but the rep makes me nervous as hell. Dragan, with his six-foot-four Serbian frame, his deep voice, usually is the one who speaks up. I find the union man too aggressive; his supreme confidence makes me feel smaller. And he stinks of cigarette smoke.

My *nervous* accent comes out and I can hardly utter a word to him that makes sense about the bad working conditions and the poor pay. The heat is unbearable in summer. A number of my co-workers talk about this affliction called RSI, but I think they are bunging it on for compo. Or so they'll be allocated a sit-down job which they can't really do, as most of them are near illiterate in written English.

Some days, after I finish my 11 pm-7am shift, I sleep in my car instead of going back home. I think of all sorts of ways to avoid the bumper-to-bumper drive via the army barracks at Glenfield. Especially if I fill in for an absent colleague on day shift and finish at 3 pm. The Mazda does not like to idle in traffic. It has a rotary engine, but I have no idea what this means. My brother thinks *a rotary engine is pretty cool,* but he has not bothered to explain to me why.

'I'd be wasting my breath, bro,' is all he said when I pushed him for more details.

I get some shut-eye between 8 am and 10 am in a laneway in Glebe and then I drive and park closer to the uni at Forest Lodge. I furtively shower at one of the uni's sporting facilities. Nobody has asked me to show them a student card except once at the cafeteria when I tried to buy a slice of pecan pie. I muttered something about having left my student card at home, but the lady simply charged me a bit extra for my slither of mostly sweet custard.

I feel dizzy with excitement whenever I sneak onto the vast campus visiting a different part of the massive uni each time. The uni is so big it has its own postcode. My favourite place, besides the quadrangle with its beautiful jacaranda and the square lawn areas that are not to be walked on, is a little internal courtyard garden slash thoroughfare with a pebbled path. It offers a shortcut leading to the smaller cafeteria by the Footbridge. If I could pitch a tent there I would. It is so peaceful with sculptures and giant sandstone and terracotta pots of maples and ferns and ground covers. It is only about fifteen metres away from busy Parramatta Road, but you can hear a pin drop in its enclosed bucolic paradise. I am convinced the courtyard has its own microclimate.

I am in the midst of things, yet I feel completely out of it all. I don't have any mates here. None of the real students know me. Nobody knows my story. I sometimes pretend I am a new international student to get out of tricky situations. Pretending not to speak English, but I doubt anyone buys my cover as I expect international students need to have some English to be accepted for study.

I daydream a lot.

I want a new life.

I want to cut ties with misery.

I want to divorce myself from my history.

Is this even possible?

Will my past haunt me forever no matter how hard I try?

I so want to escape my life. I want to break free. I am sick to death of explaining I was born in Cyprus. Yes, it is located in a gulf in the Mediterranean Sea. No, it is *not* part of Greece. If one more person asks me, *Where are you from?* I AM GOING TO DECK THEM.

I am so tired of having to explain my looks, to validate my right to be here. That we came here as refugees. I am tired of complete strangers on public transport telling me I should be grateful Australia accepted us. *Has it?* I want to challenge them. *Has it really? Or is Australia using us to do the shit jobs nobody born here wants to do?*

When I look back on my short life as I sit in traffic, I sometimes think of Maria loving me, albeit briefly. She was the one person who has ever loved me, innocently and purely. She gave me that sterling silver disc with *Je t'aime* inscribed on it. She had dark honey-black eyes that loved me, in their own way, and mine loved her back, in their own way. I wore her gift even after we broke up, like a sacred family heirloom.

When I bought the car, I hung the disc on the rearview mirror. I liked the way it glistened when the sun shone on it. It was recently looted from my old car, along with my Pioneer pull-out stereo, a birthday present from Deano. Earlier that night I'd been so excited that I had found a legitimate free parking spot just off Cleveland St, moments from work.

Making a statement, I couldn't bring myself to admit to the bored constable about my missing chain and by refusing to do so, I felt I'd repudiated any sort of connection I had had with my former girlfriend. The loss of Maria's gift was the last straw of any hope I might have had of having a normal heterosexual life. With all its privileges.

At lunch, I call my mother to see if she wants me to pick up the new issue of *Ellinis*.

'You didn't call last night. I was worried.'

'*Mitera*, I told you I'd be going straight to uni to study some days. I need to prepare if I have a shot of even getting into the preparation year course.'

'You could have called all the same Demostheni *mou*.'

'Some of the phones at uni are a little dodgy.'

'Excuses. I made *kolokasi* for you. You used to like it. I had to throw it out.'

'Sorry.'

'Are you coming home on the weekend?'

'No. I'm doing an extra shift. I need to save up to buy some new tyres.'

'*Entaxei Dimo mou*, if you can't spare half a day to be with your own flesh and blood.' I wasn't really listening to my mother's chant of passive-aggressive anger.

I see my unloved flesh every waking moment. I run my hands smoothly over my entire, naked self every day, and seek answers, but nobody provides me with these. If I don't kiss someone soon, I shall die.

I keep silent. She hates that.

'Anyway, how are things going with your studying in the big library? Any pretty girls?'

'I really wouldn't know. I'm much too busy. Look, I've got to go. Someone wants to use the phone.'

'But we've just started chatting...'

'Gotta go.'

On Sunday morning, after my shift, I drive home on the empty Hume. My mother is not looking too good. She is sick. Again. *How many hospitals haven't you been to?* I want to ask her, trying to make her face reality. The reality is that she is here now, in Sydney's maligned outer southwest. Not the Old City of Nicosia with its familiar shopkeepers and well-to-do ladies of the Faneromeni Ladies' Committee who were fearful of her reputation. Who secretly resented her renowned family's name.

Nobody knows my mother's name here.

I feel sorry for her. For me. For Dean. For Phil. I somehow cannot believe (still) that our father isn't here. What could he be doing with his life? Is he yet another victim of the popular delusion many middle-aged men have that they are still at the peak of their Lothario days at fifty? Why did he bring us here? Only to dump us? How could he do that to our poor mother? He knew that she spoke no English. She begged him to send us instead to England where she has cousins, where we'd all have some family support, but he did not listen to our poor mother's logic.

Why do grown men, not ever listen?

47

· · · · · · · · · · · · ·

I remember when I was a kid, all dressed-up like a *poupée*, a doll, waiting to be taken to Nicosia Airport. All the village relatives of my father were there too, many of them staying at our house for a week or longer.

'*Filadelfia! Konstantine! Demostheni!*' Mother would call from the kitchen. 'Your clothes are ready,' and she would carefully hand over to us the selected outfit for the day, expertly ironed by her own hand. I knew something extraordinary was happening that day because usually Mother sent her ironing out as a charitable act of kindness to Yiayia Efthimia who lived on the corner of our street. All of us were soon dressed to perfection.

When I look at old photographs, we all of us look spotless, compulsively neat. *Not a hair out of place*—that was one of the first expressions I learned here in Australia. Mother would be displeased with us if there was, even if it was the wind that had messed up our hair.

My siblings' gazes look with bland interest at the camera, but stop there. My own eyes stare direct, beyond the situation, into something else.

Did I already know then that my life's pleasures, that love, would always remain beyond my reach?

I loved going to the airport. Not so much because we would all

289

be waiting to welcome back Father (I hated *that* part of the day). I looked forward to the Airport Days, as I called them—'When is the next Airport Day, Philadelphia?' I'd ask my sister months ahead of the day—because to get there, we had to drive on the new freeway first, with its wide new road. Bright streetlights and billboards stood symmetrically, all along it.

On either side of the multiple-lane road, for what seemed for miles, stood glossy, erect, tantalizing photographs. These glamorous billboards taunted our isolated lives with pictures of far-away and exotic-sounding places and gloriously white-skinned, impeccably groomed men and blonde women in uniform, inviting us to fly British Airways or to smoke Benson & Hedges.

We used to have to wait for a long time at the airport. Usually, a grown-up (Aunt Hara I expect) would hold me by the hand, as I led her on expeditions around the exclusive boutiques and expensive shops inside the terminal. Despite my uncovered, round head and my broken nose, I pretended I was an important Arab sheik if a flight was arriving from or departing for Damascus, Beirut or Tripoli. At other times, it all depended on who oversaw me, I pretended I was the one departing and duly used to produce false tears at will. My chaperone, more used to the harsh realities of village life, would then helplessly hurl me back into my mother's arms.

'Here, take him. He's gone all strange suddenly.'

She in turn would comfort me by saying that 'Your father, will be here soon'. All I could do, enveloped within my mother's ample bosom, was to stop myself from sneezing on account of her *Soir de Paris* engulfing me in its intoxication and ponder out loud for everyone to hear:

'*Pateras*? What's that?' Mother would laugh unnerved, and the relatives would utter *Tsk, tsk*, disapprovingly, thinking I was being naughty. I was being genuine.

Today, my mother is lying in bed. Her hair is matted. She is no longer the proud owner of a string of pearls. She looks as if she has been crying for days. Her cassettes are strewn, out of their cases, all over the bedside table, next to a blue canister of Nivea. Mother is usually very particular with her music collection which would normally be neatly stacked and in alphabetical order inside the third drawer of her tallboy, the side title bar showing up.

I remain silent after greeting her. She gives me a half smile, recognising me.

I retreat to the small kitchen and make her some toast and a Nescafe with her beloved condensed milk. The diabetes can get lost today. There are no oranges to be had nor is there any fruit juice in the fridge. Since Dean left to live with his latest girlfriend, Mother's fridge is usually mostly empty. I feel immeasurably guilty for spending so much time at the university on the pretence that I am studying for my entry test. For working nights.

But I must work. Now more than ever, with Dean gone, I must keep working. The villa still has a mortgage. Father left us with a debt. Mother acknowledges my tray, my effort but does not touch the food. She sips her coffee, quietly, staring at the wall.

'Two heaped teaspoons of condensed milk,' she states in approval. I nod.

There are two A3–sized black and white photographs on the wall. Both encased in walnut frames which are in need of some repair now. One is of her engagement day and the other of her and Father as bride and groom. She looks like a Cypriot version of Anne Baxter. Her gaze is optimistic, joyful. Father, channeling Vouyiouklaki's leading men, looks displeased in both shots. As if this were an arranged marriage his mother had organised, fulfilling a dutiful promise she had made to Mother's family when he was born rather than the marriage he himself had insisted on.

Despite my mother being a city girl who would *steal him away* from his myriads of relatives in the village and make him emigrate to the restrictive behaviours of the rigid parishioners of Old Nicosia. Compel him to take on the intergenerational traditions of the reputable family he had chosen to marry into.

This is not the right time to share the secret of my pain with my mother.

It has never been the right time to share this burden with my parents.

I leave my mother alone, in the stuffy small room, and prepare a bath for her.

The next day, as I am stuck in single-lane traffic along the Ingleburn army base, I hear an emotionally heightened song called *Birdsong* by Lene Lovich on the new FM radio station. It becomes clear to me that this is how my life will be; just me, my thoughts of the past and my hunger to be loved. But the law says I cannot be allowed to love. What have I done? What Greek God have I inadvertently maligned?

48

Polixeni lies there. In the ward. Breathing in that floor cleaner smell for fresh air. Trying not to breathe. Looking downcast towards the windows. For they cannot be opened. Two of her wardmates chat to each other across their beds. One of them wears an oxygen mask but she manages. 'I'm not one to gossip,' she tells the paperboy who tries to flog her all the Sunday newspapers.

In the corner, the large and very imposing Russian woman sits silently preoccupied. No one can guess what thoughts are being filtered by her as she keeps to herself. Polixeni though is quite certain what is going on in the tall woman's mind. She, too, knows the meaning of the phrase *displaced person*. She is one. Has been one. Would rather she not be.

The Russian woman stares straight ahead at nothing, armed with a quiet dignity. Perhaps she has done one of those meditation courses in the mountains where for ten days you are not allowed to speak to a single creature? Where you eat a vegetarian diet you've all prepared in total silence. It is only eleven-thirty, yet it feels like it should be early evening at least. There is a view of the hills. Preparing those terminally ill for the open journey ahead. The hills are peppered in diluted tomato-sauce covered boxes for the working class. For those starting out. *Homes, indeed*, thinks Polixeni indignant.

Their first home. Built brand new, yes but fifty-odd kilometres from the city. How could they isolate themselves at that age? They should be travelling in Europe or the Americas not already married with a screaming child, (one if the poor woman was lucky). These young couples live in the satellite city as they have no choice; perhaps they've localised their daily lives. Their waists widening with each weekend that passes. There's been a study. Polixeni has read it somewhere—within two years of marriage both partners' weight increases. Bashing each other, telling each other off in front of the kids as they feel cheated that this is living their life. They fear there is more, that there should be more, but what it is they know not. Just that they want something more than this.

Anyway, at least they're not in here, thinks Polixeni.

She sees them driving their matchbox-sized cars, through a high-interest loan no doubt, on the winding grey stretch into their suburbs which, as yet, have not been baptised. I'm a spectator, she regrets, watching an enormous miniature game world playing at its daily grind, as I lie here, nothing to do. That damn plastic underneath the sheet. To safeguard against those hospital mishaps certainly, but a nuisance when you must lie on it all day. Polixeni may walk to the bathroom about ten metres away. No walks, however, up and down the corridors in her off- pink nightgown.

Valda's lucky. Her bed is across from the one with the mask. She even has permission to take her visitors downstairs to the visitors' lounge. She is at least ten years older than me, cries Polixeni to herself. The unfairness of life. Just yesterday morning, a group from Valda's parish church arrived all jolly and high on group singing. Probably one of those so-called modern churches where they clap and shout and all that nonsense. Really! Polixeni is not impressed with such antics. A church is a church is a proper church and nothing less.

The visitors brought with them bouquets perhaps pinched from their gathering place. But it was not on the sly, Polixeni had to admit, as the young priest, too good-looking to be holy, had come along. It was probably his idea to pinch the flowers from God's house. What do they teach them at Theological College these days?

'They serve a better purpose here,' he would have confessed at the altar, 'aiding those ailing to recuperate, appreciate life's little offerings.'

Polixeni stops suddenly. The story is put on hold as she feels dizzy. She attempts a deep breath that might cure her and make her cry 'PRAISE THE LORD' too, but her short breath only manages a piercing underneath her heart. She doesn't even bother to breathe then, rather just letting any breath to simply patronise her if it so wishes. Her eyes are fixed. Staring outside. Looking at the crowded hills.

But no. She would like to continue with the story. To have exclusive editing rights to Valda's visit and make it all flow like the traffic.

First, they had a little group prayer and Valda seemed exalted to new heights of religious consciousness. Oh, she was flying alright. Polixeni wondered if the smile on dear old Valda's face wasn't better explained by the presence of the gorgeous young man with that all too clean collar, the shiny, scrubbed skin, the rich resonant voice. All that singing. Her own priest, with long beard and grey hair, hasn't bothered to visit yet.

She is not dying (again, not yet) so he might not have the time. She understands he is busy. Preoccupied with this and that. Running a church is not easy. She knows this not from hearsay but firsthand from her membership of the Ladies' Committee. Tuesday afternoons. And Sunday mornings of course. Before and after the service.

A scrawny thing of a nurse pops her frizzy head in and announces to her kinder charges, 'I haven't forgotten you're still waiting for your pills, but we haven't been able to find the doctor.'

Good, thinks Polixeni. Find him and then lose him as if we care. We'll just lie here and recuperate on the muck you feed us, that's if you're lucky enough to get food in the first place. Honestly. Top cover insurance for years and this is what you get.

Valda's disappeared again. Further than the bathroom. Polixeni is glad she's gone. She is sick of her constant chatter. The one with the oxygen mask does her crossword now her ally is not around and has switched the piped-select on. She too has a drip, but she manages to sit up.

Polixeni's veins had been jabbed stupid by a nervous intern who knew less than she did when she was admitted, pale and suffering blackouts. Fragile like a slice of crispbread. The intern couldn't find her veins and behaved as if it was Polixeni's fault. Her now bruised arms itch terribly. The drip has been in for two days. A holiday from it on the third but mates again on the fourth. What do they know? That's why the drip, to cleanse her system so they can see what isn't functioning properly.

Take me to a mechanic and give me an overhaul, laughs Polixeni to herself. It is the kind of thing her Evagoras would have said. Bloody Evagoras. That man.

She feels light. Certain that her feet would collapse from under her like balloons bloated with water and which cannot withstand any pressure. So, the view. Yes. The hills. Speckled with the sort of anonymous yellow daisies which people tend to consider little more than weeds and which they unearth unmercifully to achieve that carpet lawn effect. Rather dull, all that unbroken sameness, decides Polixeni. ALL that green. Green is for people who have withdrawn from the world. They have done studies. It's been proven. And still, they shred those poor bloody daisies.

The 'ambulance only' driveway circles her view. She sees the big white cars cruise ever so slowly lest they spill their innards. Each time she spots one she wonders about who or what unrecognisable piece of flesh, untangled from some horrific smash, will be unloaded onto the metallic tray, left in the Casualty ward, exposed. A freakshow awaiting attendance, an audience.

Completely uninspired by anyone in the ward, Polixeni keeps to herself. The language barrier is her excuse. If she really wanted to though she would find ways of getting her messages across. A little sign here. A drawing there. A motion. A touch of the hands. But she is not one for transient acquaintances. She is a middle-aged female patient, dripping away. Slipping a little from life, 'ah, it's so sweet but we're all still miserable', not interested in the banalities the sick indulge in.

'Did you get a big serve today, Polly?' Valda questions. Mind you it's just an excuse for an opener, for her to start chatting. To talk about herself. Like people do.

'Mine is a rather small serve,' she observes. She must be getting senile, reflects Polixeni. She forgets Polixeni is not allowed solids.

Perhaps tomorrow.

Maybe the next day.

'Oh that's right, poor luv!' Valda remembers all of a sudden, and you're not sure if she's not playing some cruel game. 'You can't have food, can you? Just as well, mind,' she says, carving her slice of roast. Valda doesn't seem to observe any respectable boundaries. She is blind, unable to detect when someone has had enough of her. She continues to eat, chewing hungrily, carrying on her inane monologue. 'The food is lovely sometimes. On Sunday the roast chicken was nicely done. You might have that tomorrow.'

Oh, do belt up! God strike her down, I pray to you.

'I think it's of a Sunday and on We'nsdie it's the shepherd's pie. Fish on the Tuesday. That mushy stuff on Mondays. Pasta on Thursdays. I've never liked spaghetti that much though, I must say, no offence to you Europeans of course.'

Of course not.

'And a surprise, usually a bit of pork and vegies of a Friday.' Thank God the week has only seven days.

'And ...,' not for Valda. She's probably on a ten-day cycle. Talk, talk, talk. Blah, blah, blah.

Polixeni motions she has a headache, excusing herself. Watching Valda eat is making her queasy. She has asked for a private room. She is entitled to one. Her daughter is paying for top cover for her. But this is a public hospital, and she's stuck in it now. Here, only ancient hollow faces who are ready to pack it all in, enjoy the privilege of private living quarters. And those others, too, the not-so-old at all, the unlucky ones.

Her drip is pricking away at her, feeding her blood, pumping nutrients into her hardened veins. So, they claim. She is starving.

She feels drowsy even though no medicine has been administered. Sometimes when she looks the hills aren't there. Then they show themselves and she is left wondering how on earth she could have ever questioned their existence.

Her own husband, Evagoras, will not come tonight. After work. The other women's husbands will. Polixeni hopes he is okay wherever he might be. It's been years since she has heard from him. His depression made him run away. There was nothing Polixeni could do but allow him to find his own way to fight his demons. Still, Polixeni is aching to hear his voice. Feel his hand rest against her forearm.

Valda's husband, a thin stick of a man, always wears a bowtie and a vest made by Valda, or sometimes a jacket. His long white socks stick to his legs if he's in shorts. Valda and her husband Dick remind Polixeni of two budgerigars her brother Pericles kept in the family home, all those years ago. They used to annoy the young Polixeni more than anything, more than the neighbourhood gossips who used to gather around their dining room table (the one for visitors) and play cards and drink gin n' tonic with her mother. The birds kept her brother amused though, and he would not part with them. He would torment the poor creatures, giving them food they could not possibly digest. Rather like me, smiles Polixeni. Being given sustenance I can neither taste nor chew.

The middle-aged sister on the afternoon shift approaches Polixeni. Normally she goes on her round left to right, checking the oxygen-masked patient first. Polixeni is glad of the special attention today. She likes this woman. She is kind. Mature. She is a proper sister. Gentle enough and experienced. Has worked overseas. She is respectful. Treats you like a human being and not as just decaying meat being prepared for mushy pet food. Sister though is not cheery today, armed with a forced smile. Just goes through the motions. A bit too quiet. Polixeni knows there is something wrong. The nurse attempts a real smile, but it only serves to accentuate the extra powder on her face today.

Polixeni sees herself lying in her own tiny ward. It simultaneously makes her nervous and joyful. She sees the other patients are all still there too. The sister says, 'It's all good, Polixeni' and writes surreptitiously on her clipboard. She goes at once. Without checking the others. Valda protests. Polixeni feels relaxed. She tells her body to do what it must. She blacks out. Valda shrieks. The masked woman fumbles trying to find the buzzer. The Russian has already found it and is pressing firmly. A faint, incessant ring sounds.

The sister runs back. Soon another sister. A younger, spiked hair sort. They draw the curtains. The young one runs out. Orderlies are summonsed. Valda wipes away a tear.

Polixeni is moved to intensive care.

Dripping. Slowly. Away.

49

· · · · · · · · · · · · ·

I am driving again, listening to Depeche Mode. *My* personal Jesus isn't sitting in the passenger's seat. Where are you?

When I get home, the villa is locked. I cannot hear the cacophony of the ethnic radio Mother listens to no matter what language is being broadcast.

She's not here. She's gone. I contemplate the possibility that Father has sent for her, has asked her to start afresh in another country, maybe even back in partitioned Cyprus. I call Phil's place. Dinos answers and tells me the news as if he were sharing a funny holiday anecdote at a party. Mother is in hospital. Phil is on her way there.

I ask for her at the hospital reception. I spell my mother's surname. Twice. I wait. I then wait for the lift. She is resting in a hospital she has not been in before. It is only new. It makes for a bit of a change. Probably for her too. A heart-attack. She can't speak and I don't even know if she can hear me or if she is aware that I am by her side. I can only stay for a couple of minutes, as this is the intensive care unit. She has tubes on her face with liquids flowing inside of them. The drip gives me the creeps.

In the corridor outside the ward, on the way in, I meet up with my siblings. Phil is wearing Chanel two-piece suits these days. Dean's hair is still short at the front and long at the back. It looks as

301

if he has had the mullet permed. I can't imagine my butch brother sitting in a hair salon with perming solution and curling rods in his hair. His girlfriend must have done it at home. He wears a black t-shirt with the name of a heavy metal band I do not know emblazoned on it.

'She looks like Bella Lugosi,' is all Dean has to say. Phil's mouth twitches in disapproval yet I can detect a hint of amusement. Dean was always her favourite brother. The three of us don't talk much since Dean moved out. We don't really know much about each other's lives anymore. We can only guess from titbits we care to share. We make forced small talk out of habit and hope we have guessed correctly about what is going on in each other's daily life.

Each of us is playing the role that has been determined for us long ago. Dean's living with his girlfriend makes Mother fear there will be *bastards* soon. She has explicitly warned Dean that that would definitely kill her.

'If any grandchild of mine is not baptised Orthodox, I may as well be stoned to death by a godless mob in the depths of Africa,' is her most frequently repeated line.

Dean responds by saying, 'As if,' but I can tell he is frightened he is destined to disappoint his mother several more times in her lifetime and there's nothing he can do about it. He has never dated a woman with Greek heritage. Once, he briefly had an affair with a gorgeous Vietnamese girl, but we kept this from Mother.

It is all too late.

For all our lies.

For our pretence we are a happy, successful immigrant family.

Mother looks calm. The foreign-sounding sister on duty stares hard at me through the glass of her partition as if I am committing a crime. If Mother is ever conscious again, she will have zero chance of understanding a word the sister might say to her.

She seems like a librarian to me, making sure nobody speaks. My three minutes must be up. The windows of the ward cannot be opened. They're made of thick glass and there are no visible handles. The sprawling green hills outside seem lush with the sun's last rays. They are filled with cheap houses now. An ambulance is speeding down the winding asphalt drive. I focus on the red of its spinning siren of distress, flashing. The sound it is making is inaudible. IV machines buzz and squeal and rule the ward.

Beep, beep, the monotonous symphony continues. I wait for the rising crescendo which makes nursing staff spring to attention fiddling with the machines.

Back outside, I am sitting with my siblings again. In silence. There is nothing we could say to each other that we have not already said multiple times in other waiting rooms. We choose to not repeat ourselves. A nurse with another untraceable accent approaches us and with condescension asks: 'Is there a husband?' shoving forms in our faces. 'We'll need his details.'

'No, no there isn't,' Phil tells her finally. 'We are the next of kin.'

Soon, there will be darkness, and I am anxious my Capella's headlights will fail again and I'll be stuck on a strange highway trying to find my way back to our small and now completely silent home in pitch darkness.

50

The other day, visiting Mother in hospital took me back to the past. When I did not know much about the world. About people. When it was not up to me to decide how to spend the day or public holidays. When I was a young child, I never had to make any decision about organising something to do. Choosing where to go. Celebrations were simply celebrated with other relatives. Weekends were planned for visits or to prepare to receive visitors.

I recall all-day family picnics in large groups of family, friends and acquaintances on the edge of fields of wheat or olive groves that stretched for miles. Magic red wildflowers, *paparounes*, which I would gather, quickly wilted in the simmering heat, turning ugly, staining my hands. Mother would then slap me for messing up my clothes and I would cry and ask Aunt Hara to take me back to the village with her.

'*Vre hazo*, I am staying with you in the city tonight! How are we going to get to the village? Do you have a car? By the time we get back to the city there'll be no more buses to the village. Now, if you were all grown-up and had your own car, well, then we could do as we pleased. In the meantime, we can only do what your mother says. So, study hard, get a good job and then buy a good car we can use to go wherever we please. *Entaxei? Simfonisamen?*'

'I hate her. I don't wanna go home. Please, Aunt Hara, take me to your house. Please.'

After the midday siesta under the shade of a tree, everyone used to play games. It was then I would run away. I had not been taught any games, had not been allowed to participate, learn how to play. Mother would not allow us down from Areos 36 onto the street. I did not wish to fail at any of the games, especially in front of such a huge gathering of people. The other boys never spoke to me directly, would just grunt a *hello* when an adult tried to introduce us, hoping just because of our similar age we would instantly befriend each other and therefore get out of the way of adult conversation.

It never happened. Instead, I would go exploring on my own, around the scrub, the forest, or the valley, depending on where the picnic get-together was taking place. This was another kind of exploration, just like I used to do at the airport, only this time, I would come back with a grazed elbow or knee, the too-big safari shorts I wore torn, my eyes glistening with excitement and fear. For sometimes, I used to come across a squirrel or a small snake. I once kidded myself I saw a Cypriot deer. The marble floors inside Areos were always cold, spotless and not that interesting, did not excite me as much as the stuff I trod on and saw in what I then thought of as the Cypriot jungle.

I take the All-Stations train to Belmore (less petrol and free car parking), alight, get into my Capella and eighty minutes later I am home. I feel completely disembowelled yet somehow alive. Still able to smile as I drive past the private school, set in its expansive fields alongside the Glenfield Railway station. I had (broken) dreams of attending this school when we first settled in this godforsaken suburb. I thought my parents would soon realise I needed to go to a good school if I ever was to have a chance to go to university. It was clear to them that I was smart. Phil translated all my school reports to them in an exasperated way and nobody could begrudge me the fact that most of the comments were very positive.

When I'd get petulant asking why I couldn't go to the private school in Glenfield both my parents would refuse to even hear me out. They categorically would not even discuss the possibility with me. It became clear to me, as my parents fought over how best to distribute the handful of notes in Father's pay packet each Thursday night that there was nothing left over for school fees.

There's no sign of Mother inside. I thought she'd be resting on the sofa, watching one of her religious video cassettes.

I find her outside, busy in the small laundry. Everything about the villa is in miniature. And every light fitting, every piece of tapware, every hollow chipboard veneer wall, cheap. The kitchen, the bathroom, the three small bedrooms, the tiny courtyard at the back with the shed Dean put together, Mother's plastic pots of holy basil. The laundry is just big enough for one person to stand at the sink. Mother half-buried, headfirst, in the aging washing machine that sounds like a jumbo taking off and these days goes for a little walk-on-the-spot when switched on certain cycles.

I decide not to hassle her.

When she returns to the small kitchen, I note the evening meal's ingredients are strewn over the bare benches, awaiting preparation. The ironing board is all set up in the living room and steam is hissing. I can't help noticing the iron is a plumb phallus one can turn on or off, or excite to the point of emission, then dial down to a warm caress, a mere fondle. I am always digressing these days.

'*Mitera*, I thought you were supposed to be resting,' I admonish her.

'Yes, you are absolutely right. I *am* supposed to be resting... But tell me, who is going to do all this?' she gestures, theatrically. 'Since you've all left me here all alone. All of you have abandoned me'.

'I haven't abandoned you.'

'You're never here.'

'I am working. I am studying.'

I am depressed.

I am suicidal. My life is worse than you imagine.

I am lonely as hell.

'*Nai, Thimo mou.* You are working. You are studying,' she reaffirms, and I'm not sure whether my mother is taking the piss out of me.

'And Dean? He moves out with that Polish *skrofa*, but still brings me his laundry. *Ti tin ehein aftin?*'

'She's of Dutch heritage,' I call out. Mother waves her palm in semi-circles in the Greek way to indicate whatever heritage the girlfriend has, no good can come of it.

'Polish. Dutch. Are you sure she's not Swedish? He had a Brazilian girl for a while. He's determined to put me in my grave as soon as he can,' Mother says and even she is momentarily amused by her elder son's romantic entanglements.

I turn the TV on. We watch the screen as she irons napkins and tablecloths she has not used for a while. I have never heard my mother call another woman a *bitch* before.

'How's the university study going?'

'Good.'

'You've always been a good boy. A brilliant student, *A pleasure to have in the class*, that's what the teachers used to write in your reports.' In other words, I was a huge pain in the arse no other kid wanted to befriend. Mother is in the mood to chat. Endlessly. Always about the past.

'I wanna get a few hours' sleep.'

'Have some more *sika*.' She thrusts a handful of dried figs my way.

'I'm not hungry. I had a big lunch.'

'I'll put some *macaronia* on in a minute. I've already made a little bit of mince— more fried onions and tomato than mince— but it'll taste good with a bit of basil on top. Should be ready when you wake up from your nap.'

I go outside. It is coming on six-thirty. The pots of basil fill the air with a Greek smell, unnerving me with their scent. Reminding me of the solemnity of church. I decide to mow the tiny bit of overgrown lawn, risking the neighbours' ire, feeling the vibrations of the motor up and down the length of my arms. The sweat pours off my forehead and I sense the first blister laying its foundation. I finish and go inside.

'*Ti epathes paidi mou?*' Mother asks, knowing evidently I am not myself.

'You mow the lawn on a Thursday. You're not hungry. You've been walking around with a long face for three weeks. *Ti eheis Thimo mou?*'

No response. What can I say? A Greek child must always

do whatever it takes to please his or her parents. Make them feel proud. Make them beam with pride. A son, especially, is obligated to please his mother. His aunties. Be good to his cousins. Respect everyone even if they are not a relative. Please the priest and church. Please anyone who is older than him. Do the right thing. Never bring shame to the family.

A Greek man must always be in control. At all times. A Greek man's masculinity must never be brought into question, into disrepute. Only social death ensues if a man dares to transgress publicly. In secret, he can do whatever he wishes.

'Is some girl giving you a hard time? Don't you worry, she'll come good. Either that or she's plain dumb. A boy like you.'

'I am just tired. So tired.'

What do you mean exactly, *a boy like you?*

'*Thes ligo halloumi*?' she asks me, as if she's letting me open my birthday presents two weeks before the event when she's simply offering me the rubbery Cypriot sheep cheese I've been stuffed with since I could open my mouth.

'No thanks, I'm fine.'

'You hardly touch your food these days. How are you going to keep your energy up all night standing up, working alongside all those foreigners? Please tell me you *do* wash your hands thoroughly after handling all those packages.'

I want to get out. I feel asphyxiated. This bloody villa is too small. I hate halloumi cheese. It's too bloody salty. I want to say: *Your voice is becoming more androgynous as the years go by, your tragic droning on about doctors, x-rays, blood-tests, appointments I have to remember to take you to, your arrhythmic heart, your angina, your fear of yet another heart attack, your ulcers, your diabetes, your constantly upset stomach, your legs, the varicose veins, how little the medical fund pays back, every month the contribution is due, I know, Phil resents paying it, but what can we do?*

I switch off. I feel my blistered fingers pulsate and move from the bathroom to my room (finally I have a room of my own!) burning with the shame of my secrets, my dreams, my intense unrequited love for a faceless lover.

I leave home at eight saying I need to pop into the library to return a book. Men are very good at leaving. I should accept this. I should just leave. Aren't I my father's son? The money I spend on petrol each week could easily pay for a room in one of the boarding house terraces in Cleveland St. I could then walk to work and to the city. But who would pay for my mother's living expenses? The mortgage?

I should have learned all about leaving your family without a care from the master, my very own father. Apparently, for some men it is so easy to simply get up and go. At least for him. I should have learned something from my father's absence. I should have paid more attention to him. To study and learn his ways. For my own sake.

I go straight to work, clocking on, work like a maniac sorting and sorting quickly. Not sure whether I take in all the postcodes correctly or not as I seem to be in automation mode. When my meal break comes, at the Chinese cafeteria near Central, I find myself looking across at a Mediterranean man of a certain age who sits smoking across from me. As I hungrily eat up my rice with honey chicken dish, I am convinced this man is indeed my father.

The head of our family who left us. A man who left behind him entire paragraphs of unspoken narrative, a myriad of stories half-recalled for he was not present to correct whatever aspect of the story or anecdote he had told us that we might have recalled wrongly. A man who once led me down into a forest, greener than I had ever seen on any of the picnics the parish had organised. Told me he used to work there, in that glorious, beautiful Cypress pine forest.

But the man is not my father. He is Eurasian I realise on closer inspection.

The next evening, I get home to find my mother is unwell again. She reckons it's her stomach. She has an ulcer. Phil telephones saying she is very busy and could I just make sure to give mum her love. Dean is up the coast with his girlfriend and his mates.

'Take me to Cyprus Theo *mou*. This country is going to kill me.'

'You'll have to get a little bit better first,' I tell her.

'I want to go home. To my beautiful home. To my Nicosia.'

To our family home. Which no longer stands.

I vaguely recall summer gatherings in the courtyard, lined with potted lemon trees. The giant fig tree from next door was the tallest tree in the neighbourhood and provided us with a screening umbrella from the sun. Its thick leaves, seeping a milky substance, refused to become saturated with the water I furtively sprayed onto them time and time again. Hoping that one day I'd catch the tree unawares, and its leaves would finally be soaked, and I would feel triumphant. It never happened.

'You get better first and then we'll see...'

She drifts off to sleep.

In my room, I am eating a halloumi and cucumber sandwich.

I take out from my pocket a tattered photograph of my father in his late thirties, just before I was born. It really is only part of a torn photograph, from which I have cut out the others (men he used to work with). I recall when I was three or four my mother would tie me up, secure me with a leash, whenever we left the house. She was never a creative parent. All the time, I just wanted to break free.

Is that how my father felt too, tied down with an imaginary, all confining leash? Is that why he kept leaving us? Did Mother have him on an adult version leash? It could not have been easy to go from working in project management roles in various Middle East countries or supervising skilled welders to working as a first-rank labourer on construction sights, having been deemed *unskilled labour* on account of limited English language proficiency and absence of formal Australian qualifications.

We had learned at school through reading novels that a man's pride is all he has. On Thursday nights, in the early days of our life in the paradise of Australia, Father would desultorily go through his pay packet and Mother would ask accusingly, *What on earth are we going to do?* How must he have felt? Mother would get angrier as the money seemed to cover fewer and fewer expenses each fortnight. She would sometimes rant and scream and blame Father for bringing us here.

'Why can't you ever do something right?' she'd often ask him. Father would stay silent, and we were all frightened he would soon explode.

'What were you thinking in bringing us here?' she would finally say before going to her room, crying.

I go to the bathroom, set fire to my father's photograph and convince myself that I am a healthy young man with wonderful, unexpected pleasures ahead of me to experience. So much in life to look forward to. Good things. Ecstasy.

I should let go. I will let go of him. Now that I have set fire to the bastard, I shall never think of him again.

PART III

And then there were...

Kata ton daskalo pou paeis etsi grammata enna mathis
(Your education will depend on who your teacher is)
Cypriot proverb

51

I open my eyes.

I am still sitting in the makeshift carpark across from the Footbridge. It is just dirt but mostly cleared of bushes. The suburb is called Forest Lodge but there are hardly any trees around. Just tiny terraces stuck onto one another. A couple of feet of front yard, if any. They look like prisons or like the cubicle hotels I read they have in Japan. I cannot imagine living in one of them. What happens to your car every time it hails? Perhaps it never hails this close to the city, only in neglected suburbs far away from the CBD?

I am overwhelmed.

My face is wet, and I am sobbing. I am disturbed by the sound of my own voice. The sound is ugly. I do not recognise it. It feels like a rock is on top of me, a slab of sandstone, heavily pressed against my back, making it hard to even reach inside my pocket for an Aspro to help me relax a smidgeon.

Since we arrived here, everything has been turned upside down. Ours is no migrant success story. We have not accumulated wealth, there are no family businesses set up, there have been no new children born into this family. My father left us almost three years to the day after he brought us here on borrowed funds. Brought us here to the Lucky Country. The land of opportunity. *Streets paved with gold* our father's relatives proposed.

It had been entirely his brilliant idea. Cyprus was going to remain divided for a long time, he had said. Mother pleaded with him time and time again for us to go to England, but he was the man, he was the one who had rationed out his love to all of us. Our life was always decided on his terms. He was unequivocal in his idea to start somewhere fresh, away from my mother's extended family. Away from his own family. Far away from our divided island. Away from the sandstorms he loathed in the Middle East he had spent a decade in. Just the five of us.

But the dream materialised only for a brief period. The family, one by one, instead of integrating, disintegrated. We stopped being a true family long ago. All of us got on with the task of survival, each of us in the best way we knew how. There would be no documentary made of our success here. We made up the statistics of migrants who never make it. Who are not able to re-establish themselves in this dry continent. Who cannot recreate here the standard of living enjoyed in the past in their own countries, for they cannot manipulate appropriately the intricacies of the English language beyond a certain (low) standard. Are annihilated by the cultural system of this new adopted country. My mother never made a single good friend here.

Knowing how to manipulate the system for success is mandatory, is the prerequisite for success, for meaningful social acceptance in our adopted home. It is one thing for Australians to watch a dragon dance at the Festival of the Moon to show their tolerance and acceptance of these *foreign* people, but another matter entirely to offer their daughter's hand, to offer the CEO's position, to one of those boys inside the dragon. And to do so with an open heart. Not begrudgingly. Hoping your daughter may change her mind before any children arrive.

We remained low-status migrants. The other.

What country are you from?

Where were you born?

Where did you migrate from?

Why?

When?

How come Australia?

Are you Christian?

Foreigners. Part of a group of people who are forever frightened of the fearless Indian mynah birds who nosedive on them. People who spend a lifetime moving backwards and forwards to and from their country of birth, realising disappointingly that they are deemed ghosts of their former selves, endowed with dual nationalities, but belonging nowhere, being claimed by nobody, their place in the sun forfeited unwillingly.

Drowning emotionally in a diaspora of broken dreams.

Dean's been dead now for, is it six months already? He had to be dismantled, piece by piece, out of his beloved Monaro. He was lifeless, unrecognisable, obliterated unsparingly in a split second on the wretched Hume Highway.

So much for his sense of humour, his disdain for our mother's pain, his beloved wog chariot. Gone instantly. His life taken as if he were roadkill. The entire scene a bad take in a low-budget road movie.

I cannot believe he is no longer here.

At the macabre funeral, his father, our father, was absent. Not there to cry for his firstborn son. To honour him, to take the mantle of the man of the family, to play the part of the grieving father at the funeral. To support his wife.

Nor was he present to add a degree of solemn tragedy to the modest proceedings. What can be worse than for a parent to bury their child? What a poor substitute of a man I made in the early hours of morning, pretending to be in control, speaking calmly, my hysterical mother wailing like a cheetah, fainting in the church, making such a scene during the modest Greek Orthodox funeral.

Deano's mates did not know what to wear, what to say. None of them could understand Greek, let alone the archaic Greek texts the priest was quoting from throughout the service. My brother's friends did not know when to sit down and when to stand up during the proceedings and were always caught out. They were truly horrified, when a frozen, lifeless version of Dean dressed as a groom was revealed, as tradition dictated, when the casket was opened towards the end of the service. At precisely the same time the priest called Dean a sinner and made impassioned pleas to God to take this sinner away.

And Mother fainted again.

Afterwards, when everyone had gone home, everyone that is who could not fondly really share their memories of Dean with Mother as she still spoke no English besides a couple of greetings, Mother locked herself in her room. The telephone ringing was ignored, the delivered bread piled up on the doorstep.

In the weeks that followed, Mother coped by pretending that Dean had not really died, rather insisting that he was away somewhere. She would add to her fantasy and build on it, and as each slow day passed after the pure dread of the funeral, her ideas would get more and more fanciful. More and more absurd, more and more disturbing. At the same time, most days she sat by his grave, in a wretched, treeless cemetery in Liverpool. And yet her fantasies continued, even as she sat there.

She would also regale me with preposterous stories that Dean had moved overseas. Or that he had married a wealthy Greek girl who lived in Melbourne. That he had had two sons. Or had finally bought a beautiful home near the beach in his beloved Cronulla and that he wanted her to join him and his family one day. Her favourite go-to, was that Dean had started a business alongside our father, somewhere in the Middle East.

She would tell me fanciful things such as that Dean had set aside a room with a view of the sea, just for her. It even had its own bathroom and small kitchenette. She could move there and stay as long as she wished. Until the end of her days. If she chose to. She would tell me this over and over. The only reason why she didn't go right away was because she was waiting for her husband to come back.

I kept silent, kept my thoughts to myself, like I had always done. Mother was my responsibility now. It seemed that when we had arrived in Australia, she had given up her adult licence and had reverted to a child's learner's permit needing constant love, reassurance and attention from us. When she was supposed to have been the adult care giver. Along with our father, the person in control, the person who was supposed to provide her children with a sense of security. Financial and emotional. Parents are supposed to instil in their young the confidence they need in order to grow up healthy, well-adjusted, socialised adults. When this role is not played out successfully, there is no going back, no way out from permanent dysfunction.

Nobody, it seemed, would ever know the treacherous minefields which remained in my mind, ready to explode at any moment. It was never *the right time to tell*.

I have been abused.

I now cannot love.

I just repeat the pattern established back in the refugee camp. And in that half-finished rental. That of passive, powerless victim. Someone who does not know who to turn to for meaningful, long-lasting, life-changing help. As much as I'd like to avoid blaming my father he stands accused: he failed in his inherent paternal duty to guide, provide for and protect me. This is an undisputed fact that cannot be contested. God knows what my mother thinks of my life. She would probably die of shame if I told her the actual truth.

It's just the two of us now. How does that Cypriot saying go? *Emeinamen san ton koukoufkiaon (we're alone like an owl)*.

Phil divorced finally, encouraged by Dean's passing to make the move. It seemed losing Dean made all of us more determined to survive. I was proud of my sister's decision but displeased at her timing. Our history of losing everything and everyone who was a part of us did not bring us closer together but instead wedged us further apart. The pack was being dissipated and no amount of allegiance to the idea of Orthodox family unity would have any effect. It seemed our traumas made it impossible for us to stick together—just being in the same room seemed to reactivate all our grievances about our lives.

My brother's accident, his annihilation, was a do or die moment in our lives. We were terrified of the demonstrated risk to our own survival. Now prepared to do anything to cover our own backs. *O kathenas ton pono tou*, was the Greek saying and how true this proved in real life: everyone consumed by their own pain.

Dean had been the most successful at integrating into the archipelago of cultures his new life had brought him into contact with, but now he was gone. What kind of reward for success in your new country was premature death?

Thankfully, Phil had been preparing her escape for a while and had arranged a job teaching English in Paris. I reassured myself that Phil's leaving us was a good thing, repeating to myself, *She is following her dreams.* Youthful dreams she had abandoned for survival. Is that what all immigrants must do when they leave the country of their birth? Put all their dreams on hold? For how long?

'Australia didn't work out too well for me,' she had said at the airport in a rational manner, as if she were excusing a badly turned-out batch of over-salted stuffed tomatoes. *It gave you a free university degree* I wanted to protest but kept quiet.

'It might still work out for you, who knows' I said, without much enthusiasm.

'One day, it might be better here, for those of us who are, ahem, different, shall we say? But my dear brother, that day might not come for thirty years or more and you and I will be too old by then for anyone to give two hoots about us.'

My sister had always been right. More clear-eyed about the

inequities and ills of the world than me, a lot more pragmatic. I mumbled something about my hopes for her future, about her finding love, about the Old World treating her better and looked way, ashamed my sister evidently saw sense in her leaving and none in my staying.

Now she's gone, I do not know what to do.

I have tried tracking down my mother's husband and have made a few desperate phone calls to his sisters in Cyprus. But they are all so old now, two couldn't hear a single word I said.

Aunt Hara has been dead a long time.

Reliable Cousin Panikkos had an accident, falling down some stairs, whilst on duty at the station and he has not really been the same man since. Dimitris's sister was kind enough to write back and advise they had not heard from my father for more than ten years. Dimitris is still missing, she wrote, along with 1619 other Cypriots. Uncle Pericles, consumed as always by his polyamorous adventures, responded that he had his hands full with his young son and his new wife.

I desperately want to do something to keep my mind off my mother's predicament. There is only so much I can do for her on my own. I am not yet an adult, yet I have found myself having to behave like an adult throughout my teens. But who can I turn to? Counsellors cost money and cannot change one's past. I too need to assuage my feeling of guilt and try and survive. I do not want to end up like my mother. Abandoned.

I desperately want to feel as if I belong but society has me categorised as illegal.

I need to take action to release the emotional and physical tension which has been building up inside me for so long. To keep me from thinking of my non-event, single, abusive life. I need to be accepted into the university preparatory course, or I'll end up working in a dead-end job in some sweaty warehouse for the rest of my life.

I walk around the residential part of the campus feeling very much alone. I toss up whether I should walk up to *Maurice*'s for a falafel, up at the top end of King Street, Newtown. They have the best falafel and tabbouleh in Sydney. Instead, I sit in the Capella with the stereo off, in silence, sipping coffee from my thermos. I feel like chucking a sickie but keep on sipping my bitter coffee and it seems to settle me.

Soon enough I have closed my eyes. I'll get a falafel later and I might even splurge and also get a kebbeh roll today. *Live while you can*, should be my motto in my approach to all aspects of life: hell, I am a young man. My life is ahead of me. Yes. I affirm my life is ahead of me.

Mr Maurice wasn't getting any younger. No doubt he'd be shutting up the shop and going back to Lebanon at some stage. Whenever his son works alongside his parents, he looks miserable—I doubt he'd keep the joint open when his parents can no longer put in the long hours.

I daydream of seeing my father again. That he'll still look like he did in photographs taken from when he was in his early thirties. I've taken on my mother's delusions that everything is as it was before 1974.

I daydream of finally being looked after by him.

I daydream that he is teaching me things. He builds me a billycart. Shows me how to use an electric drill. Teaches me how to drive. Encourages me to read the instructions on how to use power tools systematically, secure in my set of skills and how to observe safety measures correctly. His reassurance quashing my anxiety that I'll mishandle them and cause damage or harm myself or others.

I daydream he has shown me how to behave, he has raised me properly, to grow into a confident young man, to be feel a part of the world. To feel entitled to a bit of the world. To be the kind of man society approves of and endorses. Giving me the tick of communal approval and all the trappings of worldly success. My father has failed in the fundamentals of parenthood. He never made me feel secure or cared for physically or emotionally; never demonstrated that I and my siblings were the most interesting part of his life; he has never made us feel admired, valued, understood through his unconditional love, accepting our limitations or imperfections.

I daydream he has shown me how to love and how to be loved.

I want to tell him: *Soon you will be dead, and you will never have acknowledged that you are mostly responsible for my downfall, my emotional stagnation. I blame you for my inability to relate to others. Specifically, my utter failure or interest to relate to happy young people my age who sincerely believe their dreams will come true. Your absence cost me my childhood innocence. My virginity.*

The version of the innocent boy I was, the boy I knew, is no longer around.

And my poor mother?

What have you done to her?

Her fears of abandonment and poverty continue to plague

her. Mother adheres to her script religiously. The plot of her life could be summarised in one paragraph: *All the men in her life keep leaving her; her father remarrying and living away from her, her husband abandoning her, her eldest son killed in a car accident, her only daughter ignoring Greek-Cypriot tradition to look after her mother when she is old and instead gallivanting around in Europe, her youngest son, remaining single, barren, not a proper man.*

But that is my mother's script.

Neither of my parents showed me I am a separate person with my own personality, interests and god forbid—desires. And that was okay whatever these interests and desires might be. So, I need to now focus on my own script. Face my own fears, in order for me to live my life as an adult. As a man. I'll be eighteen on my next birthday. I need to learn how to effectively parent myself, albeit eighteen years too late. If possible, I need to teach myself how to feel safe and loved, moment by moment.

I start the car, beautiful music fills the cabin, obliterating all other thoughts from my mind. Soon, with the window wound down, I am singing aloud, in tune to the music as best I can. I do not worry about other drivers hearing me sing badly my second-favourite Abba song, about winners taking it all.

52

I am taking a few days' break, away from the tragedy that is my mother. I am house minding for a couple at work looking after their rented tiny worker's terrace near the city in Redfern. It is approaching New Year's Eve and my Chinese workmates from Nanjing were shocked that I have lived in Sydney for almost seven years but have never seen the fireworks by the Harbour.

Outside the window where I sit, two near-black crows are courting each other in harmonies of song whilst a spider climbs steadily up the exterior wall. My workmates' rented terrace is sparse and has just the basics. The ill-matching furniture has been collected second-hand and chosen purely for functionality, not aesthetics. It feels very much like a temporary home. My feet are bare, and just like in that horrible attached terrace we rented in Waterloo when we first arrived, the soles of my feet are dark from the stained carpet. I forgot to pack my thongs.

My name is Demosthenes. The name implies vigour. Strength. It's from the Greek—meaning *citizen. Of the people.* The original bearer of my name was a great orator who gave intellectual speeches on morality. A man capable of rousing crowds to oppose Philip of Macedon and years later, his son, Alexander the Great.

What a cruel joke fate has played on my mother's aspirations for her youngest, on her life ambitions for me. She disliked the most common shortened form of my name, Demos, which translates to *municipality* in English. Finally, she relented and compromised, calling me Thimos. If she were to stress the last syllable my name, letter for letter, would mean *anger*. Most people call me Theo these days. *Theos* means *God* in Greek.

I am an angry God. What a laugh.

Perhaps I shall be almighty and heroic as I grow into adulthood?

Perhaps if I score high enough in the prep course or achieve a distinction in the year-long compulsory subjects afterwards I may be accepted into university.

I will complete a degree.

I will make it in the world.

The past is the past.

Someone may love me despite my faults, my imperfections, my sexual history. My otherness. My bitter secrets. Someday I shall take revenge on behalf of all people who have not been loved. For all people who have been abused. Who have been treated like shit. I shall make it my life's work to avenge all the dashed hopes, the constant feeling of disappointment and make up for all the lost opportunities.

My brother's death has pushed me to fight harder. I must dig deep and try and find the Odysseus in me. Pay homage to 1821 Independence heroes. I am Kolokotronis. I am Bouboulina. I am as wily as President Makarios. I am obstinate like Kissinger who ignored his long-time staff's advice and didn't give a damn about Cyprus and its people: his mission remained to just do whatever it took to gain the upper hand over the Soviet Union in the Cold War.

No mater my history of transgressions, of serial trauma, I will survive.

I shall create a beautiful life so that everyone who has treated me badly or who has not bothered to invest any of their time in knowing me well, feels I was the multi-coloured Amazonian bird that got away.

When I turn eighteen, I will get my nose fixed so I can breathe properly again. I will find a way to pay for the cost. I will be myself again.

I too am capable of loving.

And of being loved.

I may be a young man with *unmentionable tendencies* to many millions in the world, but I am just me to myself. A *me* who cannot pretend to be anything other than what my inherent nature has dictated me to be. It has nothing to do with my upbringing. Or with the bad experiences I had as a child at the hands of selfish adult men.

I am the way I was born. I cannot logically or scientifically be held responsible, be reasonably accused of any culpability. I did not choose my genetic make-up. I did not choose the colour of my complexion or my physical attributes like my height, how straight my hair is, the size of my cock, the sound of my laugh, the place I was born or the parents who created me. Did I?

53

I am starting to feel at home in the narrow terrace.

My father has been uncontactable. Untraceable. He has disappeared in a vortex of egregious abandonment. Into a time traveller's dead zone where men who leave behind their families go. But only they have permission to enter this parallel universe, this time zone separated from our normal chronology.

I have thought about him for so long.

I am biding my time. Waiting, in limbo. There is no one beside me. No one to hold me tight. No reassuring arm around my shoulder as I try to fall asleep. No one has hugged me since I was a little boy. There has never been anyone to bear witness to my life's misadventures or to forewarn me.

I have not been able to tell anyone my secret. But I am trying to deal with my past. At my own pace. In a way that doesn't make me feel worse. I am alone with my present, my past. Alone in the now. Always hiding my reality.

Some things are simply not discussed. Not even with family. I could not imagine having a conversation about what happened to me with even my own brother. Now I am older and it is too late. My brother is gone.

Mediterranean culture insists that men be physically indestructible, remain in control emotionally, remain steadfastly in control of their inner world (their sensual world too?). I am a social construct of where and when I grew up. The milieu I was thrown into. The family whose matriarch was born within the ancient city walls of Nicosia. The patriarch, a handsome peasant with one grandfather from Syracuse.

I am a product of the zeitgeist of my time. Normal heterosexual Southern European men are resolute in their innate arrogance. They draw their strength from the love of their parents and from their extended families. From generations going back two centuries. They have an entitlement just because it was predetermined by fate for them to come into the world as heteronormative males. Everywhere they look, their male gender is encouraged and welcomed.

'You are so blessed to have a son,' is a phrase that's as common as *Good morning* in most countries in the world.

Nobody ever says, 'Oh how lucky you are to have a gay son.'

Not yet. Perhaps one day this will change.

As each year moves on, becomes a memory of the distant past, I grow more and more aloof, untouchable, withdrawn. It is so safe in certain ways not being able to relate to anyone. Vulnerability is seen as an Achilles Heel. I see it as integral to being human. Open to feelings.

There is hope though. There are days and nights that I refuse to submit to despondency. I am about to become a man under the Law. The New Year will see me turn eighteen. I can make a fresh start. I am alive. I have managed to survive seven years as an immigrant, dutiful son here.

I will soon be an adult.

I am liking being so close to the city's amenities. I can go swimming in the pool four hundred metres away in Victoria Park. Be amongst other young people. Young people with vigour. Dreams. Driven by a conviction their dreams are going to come true. Youth who have never fled war, sexual abuse or poverty. Youth who are proud of their body. Youth who flagrantly flaunt their beauty.

I can go to the Art Gallery as often as I like and while away hours in the free exhibitions rooms. I can even walk there and back to save train fares. It is an easy straight walk down to the Cleveland St intersection then down Elizabeth. I take a right into Wentworth St and at the William St intersection, hang right and walk through the lower parks of the Domain, behind St Mary's Cathedral. Walking as fast or as slowly as I feel like—pretending this is my own big backyard with its glimpses and uninterrupted views of the Harbour. It surprises me not many people walk down the path, preferring the seaside walk in the Botanic Gardens.

These beautiful physical surroundings are mine.

In no time I am there. No need to spend four or five hours there and back changing trains and platforms. I can wear my Walkman and flick over the cassette when I have had enough of the same mixed tape I always listen to when I am walking.

I just have to sit out the summer.

I am thankful for having a month's break away from the misery of my mother. Last week I found the courage to go to the medical centre at the university and was strong enough to tell the doctor I needed help. She listened attentively and has given me a referral to a sexual abuse counsellor. I will save the money and in three weeks I will attend my first session. Dean's car was not worth a lot but his insurance, which took forever to come through, has meant Mother has enough to keep her going for a while, without my monetary help.

It took a few nights to get used to the fact that Ming and Zhang's tiny home has literally no front yard—you open the bedroom window, and the footpath is right there. Every time a passer-by walks past their footsteps sound too close for comfort. A group of raucous drunks walked past on Saturday night and scared me to death, as I was convinced they were already inside the house.

But it's all right, now. Just being in a home that has a different energy has been good for me. Has given me hope.

I've almost finished the preparatory course and am doing well.

I will get into the year-long programme at university in the New Year. I will manage to score a distinction in two subjects. Then, after that, if I keep studying hard, the university will allow me to enrol in a proper degree course. They will accept me. In fourteen months, the oldest university in Australia will offer me a place in its Fine Arts degree. To me. A refugee kid from the outer-western suburbs who has only been in Australia for seven years. Me, the baby of the broken family who had to learn a new language just as I was starting to use formal Greek properly. Just when I was doing so well at my school back on the island.

An island that remains divided.

Annexed without proper permission.

In two years, the villa shall be paid off and I can then find my own place, close to the city. My mother will have to decide whether to stay in the villa or find a small flat, closer to me. Where she can walk or catch the bus to the Greek deli. To the Greek church. In a suburb where she can buy herself a newspaper in her own language several times a week and feel like she has re-joined the world. A small two-bedroom unit with a balcony for her pots of basil. A small home she can lock up without concern for maintenance, if I can finally convince her to go back to our island for an extended holiday.

I must find the willpower to get through the next two years.

How the hell did I get here? To this juncture in life? It doesn't matter—the anticipation of adulthood is giving me a buzz that anything is possible.

I only must work hard.

Harder.

Remain dogged and focused on reaching my dreams.

I won't let this compulsion we all have to accumulate material possessions distract me from my meaningful goals. I can do it dammit. If people like my kind can demonstrate on the streets and can tolerate being verbally and physically abused and arrested, their names published in the newspaper, their lives destroyed, then I can surely try to do the best I can too. If those men and women protesting at that protest rally near Oxford St can put all they have on the line in the name of equality, then surely I can be brave enough to learn to come to terms with who I am? That is what makes me different to the next son of immigrants—I have multiple battles to fight against society.

But I've proven to myself I am strong. My short life in Australia has shown me that life keeps on changing and I have managed to cope.

I've underestimated myself.

I have been a good son to my mother.

I have hurt no one and never gave cheek to any of my teachers. Not even to those hopeless, clueless teachers who hated me on sight. Who hated my foreignness. Who may perhaps have perceived that I was different, not just in ethnicity.

I have helped others. I have prioritised my mother's needs.

I have been kind.

I laugh at people's bad jokes even if they are not actually funny or if I don't get the punch line. Or I just don't understand their accented busted-up English learned on the go, not in a formal class.

Hell, I am all right.

I shall study hard at university. I may or may not ever become a great painter or even ever be acknowledged as a good painter. But I know for certain I am going to be creative. Who knows? I may even become a different kind of artist.

It's all in my hands. Perhaps I may express my creative self through other means. Maybe through writing. Or performing. Writing poetry. Through landscape designing. The art of survival is in the palm of my hand. I and only I can turn the key, to allow doors to open to a myriad of opportunities. While I am alive anything is possible. I have my whole adult life ahead of me.

I shall find a way.

I will be fine.

I am fine.

There are spectacular fireworks waiting for me.

LEXICON

In order of appearance

Lotta – sow

Mitsis – the little one

Kapnistiria – incense burners

Thee mou – my dear God

Pappou – grandfather

Koritsi mou – my girl

APOEL – Cypriot soccer team

Pittes – fried flour Cypriot pastry dessert served with honey

Loukoumades – Cypriot version of doughnuts

Stete – Cypriot colloquial expression for grandmother

Kouroukla – headscarf

Horaitika – children from the city

Tsiattista – Cypriot limericks

Theia – Aunty

Mati – the Evil Eye

Kyria – Mrs

Parthena – Virgin

Einai anastatomeni – she's out of sorts/upset

Yiayia – grandmother

Karakaxa – as ugly as an old scarecrow

Flaounes – Cypriot cheese pastry

Paniyiri – festival/fete

Misismeni – the hated one

Haros – the Grim Ripper

Katharevousa – Formal Greek used by educated people in the 1960s and 1970s and still in usage to a certain degree in certain government documents, religious texts and Law Courts

Kaimeni – poor thing

Kakomazali – poor old sod

Enosi – political movement seeking unification with Greece as one nation

Ayios Savvas – Saint Savvas

Rembetika – Greek blues

Kentron – a family restaurant often located by the seaside

Ergalio – loommaker

Yiahni – a recipe with tomatoes or tomato sauce

Soot vre – Be quiet you

Theleis – Do you want

Kazani – a huge metal pot often used to wash sheets

Hristos Anesti – Christ has risen

Fourno – a mud oven built outside

Kotziakari – an old woman

Arhontiko – a house built for the well-to-do, like a manor

Ate re pigaine – go on, boy

Kleftiko – traditional dish with meat cooked in the ground

Gymnasio – high school

Bakkalis – grocer

Lountza – smoked pork neck

Kerynia, Morfou, Famagusta, Karpasi – Cypriot regions all occupied by Turkey since 1974

Mavros – Blackie

Appomeni – snooty bitch

Milas Ellinika – Do you speak Greek

Po, po, po – oh my/oh my goodness

Rezili – a humiliation

Symfrazomena – context

Kitaxtai – literally 'Look here' but used here to mean 'I assure you'

Soi – extended family clan/kinship

Einai tis ratsas – from a reputable family clan

Ayios Vasilis – Saint Basil/Greek Santa Claus

Lefkosia – Greek name for Nicosia

Paximadi – a Greek crunchy tea/coffee biscuit

Re vlaka – you idiot

Ela – come now

Mou – my, used as a term of endearment or familiarity with someone's name

Einai me to nami – his family is renowned/has a good reputation

Sou leo – I'm telling you

Faneromeni – an area of Nicosia, adjacent to occupied Nicosia since 1974

Vre – colloquial spoken word for *you*

Ohi – No

Paidi mou – my child

Efiye – he/she's gone

Keftedes – meatballs

Skase – Shut-up

Koulouri – a Greek dunking biscuit

O theos na mas voithisei – May God help us

Pista – stage

Re klais – Are you crying

Bastouni – walking stick

Ntino – shortened version of the name Konstandinos

Matsikorida – Narcissus Tazetta, wildflowers often seen on country lanes in Cyprus

O vlakas – the idiot

Kori – girl

Voithise me Ayia mou Varvara – Help me Saint Barbara

Na ftiaxo kafe – Shall I make coffee

Nai mitera – Yes, Mother

Hronia Polla – a generic expression at various celebrations such as birthdays and New Year's meaning 'best wishes', literal translation, 'Lots of years'

Mbravo – bravo

Elate vre paidia – come on you guys

Yia ton Patera sas – for your Father

Kala Hristougenna – Merry Christmas

Kolokasi – Cypriot dish using taro

Entaxei – Okay, All right then

Pateras – Father

Paparounes – Poppy flowers

Vre Hazo – you silly thing

Simfonisamen – Agreed?

Nai Thimo mou – Yes, my Thimo

Skrofa – bitch

Ti tin ehein aftin – literally, 'why does he have her' but here used 'What's the point of having her in his life?'

Sika – figs

Macaronia – pasta

Ti epathes paidi mou – What's happened my child

Ti eheis Thimo mou – What's the matter my Thimo

Thes ligo halloumi – Do you want some halloumi

O kathenas ton pono tou – Everyone is consumed with their own pain